Gray Girl

Susan I. Spieth

Gray Girl is a work of fiction. Names, characters, places and incidents either are the product of the author's imagination or used fictitiously. Any resemblance to actual persons, living or dead, or events is purely coincidental.

DEDICATION

To my mother and father, you are my foundation. To the women of West Point, you are my kindred sisters. To my daughters, you are my best work. To Bob, you are my best decision. To my Creator, Redeemer and Sustainer, You Are.

ACKNOWLEDGMENTS

I am deeply grateful to many who helped Gray Girl come into existence. Thank you, Lucian Truscott, for reading the first few chapters and advising me to start over. Lisa Bruck, thank you for reading the first draft and pretending to like it. Your feedback during our walks prompted the genesis of a better story. Thank you, David Bullock, Liz Horner Boquet and Luci Fernandez (a West Point roommate), for reading sections and encouraging me to keep going. Barb Eimer, thank you for editing the fourth or fifth version and giving me renewed hope after I had shelved Gray Girl for six months. Thank you, Jenni Moehringer ('85) and Marcia Ganoe ('84) for your encouragement. Linda Fiebig, thank you for editing what I thought was the final draft until you got your hands on it. Special thanks to my cuz, Chris Zarza, for a phenomenal cover design. Twice.

Thank you, Alex and Marlo, for many things but mainly for always asking, "When can we read it?" You can read it now. Finally, thank you, Bob. Your willingness to read each version (which isn't fair to ask of anyone), your gentle feedback, your persistent encouragement, and your patience with me (no easy task) are just a few reasons why I love you beyond words.

"A cadet will not lie, cheat or steal, nor tolerate those who do."
Cadet Honor Code, United States Corps of Cadets,
United States Military Academy at West Point, NY

Thursday, May 6, 1982
1530 hours

She felt the warm tickle begin between her shoulder blades, then glide slowly but purposefully down her spine, curling inward at the small of her back until coming to a halt at the crack of her bum. The drop of sweat stood there, like a sentry, under her Dress Gray, under the Army-issued white T-shirt, under the black webbed belt, under the heavy wool trousers, and under the Cadet Store cotton panties..

Jan Wishart stood at attention in a windowless room in front of a phalanx of thirteen young men armed not with spears but with an exacting and rigid Honor Code. Two freshmen, two sophomores, four juniors and five seniors sat across from her at three rectangular tables arranged end to end in a line. Only this was West Point, so they were called plebes, yearlings, cows and firsties, respectively. The image of da Vinci's *Last Supper* popped into her head. Two Army officers occupied another table to the left looking like courtroom deputies. Their hunter green uniforms looked downright bright and cheery compared to the dark gray wool uniforms of the cadets. Yellow legal pads and pencils waited in front of each cadet, but the bulging manila folder in front of Cadet Casey Conrad bothered Jan the most. She knew it contained all the evidence and statements against her—most of which she had not seen. She had been notified of the charges only three days ago.

Conrad, the Brigade Honor Captain, pulled a paper from the pregnant file and delivered the prepared statement to all present. "Cadet Wishart, you have been charged with two Honor Code violations regarding events on May second and third. The responsibility of this Honor Board will be to weigh the evidence and testimony and determine whether or not the Code has been breached. If we determine guilt, we will recommend your immediate dismissal from the Corps of Cadets to the Superintendent of the United States Military Academy. If we find innocence on all charges, then you will return to your company in good standing."

Without moving her head, she glanced toward her Army legal counsel whom she had met only ten minutes before reporting to this room. Major Hastings sat to her right looking down at his shoes. Jan lifted her eyes, looking for something, *anything*, that might help calm her stomach. Then she noticed the middle-aged, civilian woman sitting erect in front of what looked like a large adding machine. Something about her straight back made Jan feel slightly better.

"Do you fully understand the charges against you?" Conrad asked.

"Yes, Sir," Jan said, shaking. *How am I ever going to survive this?*

She had survived quite a lot already. Plebe year at West Point is all about making it through each day, putting one Etonic sneaker in front of the other, memorizing one menu at a time, cutting one Martha Washington sheet cake and passing it up the table before being told you are a "failure to the entire Corps of Cadets" for butchering the dessert. Every day of plebe year begins at o'dark-thirty when *Beanheads* (plebes) deliver mail and laundry to the sleeping upperclassmen. Before breakfast, fourth classmen (plebes) must memorize enormous amounts of information—the entire front page of The New York Times, the menus for every meal, various speeches, heritage, trivia and the number of days left before the high and holy days of cadet life.

This last requirement actually serves as a small help to plebes. When you fall exhausted into the rack at Taps each night, you subtract one more day from the seeming eternity until the Army-Navy game, Christmas leave, spring break and the highest of all holy days— graduation. This small, daily discipline actually instills hope in the breast of all plebes, reminding them that if they just endure, it will eventually end. One day, this shit will all be over.

"Have you received a copy of the evidence including Cadet Jackson's statement, the exhibits, and other statements from Cadets McCarron and Trane?"

"Yes, Sir."

"Sit down, Miss Wishart," the Brigade Honor Captain instructed.

Jan sat in the wooden chair at attention as required during meals in the Mess Hall—keeping her back straight, one fist distance from the chair and the same distance from the table. She squeezed her legs tightly together at a perfect ninety-degree angle from her knees.

Conrad continued, "Although I will preside over these proceedings, I have no vote. To my left are the First and Second Regimental Honor Captains, followed by their Honor Lieutenants and two cadets from each regiment." West Point consisted of four regiments, each with approximately one thousand cadets. "On my right are the Honor Captains from Third and Fourth Regiments, their Honor Lieutenants, and two cadets from each regiment. These cadets constitute the jury of your peers to hear and decide the charges before us today."

Jury of my peers? Only two plebes? No women?

"Now, Cadet Wishart, before we bring in the first witness, do you have any questions?" Conrad had to be at least six feet tall. All Brigade leaders were tall and usually white men. His class ring, a big, black onyx enveloping a half-carat diamond, set in eighteen-carat gold, weighed down his right hand. Firsties, or senior year cadets, now had their class rings, wearing them with their class crest facing the left. When they graduate, they will wear their rings the other way—with the academy crest closest to their hearts.

"Yes, Sir." She cleared her throat.

"What is it then?" he asked as he looked at his notes.

"Sir, I haven't seen a statement from Cadet Dogety in my file."

Without looking up, Conrad said, "Cadet Dogety doesn't wish to make a statement."

Dogety was Jan's Squad Leader during the first seven weeks at West Point, appropriately called "Beast," and her current Executive Officer. He could provide a statement in her favor, but he would not go against his classmate. Cadet Jackson and Cadet Dogety were also best friends since their first day of plebe year, known as R-Day. "Sir, he was a witness to the events."

Conrad flicked his wrist. "Cadet Dogety was not even present for the second honor charge. And he has the right to refuse to make a statement."

"Sir, Cadet Dogety was entirely involved in Sunday night's events and he has information about Monday morning that needs to be part of the record." Jan felt like a whining child, but she had to try.

Conrad sighed. "Cadet Dogety's actions regarding the incident have been admitted by Cadet Jackson. No one has tried to hide the fact that they were unduly hazing you. So I am not sure what more Cadet Dogety can add to the file that has not already been accounted for."

I'm taking one last shot at this. She looked back at Conrad. "Sir, Cadet Dogety knows more about the situation that has not been mentioned in any other statements so far. He has information that will help my defense and I would like for him to submit a statement."

"Well, Cadet Wishart, he has the right to refuse because he was not the one who brought the charges against you. You can still call him as a witness and you will be able to question him at that point." Conrad continued to shuffle some papers, never looking at Jan.

Not every battle is Armageddon. Save your strength for later. "Yes, Sir," she sighed.

Cadet Conrad motioned to one of the plebes who quickly rose and left the room. He returned a moment later with Jackson in tow, leading him to a small table to Jan's right. The plebe went back to his seat while Jackson remained standing.

"Cadet Jackson, please raise your right hand and repeat after me." Conrad read from a paper, "I, state your full name."

"I, Markus William Jackson," his voice was clear, strong and confident.

"Do solemnly swear to tell the truth, the whole truth and nothing but the truth...." Jackson repeated every word from Conrad.

"...in accordance with the Uniform Code of Military Justice..."

"...and the Honor Code of the United States Corps of Cadets,"

"So help me God." Jackson emphasized the last word as though his left hand had been on the Bible. He sat down in the chair, placing his gray hat on the table.

"Markus, you have charged Cadet Wishart with two honor violations. These are serious offenses. Before we begin, I must ask you if you wish to withdraw your accusations against Miss Wishart?"

"No, I stand by my statement," Jackson said.

"We have your written account, but please explain the circumstances leading up to the honor violations in question."

Jackson took a deep breath and began recounting his version of events. "On Sunday, May second, Cadet Dogety and I returned from weekend leave. We took a trip with Cadet Forthmeyer. Because Forthy was the designated driver, the Dogs and I had a few drinks. I make no excuses for our behavior when we returned to the barracks. We shouldn't have made Cadet Wishart run our errands that evening, and for that, I sincerely apologize."

Jan rolled her eyes. *Asshole!*

"However, our actions in no way justify the lies that Miss Wishart perpetrated as a result." He looked straight at Jan.

Self-righteous asshole!

"Please tell us exactly what transpired when you returned to Post," Conrad said.

"Cadet Dogety sent Cadet Wishart from H-3 to my room in B-1 with a routing envelope." Each regiment consisted of nine companies, called A, B, C, D, etc. Company H-3 was H Company in the Third Regiment and B-1 was B Company in the First Regiment. Jackson continued, "It contained a message on a legal pad from Dogety. The content of the note does not have any bearing on these proceedings. Suffice it to say, the note was meant only for me to read."

Just like the Watergate tapes were meant only for Nixon.

"Miss Wishart arrived to my room, I read the note, replied, and ordered Wishart to return the routing envelope to Dogety. We were just having fun."

"Was this during study hours, Markus?" Conrad asked.

"It started about 1900 hours but ended after study hours began, about 2030 hours," Jackson admitted.

Seven to eight thirty pm. Jan still converted military time into "normal" time in her head. The twenty-four hour military clock just never felt quite right.

"So, this went on for about an hour and a half?" The question came from the Third Regimental Honor Captain, Cadet Tourney.

"Yes, around that. Like I said, I am not proud of having taken up so much of Miss Wishart's time. We should not have continued once academic hours began. However, Cadet Wishart did not step a foot into my room after 1930 hours. Cadet Dogety also did not allow Miss Wishart to enter his room once the academic bell sounded."

Upperclassmen were not allowed in plebe rooms during study hours and vice-versa. This rule was taken seriously because it was linked to the Honor Code through plastic cards that hung inside every cadet's room indicating their whereabouts. Cadets marked these cards either "academic," "athletics," "sick call," "post," or "leave," whenever they left their rooms. If they went beyond the place indicated, it could be considered an honor violation.

"So, you sent Miss Wishart back to Cadet Dogety with a reply to his note?" Conrad clarified.

"Yes, then she came back again with another note from Dogety." Jackson said. "She made one more trip after that."

"Okay, so she made a total of three round trips from Third to First Regiments?" This came from Cadet Leavitt, First Regimental Honor Captain.

"Yes." Cadet Jackson looked down at his hat as though he felt badly about that, but Jan knew better.

2

"It is a period in which entering civilians undergo the stressful socialization process which produces a well-disciplined, motivated class of new cadets who are prepared for acceptance into the Corps as fourth class cadets... The new cadet's waking hours are completely controlled. Every activity is carefully supervised. Attention to detail and flawless appearance become second nature."
Cadet Basic Training, Bugle Notes, 81, p. 71

She knew better because Markus Jackson had been her Platoon Sergeant in Cadet Basic Training or "Beast Barracks." It began with R-day, the day that lives in infamy in every West Pointer's heart and mind. It's the demarcation line separating the comfortable, known world you left behind and the frenzied, haunted maze of shouting cadre you just marched into.

Jan Wishart spent the first few hours of R-Day paradoxically running around in circles while going from line to line. Her clothes and personal items were taken away in the first line. In the second line, she put on black shorts, a white T-shirt, black knee socks, and the ugly, black shoes she had to buy before R-Day. In more lines, someone measured her height and weight, then examined her backbone, limbs, ears, eyes, nose, and throat. Then in another line, she read the bottom row of letters and signaled when she heard a beep coming from enormous earphones.

She prayed there would not be a "pelvic exam" line. But thankfully, in the last medical line, they only asked if she took birth control pills. "Uh, no." She wondered how many girls her age actually did.

In the uniform line, a short man measured her from neck to waist, from waist to feet, and around her hips and waist. He took her breast measurement last, his face even with the tape. He then handed her a package of white V-neck undershirts, one white collared, button-front shirt, and one pair of gray trousers.

She went to more lines for more uniforms and supplies which she put in two large green duffel bags. Her arms ached from the strain of carrying the two fully loaded bags, so when she approached a firstie with a red sash after waiting in yet another line, she dropped the bags on the ground.

"Did I say you could put your bags down, New Cadet?"

"No, Sir." She picked up the bags.

"Did I tell you to pick up those bags?"

"No, Sir." This time, the bags stayed in her sweaty hands while she glanced at his nametag. *Dogety.*

"New Cadet, you will not do anything unless you are told. Do you understand?"

"Yes, Sir."

"You will not say anything unless you are asked. Do you understand?"

"Yes, Sir."

"You will keep your eyes straight ahead at all times, never looking around, not even at a nametag. Do you understand?"

"Yes, Sir."

"I didn't hear you. Do you understand?"

"YES, SIR!"

"Good. You are to report to the man in the red sash on the fourth floor of this building. He will tell you what to do next. Do you understand?"

Fourth floor? "Yes, Sir!" Jan turned to go, but Dogety stopped her again.

"New Cadet, did I dismiss you?"

"No, Sir." This time she didn't turn back to face him.

"You are dismissed, New Cadet."

"Yes, Sir."

Jan carried the heavy bags up four flights of stairs in the antique building. With its massive stone exterior and block interior, it seemed more like an old prison. *God, the first floor would have been nice.* She reached the fourth floor and saw the man with a red sash across the stairwell. *I better not screw this up.* Still she glanced at his nametag while walking straight toward him. She stopped about a foot away from Cadet Jackson, held onto her bags and didn't say a word.

"What is your name, New Cadet?"

"Sir, my name is Jan Wishart."

"Do you think we are friends, New Cadet?" He asked the question calmly, which caused Jan to question whether or not she might know him. "I'm waiting for an answer, Miss."

"No, Sir."

"That's correct, New Cadet, we are not friends. And because we are not friends, I don't need to know your first name. From now on you will be New Cadet Wishart. Do you understand?"

"Yes, Sir."

"Good. I am your new Platoon Sergeant, Wishart. That means from now on you will do everything I tell you." He lowered his voice to barely above a whisper. "You will run when I say run. You will crawl when I say crawl. You will scream when I say scream. And you will shit when I say shit. Do you understand , Miss Wishart?"

"Yes, Sir."

Then raising his voice again, he said, "In a moment, you will report to your First Sergeant. Do you see that sign on the wall to my right?"

Jan moved her eyes but not her head. "Yes, Sir."

"You will memorize that sign, and you will repeat it to your First Sergeant when you report. Do you understand, New Cadet?"

"Yes, Sir."

"Good. Now step to my right and stay there until you are called to report to the First Sergeant."

Jan took one giant step to her left as if she was playing *Mother, May I*. She read the sign on the wall, closed her eyes, and tried to say it without looking. After several attempts, someone from inside a room yelled, "New Cadet Wishart, report to the First Sergeant in room 418."

A few doors down the hallway, a huge sign on the wall outside room 418 said: "LEAVE BAGS AT DOOR." Jan figured a sign that big was meant for new cadets, so she put her bags down at the entrance, happy to give her arms a break for a few moments. She entered the room and said the words from the previous sign.

"Sir, New Cadet Wishart reports to the First Sergeant of Sixth Cadet Basic Training Company for the first time as ordered." It came out just as it was supposed to. The only problem was the First Sergeant behind the desk was a woman.

"Do I look like a SIR to you, New Cadet?"

"No, Sir."

"WHAT?"

"I mean, yes, Ma'am."

"I look like a man to you?"

"NO, MA'AM."

"That's better. New Cadet Wishart, you are entering the hardest seven weeks of your life, and in order to be successful, you need to keep a few things in mind. One, obey all orders from your superiors. Two, try your best at everything that is expected of you. Three, work together with your classmates. Four, do not give up. Five, maintain professionalism at all times, and six, keep a healthy sense of humor. Especially as a woman, New Cadet, you must make friends with your male classmates and you must earn their respect. Do you understand, New Cadet?"

"Yes, Ma'am!" But Jan didn't really understand any of that then. This First Sergeant was the only upperclass woman Jan saw that day. *She's kinda pretty. Not as good-looking as me, but not bad.*

In high school, Jan had been successful in almost everything. She had been elected Vice-President of the National Honor Society, Captain of the basketball and field hockey teams, and Senior Class President.

She was ranked fifth in her class and even gave a speech at graduation along with the valedictorian. She figured West Point would be more challenging than previous ventures but one that she would handily conquer.

"Take your bags to room 425, drop them, and report back to the man in the red sash at the top of the stairs. Do you understand, New Cadet Wishart?"

"Yes, Ma'am."

"Dismissed."

Jan turned and left the room, being sure to pick up her bags on the way out. She walked along the wall until coming to room 425. Jan placed her bags on one of the two asylum-looking beds hugging the walls. She paused a moment to look in the mirror above a sink cabinet on one wall of the room. Sweat was now sliding down her face. *Hey girl, you got this! Piece of pie! No problem!* This little pep talk drowned out another voice, deep inside, that was trying to shout something else.

She returned to Cadet Jackson, the man at the top of the stairs with the red sash. She stopped about a foot away from him without saying a word. "New Cadet Wishart, did you place your bags in your room?"

"Yes, Sir."

"Good." Jan saw him flinch slightly. Then he lowered his voice again. "Wishart, I do not cut any slack for females in my platoon. You either put up or shut up, just like all the men. I make no distinctions—you're all the same to me, and if you can't play with the big boys, then you don't belong here. Do you understand, Wishart?"

Jan looked into his brown eyes. She thought they looked a little like ones she had seen as a child but she couldn't remember where. "Yes, Sir."

"Some upperclassmen go easy on females, but don't expect special treatment from me or anyone else in my platoon. Have I made myself perfectly clear, Wishart?"

"Yes, Sir."

His voice returned to normal. "Good. You have now completed the first phase of R-day. From now on you will be taught everything necessary to succeed in Cadet Basic Training. Do you see that sign to my left, New Cadet?"

Again, she moved her eyes but not her head. "Yes, Sir."

"Those are your five responses. New cadets will use only those five responses, unless asked for further comments or explanations. Do you understand, New Cadet?"

"Yes, Sir."

"Step to my left and study those five responses for a few minutes. When you have memorized your five responses, report to the man in the red sash back at the entrance to this building. Do you understand?"

"Yes, Sir." And with another *Mother, May I* step to her right, she read a sign with bold lettering:

5 Responses of New Cadets:
Yes, Sir/Ma'am
No, Sir/Ma'am
No excuse, Sir/Ma'am
Sir/Ma'am, may I ask a question?
Sir/Ma'am, may I make a statement?

New cadets were not to say anything other than these five responses. Coming from a large, loud, animated family, Jan realized she was in trouble.

She returned to Dogety, the first red sash man. He taught her how to salute. "Place the tip of your right forefinger at the outside edge of your right eyebrow." When Jan followed that instruction, Dogety made a grimace. "New Cadet, may I touch you?"

She must not have heard him right. "Sir?"

"Is that one of your five responses, Wishart?"

"No, Sir." Her arm was still in the salute position. Somewhat.

"Then let's try that again. May I touch you?"

"Yes, Sir."

Dogety adjusted her upper arm, making it parallel to the ground. He pushed her elbow back so it came in alignment with her shoulder. Then he flattened her fingers so that they formed a straight line with her forearm at a forty-five-degree angle from the elbow. He dropped his hands to his side again and said, "Sharp corners, straight arms and hands, New Cadet." Then he sent her off to more lines where she learned how to stand at "attention," "forward march," "right face," "left face," "about face," "halt," "present arms," and stand "at ease"—which seemed a like an oxymoron to Jan.

After being sent to what seemed like a hundred lines, she was sorted into another line of ten new cadets called a squad. The first red sash man explained that he would be their new Squad Leader—their father and mother, their priest and pastor, their judge, jury and parole officer—for the next seven weeks. Cadet Dogety marched them around a huge paved area shouting, "Your left, right, left! Your left, right, left!" Because new cadets made many mistakes, he was constantly yelling, "Your other left, New Cadet!" or "What part of RIGHT do you not understand, New Cadet?" or "This isn't marching band practice, New Cadet!"

Jan kept her eyes straight ahead, thankful she had more coordination than others. *Just keep in step and don't draw attention.*

When Dogety was satisfied they had mastered the basics of marching, he led them to a barber shop beneath the huge Mess Hall. He lined them up against the wall facing twelve barbers, three rows of four chairs. Each barber held an electric hair clipper; each chair held a new cadet.

Jan planned ahead for this, coming to West Point with a fashionably short "Dorothy Hamill," a bob style haircut which had set her back about twelve bucks. She didn't need another haircut. "Sir, may I make a statement?" She shouted up to Dogety at the front of the squad line.

Dogety turned and faced the whole squad. "What is it, Wishart?"

"Sir, I already had a haircut before arriving." She knew she screwed up the moment it left her mouth.

"Is that so, Wishart?" Dogety said as he fumed down the squad line to where Jan stood, third from the end. "So you don't think you need to get a haircut like everyone else. Is that it?"

She froze.

"I asked you a question, Wishart!"

"Sir, I just thought..."

"YOU DON'T GET PAID TO THINK, WISHART!" He stood in front of her, inside her personal space. "Do you think you're special, Wishart, that you should get to skip a haircut cuz you're female. Is that what you think?"

"No, Sir." She cussed herself for being so stupid.

"Wishart, no one gets a pass in my squad. What would the rest of the squad think of you if you get out of doing what they have to do? Huh? What would they think about me if I let you get out of doing what they have to do?"

She hadn't thought that far ahead.

"So get this in your little brain right now Wishart—YOU DO WHAT EVERYONE DOES. GOT IT?"

"YES, SIR!"

Dogety lunged back to the front of the squad. Jan's eyes stung as she swallowed back the rock that had risen in her throat.

Dogety motioned each squad mate to a barber chair as soon as one vacated. Jan sat down just as another female new cadet with hair to her elbows sat in the chair directly behind her. They could see each other in the mirrors. The middle-aged barbers secured capes around their necks. Then, with shaking hands, both men picked up the electric hair clippers. Jan gave her classmate a slight smile as their faces met in the mirror. The other woman shrugged as if saying, "Easy come, easy go!"

Jan's barber combed her feathered hair straight down all the way around her head. Then he proceeded to dot the electric clippers, full circle, starting with her bangs. Jan closed her eyes in hopes that he might not ruin the feathering for which she had already paid. But when she opened them again, her hair was cut in a bowl shape above her ears. *I am a boy.*

The woman in the mirror had the very same haircut. Only it seemed much worse.

The barbers didn't try to style their hair; they just pulled the plastic sheets off both women and said simultaneously, "NEXT!" Jan stood up and read the other woman's nametag. *McCarron. Didn't seem to bother her one bit.*

After the barbershop, Jan's squad marched up the stairs, then up another set of stairs to the Mess Hall. She would have liked to take in this majestic space, but she didn't want to draw any more attention to herself. Dogety led them to a table with ten chairs. He stood behind the head chair while the new cadets fell in behind every remaining chair. He instructed them to pull out their chairs, move to the right and sit down, after the order "Take Seats" was given. He showed them how they were to sit in the chairs—with straight backs one fist distance away from the table and the back of the chair. Then, they learned a new way of slow motion eating.

Beginning with both hands on their lap, eyes straight ahead, they could use their fork to lift one morsel of food, about the size of a raisin, to their mouths. Only after placing the utensil back down on the plate and returning the hand back on the lap, could they begin to chew, slowly. After completely swallowing that bite, they could repeat the process.

Jan jumped when she heard a familiar voice shouting from the next table. "What the hell do you think you're doing, New Cadet?" It was the fourth floor man in the red sash, Cadet Jackson.

Jan froze again, forgetting for a moment that she wasn't the one in trouble this time.

"I'm talking to you, New Cadet!" He bellowed again.

"Uh, eating, Sir." The male voice sounded scared.

"IS THAT ONE OF YOUR FIVE RESPONSES?"

"No, Sir."

"Then I'll ask again: what the hell are you doing?" He asked more calmly this time. The new cadet didn't answer. "Well, New Cadet, I'm waiting?"

"Sir, may I ask a question?"

"No, you may not. Answer MY question, New Cadet?"

"No excuse, Sir."

"Damn right no excuse. That was the biggest piece of chicken I've ever seen on one fork. You some kind of pig, New Cadet?"

"No, Sir."

"You just sit there and think about that huge bite you just took. Think about how gross that looks."

"Yes, Sir."

Jan used her peripheral vision to see her squad mates taking their own unauthorized big bites. Cadet Dogety didn't seem to look up very much. He concentrated on his own plate.

Finally, the great hour of R-Day came. All new cadets changed into white shirts, gray trousers and black shoes without hats. Apparently, new cadets could not be trusted to keep hats on their heads. They lined up in squads, in platoons and in companies, and marched onto "The Plain" in front of all those spectators—family, friends and alumni. The first day hadn't even ended and Jan's calves, biceps and neck were throbbing. Throwing up was not out of the realm of possibility.

Yet, she also felt pride to be in this elite group, on this honorable field, with so many adoring spectators. In just a few hours, they had transformed from mere civilians into disciplined soldiers. They were the future leaders of the United States Army and on that glorious, sunny afternoon, the West Point Class of 1985 became part of the Long Gray Line.

Together with her classmates, she raised her right hand and took the West Point oath:

"I, Jan Wishart, do solemnly swear that I will support the Constitution of the United States, and bear true allegiance to the National Government; that I will maintain and defend the sovereignty of the United States, paramount to any and all allegiance, sovereignty, or fealty that I may owe to any State or country whatsoever; and that I will at all times obey the legal orders of my superior officers, and the Uniform Code of Military Justice."

She wondered what "fealty" meant but figured there wouldn't ever be a good time to ask. Then all 1528 new cadets, along with the "cadre," which Jan decided meant "old cadets," passed in review and presented arms.

In that glorious exhibition of tradition, as Jan's platoon rounded the corner, a male voice shouted from somewhere in the crowd, "Go home, Bitch."

3

Thursday, May 6, 1982
1700 hours

"What happened after Cadet Wishart's third time to your room?"
Conrad asked Jackson.

Here it comes. Jan dreaded this part. She hoped he would say
something that seemed out of place, anything that would raise a red
flag in their minds. *But Jackson's as cool as a carrot.*

"Cadet Wishart came back to my room while I had stepped out for
a minute to use the latrine. When I came back, I saw the routing
envelope leaning against my door. I opened it and found the note that
you have in the honor investigation file." Jackson motioned to the thick
manila folder in front of Conrad.

The Honor Board chairman opened the thick file of papers, pulled
out a clump attached with a paperclip, and distributed one to each
cadet. Major Hastings, Jan's JAG counsel, also opened a binder and
handed Jan a copy of the same paper: Exhibit A.

"Is this what you found in the routing envelope at that time?"
Conrad asked Jackson while holding up the piece of paper.

"Yes, it is," Jackson said.

Jan looked at the copy in front of her, the same one in front of the
jury of her peers. The plain sheet of paper, eight and a half by eleven

inches, contained a concise message in big, bold letters:

Quit fucking with Wishart, Assholes! If either of you messes with her again, neither of you will walk, on your own accord, across the stage on graduation day.
Signed,
Someone you don't want to mess with!

Conrad cleared his throat. A few of the other jurists fidgeted in their chairs. Jan saw smirks and grins. Apparently they found Exhibit A amusing.

"Continue, Cadet Jackson. What happened next?"

"Well, I was furious. I figured Wishart opened the routing envelope and took the messages between Cadet Dogety and me. I thought she had also written this note to intimidate us," Jackson said.

"Wouldn't that be a bit bold for a plebe, Cadet Jackson?" Tourney asked.

"Well, normally yes," Jackson replied. "But we have known Miss Wishart since R-Day. We have seen her insubordination on many occasions. It didn't seem unreasonable to me that she could have written this kind of thing."

Jan rolled her eyes again. *Right, as if I needed any more attention from you!*

"So you asked her about it?" Leavitt asked this time.

"I took the envelope and its contents back to Cadet Dogety first. He and I then went to her room and ordered her to meet us in the CQ room."

The Charge of Quarters (CQ) room, usually located near the entrance to each Company area, contained only a small desk and black rotary dial phone. One yearling, or sophomore, assigned to CQ duty every night, monitored the halls, checked cadet rooms every couple of hours, inspected and secured all common areas, and made a bed count at Taps—ensuring all cadets were in their rooms. When not going about their duties, yearling CQs sat at the desk in the small CQ room reading, studying or writing letters home. The black rotary phone was only used to communicate with the Brigade Charge of Quarters, usually a cow or junior year cadet, who ensured all the Company CQs were doing their jobs.

"Why there?" Conrad asked.

"Because the CQ room is not off limits to anyone. We figured we could question her there without violating any regulations," Jackson said.

And you could also close the door in a room without windows.

Conrad checked his watch. "We only have half an hour left before we need to break for dinner. I'm going to ask Cadet Jackson to tell us what happened in the CQ room before we break. There's not enough time for questions, so please write down any that come to mind, and we will deal with them when we resume later tonight."

Cadet Seymour, the Fourth Regimental Honor Captain spoke up. "Casey, I would prefer to ask questions as we hear the witness testify. Should we wait until after dinner before Markus continues?"

"Well, we need to get as much done as we can. If a question cannot wait until later, then of course, ask it. Otherwise, let's allow Cadet Jackson to speak uninterrupted." Conrad nodded to Jackson. "Markus, please continue."

Jackson took another deep breath and resumed his testimony. "Sam and I waited in the CQ room for Cadet Wishart. When she reported, we asked her about the routing envelope. Did she open it? Did she read our messages? Where are those pages now? Did she write the new note? Or did she know how the new note came to be in the envelope?"

Jan remembered it a little differently. Jackson continued, "She replied in the negative to all our questions. She didn't open the envelope. She didn't read our notes, she didn't write the new note, and she didn't have any idea how our messages were replaced by the new note. She denied knowing anything about it."

"Of course, we thought she HAD to have known something." He went on, "so we continued to ask her questions. Did she have the routing envelope in her possession at all times? Did she leave it at any point, at any place, in between trips to our rooms? Could she think of anyone who might have been able to open the envelope?" Jan saw a slight smirk on his face as he spoke.

"She said she had the envelope at all times, she did not have it out of her possession at any point. And no, she could not think of anyone who had access to the envelope." Cadet Jackson took another deep breath. "So you see, she denied having any knowledge of what happened to our messages and she denied writing the new note. YET, the envelope was in her custody the whole time. Obviously, something wasn't quite right."

Finally Cadet Seymour interrupted, "Was anyone else in the room to witness this questioning of Cadet Wishart?"

"Sam Dogety was there."

"I mean anyone else?"

"No, just us," Jackson said.

"What time did this questioning occur?" Seymour asked again.

"This was, oh, about 2100 hours, I guess," Jackson admitted.

"Okay, so it's an hour and a half after study hours have begun," Seymour clarified.

"Yes, but…"

"And did you consider that Miss Wishart might need to be studying, instead of being interrogated by two firsties during study hours?" Jan hoped Seymour was on to something.

"Yes, I have already said we were wrong on that account. But that doesn't excuse her for lying!" Jackson had raised his voice.

"Two wrongs don't make a right, is that it?" She began to like Seymour right then.

"Look, we were wrong. But we did not lie about it," Jackson reiterated more calmly.

Conrad interrupted, "I think we need to stop for now. We will meet back here at 1930 hours and continue to hear testimony until 2200 hours this evening. I want to remind everyone that these proceedings are strictly confidential. You cannot and will not speak to anyone about anything that has transpired in this room. If there are no further questions," he didn't wait for anyone to ask any, "dismissed."

Jan turned to her legal counsel, Major Hastings, "Any advice, Sir?" Legal counsel at Honor Boards could not speak during the "trial." He could only offer guidance and advice to the accused cadet.

Hastings said, "Well, you have already admitted that the routing envelope never went out of your sight, right?"

"Well, I did write that in my statement, but…."

"Then I'm afraid there's not much more I can say."

Well, that's helpful. Jan waited until he turned to leave before rolling her eyes again.

Jan's roommates waited anxiously while she removed her Dress Gray hat and flopped down on her bed. They had fifteen minutes before dinner formation.

"Well? How's it going?" Kristi asked.

"Swimmingly." Jan closed her eyes. "It's not good, Kissy."

Kristi McCarron, the long-haired, new cadet Jan saw in the barber shop on R-day, also ended up in Company H-3. They became roommates second semester along with Jan's first semester roommate Angel Trane. "If it comes down to his word against yours, they can't find you guilty. He doesn't have proof that you lied, just as you don't have proof that you're telling the truth." Kristi always saw things in the best possible light.

"He has proof that the original notes are missing and a new note showed up in its place," Jan said. "He has proof that only I had the envelope between his room and Dogety's. He has proof that I was previously insubordinate. But most importantly, he's a firstie, about to graduate, and five of his classmates are on the Honor Board." The plebe women sat in silence, contemplating "winning" against these odds.

Kristi practically shouted, "Well, don't go down without a fight. When I testify, I'm going to tell what assholes they have been to you. I'm going to tell everything they have done to mess you over. I'm going to insinuate, very subtly of course, that they schemed this whole thing up just to get rid of you."

"Oh good, because subtlety is your strong suit." Jan watched Kristi's face fall. "I'm sorry, Kissy. I just don't feel very positive right now."

"It's okay," Kristi said softly. "This has to be killing you."

"You know, I had to talk myself into *not* quitting all year and now that I'm in jeopardy of being kicked out, I'm trying like hell to stay." She paused before adding, "I mean, I could accept failing out or even getting booted for breaking too may rules or something cool like that. But getting kicked out for an honor violation? That would mean a life sentence of shame. I can't go home that way. I could never face my father again."

Angel, a petite black woman from somewhere in New York City, chimed in. "This is a spiritual battle, Jan. You have to fight it with prayer." Jan looked at Kristi with her lips slightly askew. "Jesus will give you the strength to fight the demons."

Despite Angel's religiosity, Jan felt deeply grateful for two roommates who still believed in her. Other classmates had already started distancing themselves. She could feel their avoidance and their abhorrence—a common reaction to anyone undergoing an Honor Board. Most would never know what really happened, but simply being "charged with honor" caused most everyone to back away. An honor charge at West Point gave you social leprosy.

"Gee Angel, I knew Jackson and Dogety were jerks, but I didn't realize they were demons," she smiled and winked at Kristi.

The plebe women rushed outside to dinner formation. As soon as Jan fell in her squad line, Dogety marched up and stood directly in front of her. Barely above a whisper, he asked, "What's happening at the Honor Board, Miss Wishart?"

"Sir, I cannot talk about it." She kept her eyes straight ahead, focusing on his chin.

"I know you can't tell me specifics, but how's it going in general?" His voice quivered slightly.

"It's an Honor Board, Sir. It's going." She refused to give him one ounce of information, especially because he refused to make a statement. "But, Sir, I would feel more hopeful if you would submit a statement."

He paused. Breathed in, then out. "I wish I could do that, Miss Wishart, but I can't."

Why? Because you're a coward? Or because you want me gone?

"Well, Sir, I will cross examine everyone who testifies." He would have to answer her questions in person if not in writing.

"I know, Wishart. I know," Dogety said softly before walking away.

After dinner, Jan brushed her teeth while standing over the sink in her room. As she rinsed the toothpaste from her mouth, a folded piece of paper flew under the door. She turned off the water, grabbed a towel, and dried her hands before stooping down to pick up the paper. It said "Jan" on one side in familiar handwriting. She flung open the door and looked up and down the hallway. The courier was gone.

SKIP, an anonymous pen pal of sorts, and Jan had been corresponding all year. She didn't know SKIP's identity, which drove her crazy sometimes. She had narrowed him down to a male cadet in her battalion, one out of about four hundred. She was getting close.

She unfolded the paper and read,

Jan,

Please, please tell me what the honor charges are. I HAVE TO KNOW...no details, just the basic charges—when and what date. All I've heard is that Jackson accused you of lying. Please give me a little more information—ASAP! This cannot wait. Write it now and tape it to your door. I'll come get it later.

I'm praying for you. Please be careful and keep me posted.
SKIP

Jan knew speaking about the details of the Honor Board was forbidden. But what about writing? Was that also not allowed? *Probably. But shit, what's the worst they can do to me??* Still, she would not say or write too much.

SKIP,
Jackson says I lied about what happened Sunday night and again

Monday morning in his room. That's all I can tell you. I didn't do anything wrong, but he seems to have the better case. Dogety won't back me up. I am screwed. You will probably need to find another pen pal.

Jan

4

"Experience has shown that a few new cadets will find the initial days of West Point a difficult period of adjustment, and a very small number may lose sight of their goals and decide to resign."
From Candidate Letter by Commandant of Cadets, May 1981

Jan received orders to have a Full Physical Exam at Fort Devens in February. The paper said she would receive a "pelvic exam," which she interpreted to mean someone would check that her hips worked properly. Her mother tried to clue her in, saying they would take a peek "down there" and maybe feel for anything abnormal.

When she felt a cold metal thing opening her vagina and pushing up inside her, she realized she had been woefully misinformed. Two assistants, acting as official knee holders, kept her legs apart. They told her to relax, but she certainly could not relax, not while the man in the white coat was *down there*. Jan tightened every muscle in her body, trying to relax. And just when it felt like her ovaries were being ripped out, the only other woman in the room snapped, "Quit moving! The more you fight it, the longer it will take!"

The white coat man finally withdrew the gut apparatus, but then inserted his fingers *down there*, with one hand, and used the other to press more on her lower abdomen. Then, he stuck another thing in her ass.

The awful ordeal finally ended, but Jan seemed to be in some sort of trance as she dressed. She could feel something seeping out of her, like a period, when she stood up. But it wasn't a period.

She waddled slowly back out to the waiting area and met her red-faced parents. They seemed embarrassed by what they all knew had taken place. For the first time in her life, she realized that there were many things they had not told her.

Beast barracks served to further Jan's education in the harsh realities of life. On the day after R-Day, well before sunrise, Cadet Dogety slammed open their door open and screamed, "GET UP, BEANHEADS! You got five minutes to get dressed and report outside for PT formation!"

Jan and her new roommate flew into their Physical Training uniforms—black shorts, white t-shirts with a black Academy crest over the left breast and brand new black Army boots over tube socks. The cadre wore the same outfits; only their black shorts, black Academy crest and black Army boots had all dulled to gray.

After rushing to pee and brushing their teeth, the new cadets pinged outside to *The Apron*. "Pinging" was the term for speed-walking that all new cadets were required to do wherever they went. Imagine Charlie Chaplin in fast, fast forward.

A gray, morning mist lingered among the ranks as they stood at attention on this large concrete slab facing *The Plain*. Jan wondered if everything was either gray or turning gray at West Point.

Squad leaders reported to Platoon Leaders, who reported to Company Commanders, who reported to Battalion Commanders who reported to the Beast Commander: "All present or accounted for." *Apparently no one left in the night.* The Stars and Stripes rose to the top of a flagpole while someone played a bugle. *It sounds kind of like a rooster which would make sense this early in the morning.* She took a deep breath, smelling the mixture of freshly mowed grass and the new leather of her boots.

Jan stood in the center of Fourth Squad, Second Platoon, Sixth Cadet Basic Training Company. She could see her roommate, New

Cadet Wright, ahead in Third Squad. First and Second Squads also had one female each.

"Second Platoon! Right, face!" Everyone turned crisply to the right in one quick move. "Forward, march!"

"Left, right, left! Left, right, left." Cadet Jackson, Second Platoon Sergeant, called cadence and kept everyone in step while marching onto The Plain. Four-foot tall platforms had been evenly dispersed on the huge, flat, grass field between the Hudson River and the grand, gray, gothic, Washington Hall. Sixth Company stopped in front of two platforms. "Right, face!" "Open ranks, March!"

The new cadets unceremoniously spread out across The Plain, screaming and shouting as they separated about five feet from each other in all directions. Sixth Company centered on the two platforms and Jan stood smack in the middle, front row.

Firsties leaped onto the platforms and began instructing the new cadets in Army exercises. "The Side Straddle Hop!" they shouted in unison before demonstrating what looked like Jumping Jacks. "One-two-three, **ONE**! One, two, three, **TWO**! One, two, three, **THREE**!" the firsties shouted as their arms went up, legs apart on counts one and three. Their arms came down, legs together on counts two and the last number.

"Sixth Company! Side Straddle Hop, in cadence, exercise!" The new cadets began doing jumping jacks in unison. "One, two, three, **ONE**! One, two, three, **TWO**!" Jan figured they'd do about twenty-five or so and then move on to the next drill. "One, two, three, **THIRTY**!"

Okay, I think we got it now.

"One, two, three, **FORTY**!"

Ah, shit, that's enough already.

The firsties' count changed tone, signaling the last Side Straddle Hop, "One, two, three, **FIFTY**!"

Thank God! That was just the first exercise.

The firsties led Sixth Company in many more drills, using the same two for one count. Just when the new cadets seemed sufficiently worn down, a new set of firsties took over the platform duties. The non-demonstrating cadre patrolled up and down the ranks making sure no one slacked off. This rotation ensured the leaders never got tired, while every ounce of energy drained from the new cadets.

Sit-ups, push-ups, leg lifts, body twists, side straddle hops, followed by more of the same. Almost an hour of non-stop, in-place drills—intended to build the body—by wearing it down completely.

Jan was in fairly good physical shape. She was an athlete—having played field hockey, basketball and softball throughout high school. Yet, she never experienced anything like West Point PT. Just when her body could not do one more leg lift, they formed back into squads by platoons by companies. "Who's gonna carry my Guidon?" Cadet Jackson asked.

"Guidon?" Jan wondered as her roommate's hand shot up.

"New Cadet Wright, post!" Wright stepped out of Third Squad and ran to the front of the platoon. Jackson handed her the pole with Second Platoon's flag.

Apparently that's a Guidon. And apparently, "post," means "get your ass over here!"

In one long line, all ten companies marched off The Plain and onto Thayer Road. Once on the pavement, they heard, "Quick time, march!" Everyone started running in step. The new cadets echoed Cadet Jackson's singing cadence. Like a drumbeat, it kept everyone in step.

Mama mama can't you see, what the Army's done to me?
They put me in a barber's chair, spun me 'round, had no hair.
Mama mama can't you see, what the Army's done to me?
They took away my favorite jeans, now I'm wearing Army greens.
Mama mama can't you see, what the Army's done to me?
I used to date a beauty queen, now I love my M16.
Mama mama can't you see, what the Army's done to me?
I used to drive a Cadillac, now I carry it on my back.

Jan did not sing. She needed all her breath just to run. She ran all the time playing field hockey and basketball in high school, but distance running in formation was an entirely new experience for her. *Dammit. I didn't prepare enough for this.* She felt herself losing pace. *Please,*

please hang on. Just stay with the herd.

The self-talk didn't help. She kept falling out of step with the platoon and the guy behind her began slapping at her heels. He finally ran around her, taking her spot.

"Wishart, move out of the formation if you cannot keep up!" Jackson shouted. She saw Cadet Dogety at the front of the squad shake his head in seeming disgust.

Oh God, not this. Not on the first run! But it was too late. She veered off to the right, just beside the formation. The platoon passed her. Then the rest of the company rushed by her. She kept running on the sidewalk, hoping to catch back up, but then Seventh Company began passing.

Now she was the worst kind of new cadet—a "Straggler." Jan felt her cheeks redden with shame as she hung her head and hoped no one would remember her face. Standing out for the wrong reason at West Point was the last thing anyone ever wanted. While she plugged away on the sidewalk, another passing platoon began singing a variance of the previous cadence.

Mama mama can't you see, look at that Straggler next to me?
Leave her behind, we don't care, go on home, you don't belong here.
Mama mama can't you see, the Army ain't your cup of tea?
They took away your favorite jeans, and you ain't fit for Army greens.
Mama mama can't you see, what the Army's sent to me?
She used to be a beauty queen, but she can't shoot an M16.
Mama mama can't you see, look at that Straggler next to me?
Go on home to your Cadillac, stay with Jody and don't come back.

The words of this cadence felt like a gunshot to Jan's spine. She could feel the bullet enter her back, move through her gut and rise up, burning in her throat. She swallowed the hot lead that tried to slip past her tongue.

Jan dropped further behind the great mass of white shirts and black shorts which at a distance seemed gray. It hadn't even been twenty-four hours since she kissed her parents goodbye. *Maybe no one will notice if I sneak down to the river, follow it upstream and find a pay phone. "Dad, I'm sorry, I just can't do it. I can't stay here anymore. Please come get me!"*

Her father had taken her three brothers to visit Annapolis and West Point, hoping one of them would get the service academy bug. He probably never expected their younger sister would be the one who applied and got in. Now she was questioning why she ever thought this was a good idea.

Her contemplations about quitting were cut short when two Department of Physical Education (DPE) officers started running next to her, one on each side. These former graduates, *really old cadre,* "brought up the rear." They made sure all the Stragglers made it back to The Plain.

The two Army officers thwarted Jan's plan to escape simply by jogging beside and coaching her: "Keep your arms still, new cadet;" "Take deep breaths, in your nose and out your mouth;" "Keep your eyes up, new cadet;" "Don't cross your arms in front of your body;" "Keep your upper body as still as possible;" "Feel the rhythm of the run;" "Pace yourself—keep cadence in your head, new cadet."

My first West Point class: Running 101.

The Company had been dismissed when Jan returned to The Plain. She pinged to the barracks. Speed walking at four times the normal pace while keeping arms straight at the sides and body erect caused many shin splints in new cadets. Jan could already feel the effects of this unnatural gait upon her leg, buttocks and arm muscles.

She entered the barracks, immediately turned right until she came to a wall, then turned left and pinged up the first set of stairs lifting her arms parallel to the ground. "Squaring off," another plebe requirement, meant turning at every corner of the stairwells or rooms. She entered the hallway at the fourth floor, pinging along the wall to her room.

"Miss, HALT!" She recognized Jackson's voice and stopped immediately. He approached and stood only inches from her face. "I don't tolerate Stragglers in my platoon." She wished he had brushed his teeth. "If you fall out of another run, you will be on my remedial running program." He leaned in closer, now only about one inch from her face. "Do you understand me, Miss Wishart?"

"Yes, Sir."

"Good. You now have five minutes to shower, change and stand tall at my breakfast formation." He lowered his voice, "I suggest you get your fat ass in gear."

"Yes, Sir." *At least I don't have camel breath.* She continued pinging toward her room.

She was ten minutes late to formation. Fortunately, Cadet Jackson was hazing someone in the First Squad. But Dogety stood in front of the last man in the Fourth Squad line until Jan fell in next to him.

"Hambin, what's the menu for breakfast?" Dogety asked her squad mate while staring at Jan.

"Sir, for breakfast we are having French toast with syrup, sausage links, home fries, hard boiled eggs, fresh fruit, orange juice and coffee." New Cadet Hambin seemed the most squared away so far in Fourth Squad.

Dogety stepped in front of Jan, looking her over from cap to shoes. "Wishart, look down at your gig line."

A gig line ran all the way down a cadet's torso from neck to crotch. The buttoned edge of the shirt was supposed to line up with the outer edge of the belt buckle and the outer edge of the fly of the pants, creating one straight line from top to bottom.

Jan dropped her head but didn't see the problem. It looked fairly straight to her. She lifted her face back up.

"Do you see what I'm talking about?" Dogety asked.

"No, Sir."

"Wishart, your shirt is puffed out. It doesn't lie flat."

"Yes, Sir." *It might have to do with boobs.*

"I want you to fix it," he commanded.

Right now?

"Did you hear me, Wishart?"

"Yes, Sir." Jan began to tuck her olive drab (OD) fatigue shirt in her pants, more than it already was. She fiddled with it while Dogety remained facing her.

Then Jackson walked over. "What's going on here?"

"Wishart is straightening her gig line," Dogety explained. Jackson walked around to her backside.

"Sam, have you seen this dress-off?" Jackson asked. "It looks like mashed potatoes."

Jan stared at Dogety while he responded, "I was getting to that, Cadet Jackson." He turned his focus back to Jan, "Are you done, Miss Wishart?"

"She can't possibly be done. Her dress-off is non-existent," Jackson barked. "Hambin and Wishart, left face!" They both turned simultaneously to the left. "Hambin, give your classmate a proper dress-off," Jackson ordered.

With Dogety now at her right side, Jackson at her left, and Hambin behind, she had only one route left open—forward. Jan unlatched her black, webbed belt and unzipped the olive drab fatigue pants. Then she slid the pants slightly down over her butt while Hambin grabbed each side of her shirt at her waistline, pulling it tight. He folded the extra shirt fabric back, holding it firmly in place, while she lifted her pants back up over his fingers. She re-zippered and re-buckled while Hambin carefully withdrew his hands. If done correctly, the shirt would lay completely flat across the back with only two hospital bed folds at the sides.

"Okay, Cadet Jackson, I'll take it from here." Dogety sounded annoyed and his eyes tracked Jackson as he walked away. "Hambin and Wishart, right face," he said quietly. The new cadets turned back to face him. "Hambin, from now on, you will report to Wishart's room before every formation to give her a proper dress-off."

"Yes, Sir," Hambin said.

But Jan didn't like it. "Sir, may I make a statement?"

"What is it, Wishart?"

"Sir, my roommate can give me dress-offs."

"Not good enough, Wishart. Your roommate is Third Squad scum."

33

Dogety nodded at Hambin. "Fourth Squad takes care of its own, right Hambin?"

"Yes. Sir," Hambin popped off.

5

Thursday, May 6 1982
1930 hours

The stenographer scowled as Jan walked to her seat in the windowless room. The two women sat in silence waiting for the males to arrive. Jan wondered how different her Honor Board would be with an all women jury. *Can't think about that. Just pray some of these guys will see the forest through the vines.*

Jan mixed up clichés all the time. She felt it showed she was a big picture person who didn't get bogged down with all the details. Yet, she needed to focus on the details now in order to find a way out of this mess. *The details might make or break my case. There, I got that one right.*

The men entered the room and took their seats. Conrad cleared his throat. "All right then, let's pick up where we left off." He looked to the witness chair. "Cadet Jackson, I want to remind you that you are still under oath. Now, tell us what transpired after you and Cadet Dogety confronted Cadet Wishart in the CQ office?"

Jackson leaned forward in his chair. "She refused to admit any blame for the switcheroo. She told us she kept the routing envelope with her at all times between trips from Third to First Regiments. She used the latrine on two occasions and stopped in her room two times where she spoke to Cadets McCarron and Trane. But she was adamant that neither of those two touched the envelope."

"Did you feel that Cadet Wishart was being truthful at that time?" Conrad asked.

"No, I thought she was lying. But I couldn't prove it. I figured someone else probably knew something that could show Cadet Wishart was lying," Jackson said, never looking at Jan. "So, we dismissed her and decided we would verify her story with Cadets McCarron and Trane later."

"Why did you think she was not being truthful at that point?" Cadet Gaskins, Second Regimental Honor Captain asked.

"Because she was sweating, shaking, acting all nervous and stuff," Jackson said.

Cadet Tourney asked, "Do you think she could have been nervous for any other reason?"

"No, not really. We have had many...uh...encounters with Cadet Wishart. She never acted like that before."

I just spent the last couple hours running back and forth between your rooms, I had no idea how the new note got in the envelope, and you had me alone in the goddamn CQ room!

"Okay, what else did you tell Miss Wishart before you dismissed her?" Conrad asked, keeping on track.

"I told her to report to my room at 0500 hours the next morning."

"Didn't she report to your room enough already?" Cadet Leavitt asked.

Jackson replied softly, "Yes, of course she did. But you have to understand. I figured she was lying about the envelope. I also felt she deserved some sort of punishment for messing with our correspondence."

Tourney spoke up again. "Wait a minute. You had already decided to do an informal honor investigation when you decided to add a punitive exercise?"

"Yes. In hindsight, we should not have added this extra requirement. But I did tell her to report to my room at 0500 the next morning."

And that's when the shit really hit the fan blades!

"What exactly did you plan for Miss Wishart at that hour of the morning?" Conrad asked.

"I was just going to have her spit shine my shoes. I figured she'd finish by 0530, giving her plenty of time to get back to her room and get ready for breakfast formation," Jackson replied. "But Cadet Wishart arrived to my room late, about 0515."

"And then what happened?" Conrad again.

"I chewed her out for being late and told her to take my shoes with her to spit shine and return them to me by 1600 hours. She acted extremely insubordinate to me at that point. She threw one of the shoes at me and called me a 'f-ing asshole.'" Jackson paused before continuing. "I reprimanded her for disrespecting a superior officer, but she just rolled her eyes and generally blew me off. So then, I told her to get the hell out of my room and that I didn't want to ever see her again in B-1."

"What time did she leave your room?" Gaskins asked.

"She left no later than 0530."

Conrad asked, "Were there any witnesses to this encounter with Miss Wishart, Markus?"

"No, my roommate moved to the regimental staff rooms at the beginning of this semester, so I have the room to myself. Unfortunately, no one else witnessed Miss Wishart's insubordination."

"Was your door open while Cadet Wishart was there?" Tourney asked.

"I believe Wishart left it open when she entered the room," Jackson said matter-of-factly.

Conrad went through his file of papers again, pulling out another clump. He removed a large paperclip and passed a stapled section to every cadet on the Honor Board. Major Hastings handed Jan two pages stapled together: Exhibit B.

Jan read the honor Investigation form 202-10. After the usual information: name, date, location, time of alleged offense, there was one single succinct statement, "Write a summary of the alleged honor violation in the box below:"

> ⸱ Cadet Wishart told several lies on May 2nd and 3rd to both Cadet Dogety and me. On the night of May 2nd, she denied having knowledge of how the contents changed in a routing envelope that was in her possession at all times. And on May 3rd, Cadet Wishart knowingly lied to Cadet Dogety about events that transpired in my room that morning. I request Cadet Wishart be investigated for Honor Charges in regards to both of these incidents.
> Respectfully submitted,
> Cadet Markus Jackson
> Company B-1

Another attached sheet detailed Jackson's allegations against Jan. The room quieted while everyone read the full report.

After a few minutes Conrad said, "Let's take a short break, use the latrine, get a coke, whatever. I need everyone back in their seats at 2130 hours. Cadet Wishart and Major Hastings, please stand fast." Everyone stood up, even the stenographer, and left the room. Only Jan, Major Hastings and Conrad remained. "Miss Wishart, I have just realized that there has been a slight oversight. You may not have been informed, but you are allowed one cadet of your choice to be present during these proceedings. Like your JAG counselor, this cadet cannot speak during the Honor Board, but he or she may take notes and provide advice. Do you have someone in mind whom you would like to have as your supporting cadet?"

Jan wondered why no one mentioned this before now. She silently hoped it might be worthy of a mistrial, if there was such a thing for cadet Honor Boards. She cleared her throat. "Sir, may I have ANY cadet?"

"Yes, as long as they agree to it."

"Then I'd like to have Cadet Dogety."

"Oh, sorry, no, you cannot have witnesses or anyone who might testify during the Honor Board," Conrad clarified.

Damn. That rules out Kissy and Angel. I can't very well call on SKIP because I have no idea who he is. Drew is not an option either. Her short list of friends was getting shorter all the time.

"Sir, I would like to ask Cadet Trane then."

"Miss Wishart, I just said you cannot ask anyone who might testify and Cadet Trane is on the list," Conrad said.

"Sir, I don't mean Cadet Angel Trane. I mean Cadet Bill Trane."

"Your Company Honor Representative?"

"Yes, Sir."

"Well, that's...unprecedented." Conrad paused to think it over. "But because he was not involved in the events, other than the initial investigation, I suppose he can be allowed." Jan figured he gave in easily to make up for the hard line he took earlier over Dogety's non-statement.

At 2130 hours, Conrad convened the Honor Board again announcing, "We are adjourning early tonight. Miss Wishart has not chosen a supporting cadet to participate in these proceedings. We will meet here again tomorrow morning at 0800 hours to give her time to ask someone of her choosing."

Did he just make it sound like it was my fault?

"Remember the confidential nature of this Honor Board. No one is to say anything to anyone. Am I clear?" There were general nods from the panel of cadets. "Dismissed."

Jan turned to Major Hastings. "Any advice for me now, Sir?" she asked hoping he might prove helpful after all.

"Nothing yet. Just try to look innocent and maybe a little vulnerable."

Oh Jaysus.

6

"The discipline which makes the soldiers of a free country reliable in battle is not to be gained by harsh or tyrannical treatment. On the contrary, such treatment is far more likely to destroy than to make an army. It is possible to impart instruction and to give commands in such manner and such a tone of voice to inspire in the soldier no feeling but an intense desire to obey, while the opposite manner and tone of voice cannot fail to excite strong resentment and a desire to disobey."
Schofield's Definition of Discipline, Bugle Notes, 81, p.51

"ATTENTION TO ORDERS!" The booming voice commanded all cadets in the Mess Hall to stop eating. After several other announcements, the OZ-like voice said: "All female new cadets will report to Thayer Hall, Room 519, immediately following breakfast."

The new cadets filed out of the four wings of the Mess Hall through massive, oak doors. Ninety percent headed to their barracks to shine shoes, memorize "poop" (the term for everything new cadets were required to memorize), or do anything their Squad Leaders wanted. The women headed to Thayer Hall, Room 519.

Jan took a seat in one of the middle rows of the large lecture room, safely not too close nor too far from the speaker. A familiar face came up the steps. Her nametag read, "McCarron." She chose the seat next to Jan.

While the room filled with new cadet women, McCarron whispered, "three guesses—sex, birth control or hygiene—not necessarily in that order." Jan smirked but hoped this meeting wasn't about any of those things.

A female officer, the first they had seen at West Point, entered the room. Extremely physically fit, Jan thought she could pass for a man in the right light. Captain Milliford started speaking, "It's not uncommon for young women to stop menstruating at West Point."

"I knew it," McCarron whispered.

Captain Milliford continued, "We have found this to be true especially during Beast and often throughout plebe year. Most of you will stop menstruating for a few months. Some of you will not have a period for six months."

Fine with me! Jan figured this might be the *one* benefit of Beast.

"Due to the physical and emotional stress of Cadet Basic Training and the Fourth Class System, it is perfectly normal to lose your period for the entire plebe year."

Can't be gone too long for me! Jan hoped she'd be in the full year category.

"So don't be alarmed if you stop menstruating," Captain Milliford continued, "It will return eventually."

Oh damn.

The captain ended her talk saying, "The technical term for the cessation of the menstrual cycle is *'Amenorrhea.'*"

They were dismissed. Jan stood and whispered to McCarron, "I think she meant to say *'Amen-oh-yay-ah!'*"

McCarron giggled.

The Second Platoon women: McCarron, Plowden, Wright and Jan, returned to the company area, but the rooms, hallways and latrines were empty. No Platoon Leader, no Platoon Sergeant and no Squad Leaders.

"Did anyone hear where we were supposed to go after the lecture?" Plowden asked when they had gathered in Jan and Wright's room. They hadn't been told where to report.

"Is this a girl scout meeting?" The four women popped to attention and turned toward the door. Cadet Trane, their Sixth Company Commander, stood in the hallway, smirking.

"No, Sir," McCarron said.

"Sir, may I make a statement?" Jan asked.

"Yeah, go ahead, Miss Wishart."

"Sir, we just returned from the lecture at Thayer Hall and we don't know where the rest of the platoon went."

"Oh, that's easy. You'll find them in the dayroom," Trane said, before sauntering off.

The four women filed along the wall, pinging and squaring off until they reached the basement. They barged into the dayroom, Wright first, followed by Plowden, McCarron and then Jan.

The entire platoon sat on dilapidated couches and on the floor throughout the room. Dogety and the other Squad Leaders leaned against one wall. Jackson stood in the center of the room. "Oh look, men, it's your female classmates, back from their special lecture," he announced. "Nice of you females to join us."

Jan saw Dogety shift his weight from one foot to the other. Jackson kept going, "But because you are late to *MY* lecture, you will have to wait outside in the hallway until we are finished."

Hambin furrowed his brow. It was hard to tell what anyone else was thinking. She saw a mixture of satisfaction, confusion and perhaps distress on some faces.

"Did you hear me, females? OUT!" Jackson shouted.

Plowden exited immediately. But Jan, Wright and McCarron all stood fast for a moment longer before leaving. When Jan turned to go out of the door, she did her best "screw you" face and made sure everyone saw it.

The rest of the week dragged, with PT every morning, followed by room organizing, cleaning and inspections which resulted in more room organizing, cleaning and inspections. They reported to many formations every day for uniform, shoe, boot and personal hygiene inspections which resulted in more uniform, shoe, boot and personal hygiene

---

inspections. They marched everywhere: to lectures at Eisenhower Hall, to the Mess Hall three times a day, and to The Plain for almost everything else. They were taught to disassemble, clean and reassemble their M-14s, and march with these heavy wooden rifles. "Right Shoulder, Arms!" "Order Arms!" "Port Arms!" and "Present Arms!" became familiar commands in less than one week.

Jan still wasn't making the morning runs, but Jackson seemed to be unaware of it or just too busy harassing someone else. Either way, Jan didn't mind the break from "Jackass," as she began calling him.

The first weekend wasn't a weekend. Every minute continued to be under the control of the cadre with only a couple of free hours Sunday morning for those who wanted to go to church. Jan never went to church before, so she didn't see the point in starting that habit. She regretted the decision, however, when Cadet Dogety ordered the non-churchers to assemble in the day room for a boot shining lesson.

Jan's luck with Jackson ran out when she fell out of another run in the second week, which made her late again to breakfast formation. He was waiting for her. "Wishart, you will begin remedial running tonight. Report to my room at 2100 hours in PT uniform."

"Yes, Sir."

"And what's for dinner?"

"Sir, for dinner we are having steak, baked potatoes, green beans, rolls, lemonade and Martha Washington Sheet Cake."

"Wishart, you didn't make the run again this morning. You better give careful thought to how much you eat." His gaze moved down her body. "Running is much easier for thin people."

Is he saying I'm fat? I'm not fat. Am I? "Yes, Sir."

At dinner formation that evening, Dogety walked down the squad line, stopping in front of each new cadet. He asked them all the same question and wrote the answer on a clipboard. "Did you have a bowel movement this week, New Cadet?"

Why does he need to know that?

Everyone responded in the affirmative until Dogety reached her. "Wishart, did you have a bowel movement this week?" He didn't look up from the clipboard.

Oh my God! "No, Sir."

"No?"

"No, Sir."

"Wishart, it's been seven days."

And what exactly do you want me to do about it?

"Wishart, you need to have a bowel movement. If you don't have one in the next few days, you will have to go on sick call. And you don't want to go on sick call. Sick call is for sissies."

Are you shitting me?

"So, I expect to hear a 'yes' next time. Understand, Wishart?"

"Yes, Sir." *Jaysus.*

Jan sat in the Dessert Corporal chair, the left end seat of the ten-person table. While holding up the cake, she announced, "Sir, the dessert for tonight is Martha Washington Sheet Cake! Does anyone not want Martha Washington Sheet Cake, Sir?"

"I don't want any," Dogety stated. Jan could cut nine slices, one for each remaining new cadet at the table. However, because it was always easier to cut an even number and because Jackson implied she was fat, Jan chose to cut only eight slices.

Many new cadets designed a template for this task, but Jan eyeballed it. Each piece had to be exactly the same size and the cuts had to be smooth. She took her time knowing Dogety would inspect it. "What's taking so long, Wishart? Haven't you finished yet?"

"No, Sir."

"Well, hurry up. We haven't got all night."

"Yes, Sir." She made one slice all the way down the center, cutting the cake in half. Then another cut right through the center of that line, making fourths. Then two more lines down the center of each quarter, making eight perfect pieces. The lines were straight, the pieces were even, but small pieces of cake had come up with the knife on each slice.

Can't help that. She held the cake up and announced, "Sir, the dessert has been cut and is ready for inspection, Sir!" She passed it to the new cadet to her right who passed it to the next one and so on until it reached her Squad Leader.

Doegty's face contorted as he inspected the cake. "New Cadet Wishart, you just butchered my Martha Washington Sheet Cake! How did you screw this up so badly?"

"No excuse, Sir!"

"Gawd, it's been raped!" The table was silent as Dogety showed the Martha Washington Sheet Cake to Jackson at the next table. "Look what Wishart did to this poor cake."

Cadet Jackson made a disgusted face and said, "Glad she's not on my table, man."

"Wishart, what were you thinking?"

"No excuse, Sir!"

"Damn straight, there's no excuse. It's a good thing I didn't want any! Otherwise, I'd really be pissed off."

Jan knocked twice on Cadet Jackson's door at 2100 hours. "ENTER!" Jan opened the door but stood in the hallway.

She saluted and said, "Sir, New Cadet Wishart reporting as ordered."

Jackson had been sitting at his desk. He stood up wearing the black shorts and white Academy crest t-shirt. Then he sat back down on his bed to put on his socks and running shoes. He stood up again, walked to the sink counter and combed his hair. Then he brushed his teeth. He finally whisked past Jan and said, "Follow me, Wishart."

In darkness, he led her across Central Area, past The Plain, onto the road that runs all the way up to Lusk Reservoir. He stopped just past the statue of Eisenhower. "Wishart, we are going to run every night until you start staying in the morning formations. This will not only build your stamina, it will give you incentive to finish the runs with the platoon. And it may help with your weight problem."

They began running. Jackson talked about the great ones of West Point: Grant, Lee, Pershing, Patton, MacArthur and Eisenhower. "They are turning in their graves now," he said, "because you are here."

Jan said nothing, thinking about her classmates shining their boots, memorizing poop, or finishing other duties.

"These great ones who came before us—their honor, their sacrifice and their spirit—are still here," he continued, "but you are tarnishing that legacy."

Jan remained silent.

"And it's my duty now, and the duty of all of us in the Long Gray Line, to ensure that this legacy remains unsullied."

Not a word.

"You will not make a mockery of this great institution."

Silence.

"Do you understand me, Wishart?"

Damn. A question. "Yes, Sir." And she did understand. She understood that Jackson was a *freaking asshole*.

They ran for three miles and returned the back way, coming to a walk at the underpass behind the Mess Hall. This was a noisy, bustling hub of activity during the day, but at that time of night, it was deserted and dimly lit. They reached a spot between the streetlights where it was completely dark.

"Halt, Miss Wishart."

Jan stopped. *Uh-oh.* She couldn't see a thing. Not Jackson, not the loading docks which were on the right, nor the solid rock wall on her left. But she heard him circling around her.

"It gets dark in battle, Wishart." He continued to circle in a wide arc, probably five feet away from her. "Sometimes you won't be able to see anything. You can't see the battlefield, you can't see your commanders, you can't see your troops and you certainly can't see the enemy."

No question. No response.

"This is what it's going to be like, Wishart," he continued. "You're gonna find yourself all alone in the dark."

No question. No response.

"Are you scared, Wishart?"

Dammit. "No, Sir."

"No?" He stopped circling. He remained silent for what seemed like a minute but might have only been twenty seconds. Then she felt him right behind her and she tensed. He leaned toward her left ear and whispered, "because in the dark you have no idea who's gonna sneak up on you."

No question. No response.

"ARE YOU SCARED, WISHART?"

She jumped. "NO, SIR!" But she was, actually.

He stepped back away from her. "Well, you should be, Wishart. You should be very afraid. Because in the time it took to have this little chat, you would have been killed in combat. Or worse."

Then she heard him take off running. He left her there alone in the dark to contemplate the worse part.

7

Thursday, May 6, 1982
2140 hours

Jan pinged back to her barracks, straight to Cadet Trane's room. She knocked twice, not loudly, not softly.

"Yeah!" A masculine voice yelled from inside. Jan opened the door but stayed standing in the hall.

"Sir, may I ask a question?" Trane sat on his bed in gym shorts and a white t-shirt. He was older than most firsties, very old in fact. He left enlisted ranks to enter West Point at the age of twenty-one. Now, at twenty-five, he was considered the "Grandfather" in H-3. But what made him special to Jan was that he openly dated a female cadet.

Her name was Cadet Williams, from Company I-3, another tall redhead. But Williams had curly hair, almost fuzzy, unlike Jan's straight hair. Williams also had enormous breasts. Too big, Jan thought, for a woman in uniform. And while Williams was mildly attractive, Jan didn't like her. Probably because she felt Cadet Trane could do better. *Cadet Williams probably has a great personality. Then again, it could be the boobs...*

Jan wished she had been in Trane's class. She felt certain she could have turned his head away from Cadet Williams, even without the boobs.

Trane was about six feet and probably weighed in the vicinity of one hundred and eighty pounds. He had the face of a thirty-something year old: seasoned, strong, yet a little soft around the edges. His hair was light brown, perhaps even slightly gray at the temples. He had a muscular build, without being over the top. It seemed he just came with that strong, wide chest, as opposed to having earned it in the gym. His lovely chest narrowed down to a perfectly tight waist. *Funny, women look for similar traits in men—big chests and small waists. Yet, the most attractive thing to me is kindness.*

Cadet Trane was kind, Jan could tell. Even when he hazed plebes, he did it with a slight smile. He never seemed to enjoy the yelling and screaming, as if hazing was beneath his personal standards of decorum.

Dating Cadet Williams, openly and unabashedly, gave him the most credibility. In Jan's estimation, he must have some sympathy or understanding for female cadets.

"Have they acquitted you yet?" he asked.

"No, Sir. Doesn't look like that will happen."

"Well, then, what can I do you for?" He often sounded like an old First Sergeant, the way he said things.

"Sir, I am allowed to have one cadet of my choosing to sit with me on the Honor Board, to provide support and advice, but I cannot ask anyone who is involved or will testify, so that rules out McCarron and Trane, and I cannot ask Cadet Hambin either, so, Sir, that leaves you." She took a deep breath.

"Whoa, there, Kemosabe. Slow down and run that by me again." Jan made her request again, calmer and slower. "Wait, are you asking me to be your cadet counsel at your Honor Board?" Trane asked.

"Yes, Sir. I think you would be very helpful to me."

"You do realize, Miss Wishart, that we are about to enter final exam week?"

"Yes, Sir."

"And you do realize that being on an Honor Board takes a considerable amount of time?"

"Yes, Sir."

"And do you realize that if I become your cadet counsel for your

Honor Board, there is a good chance I will not study adequately for my final exams and therefore jeopardize my own grade point average and put my own graduation in peril?"

"Yes, Sir."

"So you are asking me to sacrifice my well-being for your well-being, is that it, Miss Wishart?"

"Yes, Sir."

"Good. I hate goddamn exam week anyway. When do we start?"

"0800 hours tomorrow, room 413, Mahan Hall."

"Great, let's do it." This is why she was in love with Cadet Trane.

Jan returned to her room, changed into her shower uniform—gray polyester bathrobe over flip-flops with towel folded over one arm—and proceeded to the latrines. Alone in the white-tiled room, she turned on one of the six shower heads, removed her bathrobe, and hung it on one of the six hooks lined up on the opposite wall. She stepped under the hot spray of water and let it soak through her thick, short, straight, red hair. She opened the shampoo bottle and squeezed a dollop onto her palm and rubbed the gelatinous substance all through her hair until it became a big wad of foam. She massaged her scalp, neck, ears and face before tilting her head back under the water spray. The white bubbles cascaded down her face and neck, over her breasts, stomach, hips and thighs. She watched as the foaming stream continued its journey down her long legs and onto the white tiled floor where it swirled around in circles until it found the drain. The churning bubbles seemed to say, *"There's an inevitability to things."* Jan sensed the bubbly flow speaking to her, *"Water flows downstream, not up. Gravity pulls objects to the earth, not away. Honor Boards bend toward finding guilt, not innocence."*

The laws of the universe were not going to change for her. Two hundred years of brotherhood would not step aside so she could pass. Only one thing could change the tide. Jan wept huge, silent tears of anger, frustration and defeat, for she knew she didn't deserve a miracle.

"Kristi, no matter what happens, just tell the truth tomorrow," Jan said after Taps had played over the Corps-wide PA system. The three roommates lay awake in bed with the lights out.

"I will, Jan. I just wish I had looked more closely at you Monday morning. I wish I had noticed something was wrong and asked you about it before the day slipped away," Kristi said.

"You had no way of knowing anything. Hell, I had no idea he would bring honor charges on me. I should have. He had to cover his ass."

"Jan, if they find you guilty, I'm going to talk to my dad." Kristi meant her step-dad, the man who raised her.

"Okay. I'm sure he will be helpful." Jan figured Kristi would seek his counsel, comfort, or wisdom as any good father would provide.

"Yeah, I think he will be able to do something. What good is a presidential appointment if you can't use it once in a while?" Kristi said.

Jan hadn't fully computed Kristi's last sentence when Angel chimed in, "Kristi, is your dad in politics?"

"Not really. He was a business man before being appointed as an ambassador."

"Your dad's an ambassador?" Jan asked the question, but it came out more like a shocking statement.

"Yeah, didn't I ever tell you guys that?" Kristi asked.

"Uh, no, you neglected to mention that fun little fact," Jan said.

"Oh, sorry. I thought you knew. My real dad died in Vietnam. I told you that, right?"

"Yes, you told me that, but you never mentioned that your step-father is a freaking ambassador? To Germany, I suppose?" Jan couldn't believe it.

"Yup." Kristi said like it was no big deal.

"Jesus H. Christ, Kissy, all this time I had no idea you were so high up the food chain," Jan said.

"Well, it's really not that glamorous. But still, I do hope he can help out if things go badly here," Kristi said.

"Thanks, Kissy, but if I am found guilty, there's NO way I would stay, with or without your dad's influence. I mean, I appreciate the offer, but think about it, Kissy."

A guilty verdict from an Honor Board was rarely overturned,

although the Superintendent had the authority to do so. The few cadets who did return to the Corps after being found guilty of an honor violation basically lived in solitary confinement. Most other cadets would not have anything to do with the dishonored cadet. The "get-over" would room alone, eat alone and study alone. It was only slightly milder than the old silencing when cadets found guilty of honor and returned to the Corps, for whatever reason, were segregated completely into separate barracks, classes, formations and meals. "There's no future for me here if this thing goes badly," Jan said.

8

Q: What is Murphy's Law?
A: (1) Nature always sides with the hidden flaw.
       (2) Things, if left to themselves, go from bad to worse.
Heritage, Bugle Notes, 81, p. 246

Jan probably should have reported what "Jackass" had done on the remedial run, but any complaints would have to go up the chain of command which meant she would have to tell Dogety, then Dogety would tell Jackson and that's where it would stop. Or worse, "Jackass" might accuse her of lying because there weren't any witnesses. It was her word against his and he had all the power and influence in the situation. Besides, she was fairly sure she could handle him next time. Next time, she would just keep running until she reached the barracks. So, it seemed reporting the incident would only make things worse.

Things got worse anyway. Jan and Wright prepared their room for the first SAMI—Saturday AM Inspection. They tightened their beds and opened their closets displaying their uniforms on hangers exactly two inches apart. Their highly polished shoes and boots were lined up from tallest to shortest, left to right. Below the closet, two large drawers held their foldable garments, displayed according to the regulations manual. Underwear folded in thirds, left side over right, then crotch tucked underneath, lay folded side down. Bras looked like small hills among the panties, with one bra cup tucked into the other, clasp end stuffed into the hollow of the cups and displayed with cup opening down. They also swept, dusted and emptied the trashcan.

Two loud knocks announced the inspectors' arrival. "ENTER, SIR!" Cadets Dogety and Jackson sauntered into the room. Dogety inspected the sink cabinet and laundry bins while Jackson made a cursory look around the room dragging his finger along Jan's desk and shelves. He dropped down into a squat to peer under her bed for dust bunnies.

So far, so good.

Then Jackson proceeded over to the drawers beneath the closet. Looking down at Jan's underwear drawer, he picked up a bra holding it up by the strap with his forefinger and thumb. "What the hell is this, Wishart?"

"Sir, it is a bra."

"I know that, Wishart! What the hell is it doing on display?"

"Sir..."

"You think I wanna see this crap?" He threw the bra back in the drawer and slammed it shut with his foot. "I don't wanna see any goddamn bras or panties or tampons or sanitary pads. I don't wanna see any female shit. You understand?"

"Sir, the regulations...."

"IS THAT ONE OF YOUR FIVE RESPONSES, WISHART?" Jackson screamed.

"No, Sir."

"I don't give a shit what the REGs say. I DON'T WANT TO SEE THAT STUFF. YOU GOT ME, Wishart?"

"Yes, Sir."

"That goes for you, too, Wright!" Jackson added. "AM I CLEAR, BEANHEADS?"

"Yes, Sir," both roommates responded.

Jan began hiding underwear in her laundry bag and footlocker. Her tampons and pads, which she hadn't needed to date due to "Amen-oh-yay-ah," went in a woman's locker from Third Platoon. Every sign of femininity disappeared from her room and locker. She never asked Wright what she did with her female items; she wasn't sure Wright ever had that stuff.

About halfway through Beast, Sixth Company began having weekly "weigh-ins." Cadet Jackson sat behind a desk at the end of the hallway where a scale with adjustable weights had been placed. Cadet Dogety assembled Fourth Squad along the wall facing the scale and called them, one by one, to step on the scale.

"Pope, step up," Dogety yelled. New Cadet Pope stepped on the scale and Dogety adjusted the measurement. "172 pounds!"

"Pope—172 pounds!" Jackson repeated for clarification, apparently, and recorded it on a piece of paper.

"Not bad, Pope," Dogety said. "Now get off my scale. Jones, step up." Dogety fiddled with the weights again. "149 pounds."

"Jones—149 pounds!" Jackson said.

"You could stand to eat a little more, Jones."

"Yes, Sir." Jones replied.

"Now, get back against the wall. Wishart, step up!"

Oh damn. Please, please, please...don't let it be too high.

Dogety adjusted the weights. "160 pounds!" Dogety's voice sounded venomous.

"Wishart—160 pounds." Jackson repeated as he looked at Dogety, shaking his head slightly.

Does he really have to do that?

"My God, Wishart, what the hell have you been eating?" Jackson asked loudly enough for the whole hallway to hear. Jan couldn't think of a good answer. "Well, answer me!"

"Not much, Sir!"

"Is that one of your five responses?"

"No, Sir!"

"Then, I'll ask again. What the hell are you eating, Wishart?"

"No excuse, Sir!"

"Damned right there's no excuse! You're turning into the Pillsbury Doughboy! No wonder you cannot run worth a damn. I better start seeing this number go down. Do you understand me, Wishart?"

"Yes, Sir!"

"Now get the hell off my scale."

"Yes, Sir!" Jan turned, red faced and close to crying, to take her spot back against the wall with all nine of her squad mates.

"Teady, step up!" Dogety shouted.

And this is how Jan began to despise her beautiful, healthy, strong body.

Jan's table Commanders most often were either Dogety or Jackson, making it practically impossible for her to eat a decent meal. Yet, she didn't lose weight during Beast. In fact, she gained weight. She never understood how someone could eat so little, move so much, and put on weight. Still, she felt hungry most of the time in Beast.

That's why she went to church.

New Cadets had one *free* hour after dinner on Wednesday nights to attend Chapel. Jan wasn't sure what Chapel meant, being that she was raised in a good, lapsed-Catholic family. But if Chapel could get her away from the cadre for an hour, she would be more than happy to learn all about it. The real incentive, however, were the cookies. Cookies were given out at Chapel.

Exiting the huge Mess Hall doors opening onto The Apron, Jan pinged to Trophy Point beyond the far end of the Plain, on the bank of the Hudson River. As she moved away from the massive, gray, gothic structures toward the open beauty of the river and the surrounding hills, she felt an ever-so-slight lightening. Facing the blue water and sky had a calming effect.

She scarfed a few Oreos and sat in one of the folding chairs. Another new cadet sat next to her with about five cookies in each hand. She was glad to see someone else had come for the goods. Jan wished she had thought to grab a few extra. The guy must have read her mind as he leaned his left hand in front of Jan, offering cookies. She hesitated, knowing the Dogety/Jackson duo would not approve. *Wait! This is insane. I'm not going to let those jerks decide if I can eat cookies!* Jan reached over and took two of the offered cookies, smiling at the young man's kindness.

"I hope we can grab a few more before leaving," he said in a quiet voice.

"Me, too!" Jan admitted.

Someone started playing guitar, others started singing—and that's when it began to get awkward. But Jan figured this was a small price to pay for more cookies. The guy next to her sang beautifully. His voice soothed and comforted her, almost painfully so. Jan knew she might cry if she wasn't careful. For that reason, she stared straight ahead as if she were standing at attention.

The singing stopped and the man called "Chaplain," another unknown word to a lapsed-Catholic girl, began to speak. Jan could not remember anything he said that evening, except one sentence: "I lift mine eyes to the hills from whence cometh my help."

Her brain locked onto this sentence, and as Beast progressed, she said it over and over again. When doing leg lifts on The Plain, when running in formation, when marching in full combat gear, and when staring at her barely-eaten plate full of food in the Mess Hall, it became her mantra of sorts. Along with Jim Croce's song, "New York's Not My Home," this verse somehow comforted and sustained her.

"I will lift mine eyes to the hills from whence cometh my help," followed her like a prayer.

After Chapel, just as she and Wright began polishing their boots and quizzing each other on poop, they heard two loud knocks on the door. *It's probably Dogety or Jackson wanting to know how many cookies I ate!*

The two roommates popped to attention and yelled in unison, "ENTER, SIR!" The door flung open and Wright's Squad Leader stood at the door. He held out a whole, uncut, Martha Washington Sheet Cake.

"Just happened to have an extra one of these. Thought you two might want it." Jan and Wright stared in disbelief at this unexpected offer. Jan also wondered what the catch might be. Was he teasing them? Yet, the firstie simply stepped into their room, put the cake down on the sink counter, then turned and walked out.

First the guy at chapel offered her cookies, now this. *Well, maybe not everyone thinks I'm fat.*

9

Friday, May 7, 1982
0330 hours

The blueberry pie is sailing through the air in slow motion. It looks like a Frisbee, but she knows what it really is. The sweet scent floats toward her, closer and closer. She shuts her eyes and breathes in the perfume of warm blueberries. Her mouth waters in anticipation of that first bite.

The pie smashes into her face. Ah shit, how'd that happen? The blueberry goop drips from her nose and chin; somehow though, it looks like camouflage. She stands up. The entire Mess Hall is silent. Everyone is watching the girl with the blueberry face. She hopes they will assume that she's covered in combat paint, yet she cannot tell what they see. She turns to run away from the table, but her body feels like it's underwater. Her feet seem to have grown roots into the floor. The muscles in her legs ache with every arduous step. She keeps running, slowly and painfully, until she reaches the massive, oak doors. With the speed of peanut butter, she descends the granite steps.

She hears Cadet Jackson laughing from his table inside the Mess Hall. Then Cadet Dogety starts laughing even though he is at the opposite end of the Mess Hall. Another cadet begins to laugh from the third wing, then another joins in, and then another. Soon the entire

Corps of Cadets is laughing. Even the waiters are laughing. She knows they are laughing at her.

She keeps running toward her room and finally arrives just as the two-minute bell is being called. She must report to formation. But her Dress Gray is ruined. Blueberry goop has stained all of her uniforms. There is nothing she can wear. The minute caller leaves his post. She has to go to formation. Now.

She pings back outside and stands in the squad line. Everyone is staring at her. The Commander shouts, "Forward, March!" She begins marching in formation with her Company onto The Plain. All the other companies are already there and formed into a large circle. Company H-3 marches into the center of the huge circle. The Commander shouts, "Wishart, stand fast!" The rest of H-3 marches away toward the outer ring of cadets. Alone, in the center of the circle, Jan stands at attention, completely naked.

10

"Cadets cultivate the habit of not offering excuses. There is no place in the military profession for an excuse for failure. Extenuating circumstances may be explained and submitted, but, even if accepted, such explanations are never considered excuses."
The Fourth Class System, Bugle Notes, 81, p.72

The last week of Cadet Basic Training finally arrived and began with a grueling 14-mile road (and off-road) march in full gear to Lake Frederick. The new cadets and cadre wore the OD green, Army fatigues, helmets and Load Bearing Equipment (LBE) which held the water canteen, bayonet, compass and other necessary items. Then the rucksack went over everything—holding socks, underwear, personal hygiene items, sleeping bag, pup tent and various field training equipment. They also wore their, now worn in, Army issued combat boots and carried M-16 automatic rifles.

They had completed plenty of marches in full gear, but none more than five miles. This last march would be more than double the length of any previous marches. "You WILL NOT fall behind on this march," Dogety told Jan a few days before. In fact, he informed the entire squad that no one would be allowed to quit the march to Lake Frederick. For any reason. Period.

He also warned them about "Bear Hill" near the end of the march.

"It's a do-or-die hill," Dogety told the entire squad. "You will either make it to the top of this hill or you will die trying. Especially you, Wishart."

"Yes, Sir." Jan could march with the best of them. As long as the formation didn't break into a run, she knew she would make it.

"Everyone who ascends Bear Hill successfully will be welcomed into the Corps of Cadets. Those who don't, well, they just aren't cut out for the Academy." Dogety reiterated this sentiment on several occasions before and during the march.

The first six miles went smoothly for Jan. They stopped every couple of miles for a brief water break. At some of those water breaks, they were ordered to take off their combat boots and change their socks.

At the seventh mile, Jan began noticing a pain in her left big toe. She didn't mention it to anyone knowing that Dogety would tell her to "suck it up" anyway. Besides, a little blister could not, and would not, keep her from marching. However, by the tenth mile, her toe began throbbing. At the next sock change, she took her boot and wet sock off to discover a massive blister. A soft liquid-filled lump bulged on top of a larger, harder lump.

As she examined her toe, Dogety walked over and saw the bulbous growth. "Wishart, why didn't you say something? That's the biggest blister I've ever seen." He yelled for the medic.

"Sir, may I make a statement?"

"What is it, Wishart?"

"Sir, it's fine. I can march just fine."

"Yeah, well, that looks like it's infected. It needs medical attention, ASAP."

"Sir, I don't want to stop..."

"I know, I know, Wishart. But you gotta do what you gotta do. And that thing isn't going away on it's own."

Dogety walked away as a young Army specialist assigned to Sixth Company came running over. He took one look at her blister and said, "I gotta drain it."

"How do you do that?" Jan feared he might have to take her

somewhere which would cause her to lose her place in the squad.

"I'm going to lance it and push out the puss. Then I'll clean and bandage it and you should be good to go."

"Can you do it fast? I've gotta stay with my squad."

He was fast and good. He made a small cut with a tiny surgical tool, and then he pushed on her toe with his fingers. Jan had never seen anything so disturbing in all her years. The bump exploded. A gush of ooze came shooting out of her toe. She wasn't sure it was still her toe or some alien creature. He continued to squeeze until every last drop of the evil fluid emptied. Then he wiped it with an antiseptic pad and wrapped it with gauze and tape. He told her to have it looked at again once she got to Lake Frederick.

"Will you come take a look at it?" Jan asked. He smiled and said he'd try to find her. She decided there should be a merit badge for any man who could push that kind of goop out of a body and not throw up.

The line was back up and moving. Jan returned to her spot in the middle of the squad where Dogety had positioned her so that the "front could pull and the back could push her," if necessary.

Her toe felt amazingly better and she marveled at what seemed to be a miracle cure. The pain of the cut and the pushing on the toe were nothing compared to how it felt when it held all that crap inside. Once released, the toe was free to be a toe again—instead of a putrid vessel. For some reason, she thought a long time about that blister. *Once it was cut open and drained of the bad shit, it immediately felt better. And it works again without pain!*

At mile thirteen they stopped for the last water and sock change. Dogety came down the squad line and stopped in front of Jan. "Wishart, we are about to ascend Bear Hill." He looked directly at her. "You know what that means?"

"Yes, Sir."

"Well, just to be safe, I am going to march right in front of you. As I have already said, I am not going to lose anyone to this hill, not even you, Wishart."

"Yes, Sir."

"If you start falling behind, you are to grab onto my rucksack. I will carry your ass up that hill if I have to."

"Yes, Sir." But Jan cursed him in her mind, saying to herself, *"There's no freakin' way I'm going to touch him."*

She soon discovered Bear Hill was neither particularly high nor steep. As they climbed upward, the pace picked up. And then she understood why it was called "Bear Hill." Not because of its size but to see who could *bear* it. About halfway up at this faster pace, to her great dismay, she started breathing heavily and falling behind. *We're practically running this damn hill!* The squad mate behind her began stepping on her heels. She realized this was not a good time to die on her sword. With much reservation and humiliation, she grabbed Dogety's rucksack. As bad as that was, it was better than failure.

Strangely enough, Dogety seemed pleased that she had taken him up on his offer. While never dropping the pace, he turned his head to the side and shouted, "That's it, Wishart, hang on."

For one moment, halfway up Bear Hill, he became her *Knight in Drabby Green.* Yet, she detested him even more for it, so she pretended he was that nice medic instead.

The whole squad made it to the top of Bear Hill and Cadet Dogety was briefly proud of his little charges. They all marched to Lake Frederick as one squad and began setting up their pup tents. The field soon began looking like something out of the Civil War with some eight hundred small tents all lined up in rows.

"Look across the field, Wishart, at that deuce-and-a-half pulling up," Dogety said, pointing to a truck carrying a dozen or so new cadets. Jan watched as they hobbled out from the back of the vehicle. "Do you see them, Wishart?"

"Yes, Sir."

"Those are the ones who didn't make the march—the weak, the lazy, the pathetic. Aren't you glad you're not one of them?"

"Yes, Sir." And she was.

Jan had not had a period since before R-Day, which was *perfectly normal* and perhaps the best thing to happen during Beast barracks.

But she broke out in a rash covering her back, chest, legs and arms. It had spread to her face by the time they reached Lake Frederick. Dogety noticed the next morning.

"What the hell, Wishart? You look like you have chicken pox. What's going on?"

"No excuse, Sir."

"Seriously, you put something on your face or what?"

"No, Sir."

"Well, what happened? You look like you got some rare disease."

"Yes, Sir."

"I ASKED WHAT HAPPENED, WISHART?"

"I don't know, Sir."

"It was probably something you ate."

Day three into Lake Frederick, Dogety handed Jan a padded helmet attached to a goalie mask. "Wishart, put this on!" He tossed her a padded vest, like a baseball catcher's. "This, too."

"Sir, what is this for?"

"You're first in the Pugil Boxing ring."

What? Pugil Boxing? Dogety led his squad to an open area with a ring of stacked sandbags. The other squads from Second Platoon were already seated on three quarters of the sandbag ring. Fourth Squad filled in the remaining quarter. Dogety motioned for Jan to step in the ring.

Jan stood in the center of the makeshift ring, wondering what she was supposed to do. Dogety handed her a long stick with padding on each end. "Don't embarrass me, Wishart!" he said before stepping out of the ring.

Before Jan could contemplate the situation any further, she heard a familiar, wild scream. She twirled around just in time to see Wright leaping over the sandbag wall between two seated new cadets. She wore the same outfit as Jan—padded helmet with mask, chest vest and the long padded stick. *Oh shit! Not Wright!*

Wright immediately began pummeling Jan with the Pugil Stick.

Cheering rose up from the circle of new cadets—mostly yelling for

Wright. But one voice shouted, "C'mon Wishart! You can do it!"

Do what? Jan began to hit back. She took a few jabs at Wright, who was clearly the Alpha dog in this fight. Jan felt sick to her stomach. Her mind raced back to the first time she rode a roller coaster. *I just want it to be over! Please let it be over!*

Wright's smile, beaming through the facemask, belied her intent. A left jab, out of nowhere, knocked Jan off balance. Then another on her right sent her falling backwards. She found her footing and swung back, but Wright ducked and came up with another blow at Jan. The circle of new cadets continued to cheer for Wright except for one voice shouting for Jan. With jellied knees, she swung a few more times, once hitting Wright in the arm. Still, it wasn't even close. Wright pummeled until Jan fell down on both knees. Wright was declared the victor and two more new cadets were chosen to do battle in the Pugil Boxing war.

Once everyone took a turn in the Gladiator ring, Cadet Jackson dismissed the platoon for dinner. "Wishart, stand fast," Dogety barked. Jan stood at attention by the sandbag ring while everyone else ran off. "You gave up, didn't you?"

How should I answer that? Jan didn't want to say yes or no. Neither one would be quite right.

"Didn't you?" Dogety asked again.

"Yes, Sir."

"What the hell, Wishart? Why did you give up without even trying?"

Um, maybe because I don't know how to physically fight? Or because Wright scared the shit out of me. "No excuse, Sir."

"You continually perplex me, Wishart! Why are you even here? Where do you think you are exactly?" Jan couldn't think of a good answer. "Do you think you can just give up in war when the enemy seems to have the advantage? Geez, Wishart, you aren't at Girl Scout camp for God's sake!"

I know, I know, but....

"Do you have anything to say for yourself?"

"No excuse, Sir!"

"Wishart, sometimes you are a sorry piece of shit."

"Yes, Sir."

Last in line again for the dinner meal, she picked up a tray and entered the Mobile Serving Station. An Army specialist plopped what looked like chili into a paper bowl and passed it to her. Another specialist pushed a paper plate with cornbread toward her. She picked up a pint of milk, passed on the chips and brownies, and walked out of the other end of the vehicle.

At Lake Frederick, the cadre ate with cadre and the new cadets ate with their squads. Both Dogety and Jackson, sitting on a patch of grass near the exit of the serving station, looked up when she emerged.

"What's on your plate, Wishart?" Jackson asked.

"Chili, cornbread and milk," she answered.

"Chili, cornbread and milk, WHAT?" Dogety demanded.

"Sir! Chili, cornbread and milk, SIR!" she said *with attitude* as her mother use to say.

"Do you really need to eat that cornbread, Wishart?" Jackson asked again.

Suddenly she had had enough. "Sir, you can have my damn cornbread," she said as she threw it at him.

"What the hell!" Jackson jumped up and stormed toward Jan.

Dogety got to her first. "Wishart, go inside the mess station, NOW." Jan turned and ran up the three steps. Dogety stood at the bottom of the steps while Jackson tried to push past him. "Markus, leave it alone," she heard him say quietly to Jackson.

"What the hell are you doing, man? You saw what she did," Jackson yelled at his friend.

"Yeah, I saw it, and I'll deal with it," Dogety said.

"Like you've been doing? Your plan ain't working so well, Sam. I'll deal with her myself."

"Settle down, Markus. She's in my squad. I'll take care of it." Jan had never heard Dogety defend her before.

Jackson stared at Dogety in disbelief for a moment. Then he said, "You're pussy-whipped, aren't you, Sam? She giving you something, is that it?"

Dogety grabbed Jackson by his shirt with both hands, "I said that's enough. Let's not make this worse than it is." Jan watched as the two firstie friends seemed locked in a trance. Then Dogety let go of Jackson's shirt.

"You're an idiot," Jackson mumbled as he turned away.

Dogety looked into the mess station and said, "Wishart, come here." Jan ran down the three steps, still holding her mess tray with the chili and milk. "Don't ever pull that kind of shit again, you got me?"

"Yes, Sir."

"You could have been in a truckload of trouble if Jackson wanted to push it. I plan to finish Beast with my entire squad intact. That includes even you."

"Yes, Sir."

"If you pull another stunt like that, I will not be able to protect you. You got me?"

"Yes, Sir."

"Now go eat with the rest of the squad."

"Yes, Sir."

She approached her squad, nine male new cadets sitting nearby on the grass, all of whom had witnessed the mess station incident. Without an opening in their circle, she sat down just outside the loop. She hoped someone would move over, making room for her to join, but that didn't happen. After an awkward minute of silence, they resumed their talking and laughing.

Well, now they must love me even more.

She observed the other squads with women. Wright laughed in the midst of her squad. Plowden and McCarron seemed fully engaged with their squads. *And here I am sitting by myself, talking to myself. Maybe it's just me. Maybe I'm just never going to fit in here.*

At that very moment, New Cadet Hambin turned around. "Hey, Wishart, what the hell just happened?"

"Oh, I just threw my cornbread at Jackson."

"Whoa! That's gutsy—throwing your food at Jackson!"

"Yah, well, I just got sick and tired of his shit."

"Did Dogety save you?" Hambin asked.

"I guess so. He's never done THAT before."

"Maybe he feels bad about the pugil boxing."

"Well, he should. That was miserable." Jan admitted.

"I thought you did fine. I mean, I wouldn't want to go up against Wright either!"

"Thanks, but it was no contest really. I kind of gave up."

"Well, I was cheering for you!"

"I thought I heard one fan in the crowd!" Jan smiled at him.

"You didn't do any worse than some others." Hambin said.

"Thanks, I'm just glad it's over."

"That makes two of us!"

Andrew Hambin, called Drew by friends and family, grew up on a farm in Oklahoma. Beautiful would be an understatement for Drew Hambin. He was model gorgeous, stunning actually, at about five feet eight inches tall with blonde hair and blue eyes. Jan mostly noticed his long fingers. She wondered how he could be both gorgeous and nice. Those qualities usually didn't go together in most men, Jan believed. But there they were in Drew Hambin, an enormously handsome AND kind young man. He even agreed that Dogety and Jackson seemed to take a particular interest in hazing Jan. Then she knew that it wasn't *all in her head.*

The Land Navigation Course was the final challenge of Lake Frederick week. Armed with a compass and a map, the new cadets had to find ten stamps matching the ones on their checklist. At least fifty different stamps had been set across the thousand or so acres of wilderness surrounding Lake Frederick. Once all ten stamps were found, the new cadet could then proceed to the finish point. Cadets had two hours to complete this challenge.

Jan found herself alone for the first time in seven weeks. She slowed down to enjoy the quiet of the forest and the precious moments of solitude.

"What do you think you're doing, Wishart? This isn't some nature walk!!" Jackson seemed to sneak up on her, again.

Where'd he come from? "Yes, Sir."

"Have you found all your stamps yet?"

"No, Sir."

"Then why are you bird-watching? Do you think the stamps will find you?"

"No, Sir."

"Wishart, did you think you could just blow off this last challenge?"

"No, Sir."

"Then get your ass moving and find the rest of your stamps, Wishart! I want you double-timing this course!"

"Yes, Sir." Jan began jogging in boots, helmet, rucksack and rifle.

Not satisfied, Jackson ran behind her and screamed, "PICK UP THE PACE, WISHART!" She felt him on her heels right before he shoved her forward. The force of his push knocked her onto the ground. The M-16 flew a few feet ahead while her helmet dropped down over her eyes.

Jan assessed the situation: she was on her knees in the middle of the woods with Jackson standing over her. *Shit.* But this time, she didn't feel afraid. She wasn't the least bit scared. Nope. Only pissed off. Goddamn angry.

She stood up slowly. Even more slowly and dramatically, she turned around to face Jackson. If he thought she was about to lose it, he would have made a good assumption. She stared at him for a few long seconds, gathering her rage, reining it in. Then calmly, with complete control, she said, "Jackson, if you ever touch me again, I will make sure you regret it for a very, very long time."

Jackson stood still. He seemed unsure of what to do. Then, as if clearing an image, he shook his head and seethed, "If you ever try to humiliate me again, Wishart, YOU will regret it. I promise you that!"

Neither one moved. They were locked in a staring trance for another long moment until Jan bent down and picked up her M-16. Then turning her back on Jackson, she walked away, realizing the power of anger.

11

Friday, May 7, 1982
0800 Hours

Cadet Trane held the door for Jan as they entered room 413 of Mahan Hall. *When's the last time THAT happened??* She wondered if she would ever meet another man like Trane and secretly hoped he *would* fail his final exams. *Maybe then he'll have to repeat firstie year and I could snag him while Cadet Williams is stationed in Korea.*

Everyone sat in the same seats. Cadet Trane took the chair to Jan's right, closest to the witness. She heard Jackson say "Morning, Bill." She saw Trane nod in return without saying anything. She hoped that meant he didn't like Jackson either.

Conrad opened his thick file and cleared his throat. "Welcome back, everyone. We have a lot to get to today and I want to keep on track as much as possible. Because final exams begin Monday, I hope to finish by today or tomorrow at the latest. We will continue to be thorough in all we do, of course."

Of course you will.

"So at this point, Cadet Wishart may now question Cadet Jackson," Conrad said as he waved his hand in Jan's direction.

Jan knew Jackson would not betray his own testimony. She couldn't expect him to change his story, even if confronted with her version of events. Yet she decided she would highlight some of the discrepancies in their statements. Maybe she could draw him out, even a little, from what he said happened. She also wanted him to verify, confirm and solidify other parts of his statement—in hopes that it could be contradicted later.

She turned to face Jackson although it hurt her eyes to look at him. "Cadet Jackson, you stated that I had the routing envelope at all times between Cadet Dogety's room and yours."

"Yes, you said as much yourself," Jackson said.

"You also admitted that you were in the latrine during my last trip to your room when I left the routing envelope leaning against your door where you found it."

"Yes, that's right, but it could not have been there for more than two minutes. I only took a leak, Miss Wishart, not a dump." A few chuckles punctuated the room.

They think this is funny. "But you have to admit, Cadet Jackson, that the routing envelope was unattended for a time when it was not in my possession."

"Yes, like I said, I doubt anyone could have changed its contents in the minute or two it sat at my door—or that anyone else would have a reason to change its contents."

"Except if someone really wanted to mess with me, they could have done it at that time, right Cadet Jackson? If someone wanted, let's say, to teach me a lesson, to get me in trouble, or to make me look insubordinate?"

"Cadet Wishart, if you are insinuating that I had something to do with writing that note, just to get you in trouble, you are going down the wrong rabbit trail."

"I simply want to verify that the envelope was out of my possession for a time before it was in your possession," she clarified.

He said, "Yes, for probably no more than two minutes."

"And then, when you found the envelope, how long was it before you brought it to Cadet Dogety's room?"

"I took it over right away...maybe about 2045 hours."

"Did anyone else see or touch the envelope in that time between

71

your room and Cadet Dogety's room?" she asked.

"No, just me."

"Okay, so just to be clear, you had the envelope for approximately fifteen minutes after it left my possession and before Cadet Dogety saw it."

"About that, yes. But I didn't write that note Wishart, and you know it."

"I just want to clarify that the envelope was NOT ALWAYS in my possession that night." She looked over at the *jury of her peers.* Their expressions gave nothing away.

"Okay, Wishart, it was in my possession while I walked it over to Cadet Dogety's room. Happy?"

"And when you and Dogety questioned me in the CQ room," Jan continued, "would you say the tone was 'conversational' or 'adversarial?'"

"When was the last time any firstie was 'conversational' with you? Despite being this close to Recognition, most firsties are still not 'conversational' with plebes." He raised his voice slightly.

That's it, Jackson. Show your anger. "Exactly, Cadet Jackson," she refused to call him Sir. "So you would characterize the CQ room questioning as adversarial?"

"We questioned you the way firsties question plebes. Is that what you mean?"

"Yes, you had me standing at attention against the wall and screaming at me about two inches from my face, correct?" This was not unusual plebe/upperclassman interaction, but she wanted the Honor Board members to picture it.

"We were angry with you. You screwed up AGAIN. So, yes, we had you in the smack position which was appropriate given the circumstances."

"Okay, but only *you* screamed in my face, right? Cadet Dogety did not scream at me in the CQ room. In fact, Cadet Dogety asked you to calm down, didn't he?"

"I don't recall that."

"You don't remember screaming in my face or you don't remember

Cadet Dogety asking you to calm down?"

"I recall screaming at you, maybe in your face, as you put it. But I don't recall that Cadet Dogety didn't do the same, or if he asked me to calm down."

"He asked you to calm down or quiet down at least three times. You don't remember any of that?"

"No, I don't recall that."

"One last thing, Cadet Jackson. When I came to your room at 0515 hours, you were still in bed, correct?"

"I was sitting on my bed, yes. You were late, remember?"

"Yes, I was late, but you were still *lying* in bed when I arrived. Do you not remember that either?"

"I DO remember that, Miss Wishart. I was sitting up and waiting for you to arrive."

That was the crux of the problem. Jan's version and his version of that morning were entirely different. And no one else witnessed what really happened.

Cadet Trane slid a piece of paper in front of Jan. She read his handwriting which was not at all easy to do. *That's enough for now. You will piss everyone off if you keep pushing him.*

"That's all I have, Sir," Jan stated as she looked directly at Cadet Conrad.

12

Q: Where do plebes rank?

A: Sir, the Superintendent's dog, the Commandant's cat, the waiters in the Mess Hall, the Hell Cats, the Generals in the Air Force, and all the Admirals in the whole damned Navy.

Heritage, Bugle Notes, 81, p.243

They marched back from Lake Frederick to the gray walls of West Point where the ratio of upperclassmen to new cadets tripled. With yearlings and cows back from their summer training, plebes never stopped saluting and shouting, "Good morning, Sir," "Good afternoon, Ma'am" or "Good evening, Sir" while pinging and squaring off, from reveille to taps. The new cadets also received their first promotion—to "cadets." They were still plebes, so it was like going from "private" to "private first class." They were still the lowest things around.

Another transition from Beast to the academic year required moving to new companies. Perhaps because the military lifestyle is one of constant transience, West Point didn't allow anyone to stay in one place very long. Plebes were scattered from the ten Beast companies to the four regiments—called First, Second, Third and Fourth Regiments respectively. Each regiment had nine companies—Company A through Company I. Jan was assigned to H-Company, Third Regiment, the *H-3 Hamsters.*

Angel Trane introduced herself to Jan. The petite, soft-spoken, black girl from Queens, New York seemed shy and introverted, not anything like Leslie Wright. *And she looks like she might fall over on a breezy day.*

"I'm Jan Wishart," her voice cracked. Saying and hearing her own first name for the first time in seven weeks choked her up. She never liked her first name. It was plain and boring. 'Jan' wasn't even short for Janice or Janet or Janiqua. Still, she almost cried when she said it aloud to Angel.

With very little talking, the new roommates began to put their room in order for inspection. They were fast at work when they were interrupted by the telltale knock of an upperclassman—two loud thumps—like he was trying to knock the door down.

"ENTER, SIR!" the roommates yelled simultaneously while popping to attention. The door slammed open. There stood a familiar firstie— the cream of the crop, the best of the best, a demi-god in their eyes, a perfect specimen—his gig line absolutely straight, dress-off tight, shoes sparkling, saber gorgeously at the hip, and white gloves in hand.

Stunning piece of work.

"So, I take it you are Trane?" Cadet Trane nodded to Angel.

"I am, Sir," she replied.

"Oh."

Silence.

"Well, my name is also Trane," he said, "and I thought we might be related."

Pause.

Jan bit her lip trying not to laugh.

"Guess not, huh?" Trane was probably of Irish or English descent but certainly not African.

"No, Sir," squeaked Angel.

Cadet Trane started laughing. The two women looked at each other and tried not to laugh, but they started chuckling anyway. They quickly recovered their composure, unsure how this firstie would react to their lapse in decorum. Cadet Trane kept laughing. So they smiled with him.

75

Leslie Wright was sent to I-3 while Kristi McCarron and Debra Plowden became roommates in H-3. Having Kristi in the same company almost made up for the presence of someone Jan hoped would NOT be in her new company—Dogety. *At least Jackson is far, far away from me in B-1!*

Drew went to G-3, but because G and H companies shared a floor, he ended up in the room next to Jan's. They became even better friends, winking to each other when passing and stopping in each other's rooms for supplies, questions or advice. If roommates weren't available, they gave each other dress-offs and checked gig lines. They often studied together in Jan's room because Drew's roommates didn't like having females in their room. The door had to remain open whenever the opposite sex was present. An open door was also an open invitation for upperclassmen to harass them from the hallway which most plebes wanted to avoid whenever possible. Jan and Angel didn't mind that though. They figured Drew's presence trumped any threat of hazing.

Jan arrived at her first class two days later and sat at a vacant desk in the middle of the classroom—not too far, not too close. She looked around the room. *No other women.*

"CLASS ATTENTION!" The cadets popped out of their chairs as the professor entered the room. The Army Captain walked to the "P's" desk and dropped his three-ring binder and books. Then he went through the room, inspecting shoes, haircuts, gig lines, dress-offs and any other aspects of the cadets' appearances.

"Cadet Jamison, did you shave this morning?" Captain McGinn asked.

"Yes, Sir," Jamison said.

"Well, it looks like you missed a few spots. Make sure you come to my class with a clean-shaven face next time."

"Yes, Sir."

The professor found some fault with each one of them. "Your shoes haven't been shined, Mr. Trawick."

"Yes, Sir."

"They better be sparkling for the next class."

"Yes, Sir."

Captain McGinn came to Jan's desk and walked completely around her. When he faced her again he asked, "Miss Wishart, when's the last time you had a haircut?"

"Just yesterday, Sir."

"Well, they didn't take enough off. Your hair is below the bottom edge of the collar of your shirt."

Jan didn't comment because he hadn't asked her a question. Captain McGinn moved his eyes down her body until he reached her shoes. After a longer than normal pause, he said, "Miss Wishart, don't expect special treatment from me. I don't play favorites with female cadets like some of my colleagues do."

She decided she didn't need to respond to that either. But then he asked, "Do I make myself clear, Miss Wishart?"

"Yes, Sir."

Captain McGinn finished examining his new students and said, "Take seats!" The cadets sat down behind their desks which had been arranged in rows and columns. The professor walked to his desk and picked up the binder. "Now, everyone stand back up," he said. "When I call your name, I want you to pick up your desk and move it to form a line starting on my right, your left. Andress!" Cadet Andress picked up his desk and placed it down on one side of Captain McGinn's desk. "Clarbonne! Ferguson! Juten! Laramore!" He continued to name cadets. Each one lifted his desk and placed it in the line. The desks turned at the corner of the room, forming an open rectangle.

The entire class had been called except for Jan. She continued standing behind her desk, now enveloped on three sides by her classmates. Captain McGinn closed his binder, placing it back on his desk. Jan was not about to move without being told.

"Miss Wishart, take your desk and move it to my left, your right," he said. She lifted her desk and placed it in the very last spot in the three-sided rectangle.

Captain McGinn put down his binder and picked up the teacher's edition of the history textbook. He walked to the left of his desk and sat down on top of Jan's desk. Facing everyone else in the class, he said, "Open your textbooks to the table of contents." Jan opened her book and laid it on her lap because Captain McGinn's ass took up her entire desktop. "I expect you to read three to four chapters for every class," he said. "And sometimes more. There will be pop quizzes whenever I feel like it and weekly exams on the reading every Friday."

Jan could hear Captain McGinn quite clearly although she could only see his back. He stood up and wrote the homework assignment on the chalkboard, then he walked fully around his desk before sitting back down on top of Jan's desk.

This was just part of the game. Jan learned a thing or two from Beast and her strategy for this professor would be the same. Keeping a blank facial expression, she would not belie her thoughts. Other than the customary "yes, Sir" or "no, Sir" during the inspection, she would not speak in class. She resolved to keep her head down and never show emotion. *I am a stone.*

West Point required all cadets to participate in athletics, either on a Corps (Varisty) team, a Club team or an intramural team. One could never just hang out, go for a walk, meditate, or—*God forbid*—take a nap. Down time was frowned upon.

Angel Trane made the rowing team as the coxswain because she weighed a hundred pounds soaking wet. Debra Plowden had been recruited for the swim team. That left Jan and Kristi as the only plebe women on the H-3 intramural soccer team. It was either that or intramural lacrosse which involved a stick. After the pugil boxing experience, Jan never wanted to touch anything resembling a stick.

Neither woman had ever played soccer and it showed. They couldn't kick the ball worth a damn. The team soon learned to keep the activity away from them, and they soon learned to stay out of the way. It was a good understanding.

All through September and most of October, after classes on Mondays, Wednesdays and Fridays, Jan and Kristi marched to the soccer field for an intramural match which Jan renamed "intra-murder." While everyone else played soccer, Jan and Kristi talked. She was not sure why she started calling Kristi, "Kissy," but since Kristi didn't object, the name stuck.

Jan learned that Kristi's real father died in Vietnam when she was five years old. Her mother announced, "Your father is dead," and that's all she was told. No one in the family ever mentioned his name again. In high school, she finally researched how he died.

"Helicopter crash. He was the pilot. Most likely shot down. Never saw it coming. Four other men on board." Kristi rattled off the facts like she was reading a list of ingredients.

Jan could not imagine losing a parent. Her family completely intact, both parents still married, all siblings alive and accounted for. She remembered the Vietnam War, of course, and the body counts each night on the news. The Wishart parents tried to shelter their children from the coverage, but Jan heard it anyway. Yet, she never actually knew anyone who went to Vietnam, never mind anyone who died there. Kristi seemed to have lived through the war, while Jan just lived through the news of the war.

Every Wednesday evening at 1900 hours, the H-3 plebes assembled in the Company dayroom. The 1976 cheating scandal, still an open wound for the Academy, resulted in weekly honor classes for plebes. Using scenarios, role-playing and hypotheticals, they dissected the Honor Code's succinct statement: "A Cadet will not lie, cheat, or steal, nor tolerate those who do."

A "lie" not only meant telling an un-truth but also quibbling, making evasive statements or embellishing stories. "Cheating" was not limited to copying someone's paper or stealing answers to a test. It included cutting corners in any area of life—to take something away from the full experience of a duty, sport or task. "Stealing," meant taking something that did not belong to you or taking something without paying for it. It could also mean taking credit for someone's words, ideas or creativity.

Jan sat on one of the four, worn out, burnt-orange couches in the dayroom next to Kristi McCarron. Plebes were still not allowed to speak to one another in public so Jan nodded and smiled at her new friend and Company mate. Then Kristi whispered, "How's the 'amen-oh-yay-ah' going?"

"Great!" Jan whispered back, "You?"

"Perfect! I could get used to this!"

Cadet Trane, the Company Honor Representative, handed out papers to the H-3 plebes. "Take a moment to read over the first scenario," he said. Jan shared a paper with Kristi as they read silently:

```
Two brothers, both cadets, were home on
leave.  One brother brought his girlfriend to a
nightclub where she used a fake ID to gain entry
and to purchase alcoholic drinks.  When the other
brother found out, he thought this could be an
honor violation. What should he do?
```

He should get his own damn girlfriend.

"Alrighty then. Everyone finished reading the first scenario?" Cadet Trane asked. "What do you think? Was this a violation of the Honor Code?" The plebes remained silent for a few moments. "Anyone care to comment?"

"Sir, yes, the Code has been breached," Cadet Winnans answered.

Tool! Jan hated when some cadets gave the "correct" answer instead of a real answer.

"Why's that, Cadet Winnans?" Trane asked.

"Sir, the cadet obviously knew his girlfriend was lying and cheating. She lied about her age and cheated the nightclub which had a responsibility to serve only legal adults."

Are you shitting me?

Another H-3 plebe spoke, "Well, I think it really depends on what she looked like." Laughter lit up the room. Jan glared at Rick Davidson, trying to decide how she felt about him. With Winnans, it was clear—he was an idiot. Rick Davidson, on the other hand, was harder to judge. He was prior service like Cadet Trane, but with one major difference. Davidson earned a combat patch for participating in the doomed Iranian hostage rescue mission.

Operation Eagle Claw, a highly risky operation, ran into a series of unfortunate events, which led to then-President Jimmy Carter's decision to abort. On the return flight, a refueling helicopter kicked up sand which flew into the nose of a transport plane causing it to explode. Eight men died. No one seemed to know Rick Davidson's exact role in the experience, but everyone knew he had been there.

"Or maybe it should depend on what HE looked like," Jan blurted out. *He's just another plebe like the rest of us.*

Cadet Trane brought the discussion back, "Well, he's on leave, right? He's not responsible for his girlfriend, is he?" Jan detected a hint of "pissed-off-ness" in his voice.

Maybe Trane thinks this scenario is ridiculous, too!

"Sir, he was aware of her false actions. He knowingly allowed her to lie and cheat. That makes it an Honor Code violation," Winnans insisted.

"What are you talking about?" Kristi McCarron practically shouted. "Was he supposed to hold her hostage until she gave up her fake ID? She is not his property! She can do what she wants!"

Rick Davidson said, "Well, not if he's paying." Laughter erupted again.

Winnans is a tool which he probably can't help. But Davidson is just being a jerk. "So if you are paying, your date has to do whatever you want? Is that how you work, Davidson?" Jan locked into eye contact with him.

No one else had challenged him before, and everyone could tell Jan was not joking. She resented that Davidson seemed to get "a pass" most of the time. No one argued with men who had combat patches which Jan somewhat understood. *Still, we are all equals here.*

"Whoa, easy there, Wishart. I'm just joking," Davidson said. Her Company mates went quiet. Jan felt a rush of blood in her neck and cheeks.

"Okay, back to the issue here," Trane said. "Miss McCarron has a point. Contrary to Mr. Davidson's thoughts, the woman has a right to do what she wants."

81

"Yes, but her boyfriend should not have participated in her actions. He should not have even gone to the bar knowing she would use a fake ID," Winnans argued.

"Right! And who are we, the morality police?" Kristi asked, getting as fed up with Winnans as Jan had with Davidson.

"Okay, so what should be done?" Trane asked.

"Sir, the other brother needs to report the honor violation to his Honor Rep," Winnans continued.

"What?" Kristi had had enough. "Would you turn in your own brother?"

"If it was my duty, yes."

What a freakin' idiot!

"Well, I'm glad I'm not related to you!" Kristi exclaimed. Jan let out a chortle.

"What's so funny, Miss Wishart?" Trane asked with a slight smile.

"Nothing, Sir," Jan replied, not wanting to say anything more.

"Well, it must have been something or you wouldn't have snickered."

She sighed, "Sir, I think it's more unethical to turn against your own brother than anything else."

"Please elaborate," Trane said.

"Well, Sir, it seems to me that you have to be a pretty big jerk to turn in your own brother. I mean it's not murder. It's not embezzlement or anything that really hurts anyone else." Jan felt a little bolder now.

"But is it an honor violation?" Trane pushed for an answer.

"If he were my brother, I would talk to him. I'd tell him that *it could be considered* an honor violation. And for that reason, don't do it again. But I don't think I'd turn him in. I would quit first."

"Amen, Sista!" Kristi shouted and held up a palm for a high five. Jan felt awkward but high fived her back anyway.

"Loyalty isn't one of the three hallowed words," Winnans protested. Everyone knew what he was talking about, of course. All plebes were required to memorize part of a speech given by General Douglas MacArthur to the Corps of Cadets in 1962. This quote, more than any other, is the epitome of West Point values:

"Duty—Honor—Country. Those three hallowed words reverently dictate what you ought to be, what you can be, what you will be. They are your rallying points: to build courage when courage seems to fail; to regain faith, when there seems to be little cause for faith; to create hope, when hope becomes forlorn."

Cadet Trane smiled, cleared his throat and said, "Well, it says here that this is, in fact, an honor violation."

"You're kidding me," Jan mumbled.

Cadet Trane read from the teaching plan. "The non-offending brother is duty-bound to report the honor violation to his Company Honor Representative." Trane continued reading, "Although this would be a difficult task, a cadet must always choose to do the harder right over the easier wrong. The cadet with the girlfriend was an accomplice to a lie, and therefore, is guilty of violating the Honor Code. While the young woman in question is not a cadet, the code clearly states, 'A cadet will not lie, cheat or steal, nor tolerate THOSE who do.'" Cadet Trane looked up from the paper.

What bullshit! I would never rat on my brother—even if he robbed Fort Knox!!"

The room fell silent until Kristi spoke, "Sir, that's ridiculous."

"I don't like it much either, Cadet McCarron. But this is the hard truth about the Honor Code. All of us have to abide by it or we can transfer to the Naval Academy." A few uncomfortable chuckles punctuated the room.

After the honor class, Jan and Angel scrambled to their room as screaming spread throughout the Corps of Cadets. The roommates quickly changed into the strangest non-uniform they could pull together. Jan chose to wear gray bathrobe over t-shirt with fatigue pants (solid, olive drab, field uniform) and the full dress hat, called a "tar bucket" by cadets. They ran out of their room, screaming, to join the "mandatory fun" happening in Central Area which consisted of several hundred pent-up plebes milling around in all manner of dress and undress. It wasn't exactly a keg party, but to a fourth-class cadet, it was a little bit of heaven.

They returned from the rally to find a folded piece of paper with Jan's name written on it taped to their door. She sat down on her bed and read its contents.

Dear Jan,

This is just a short note to encourage you. Not everyone here is as stuck up as you might think. There are a few of us left. We are banning together to plot a counter-revolution. Some time in the future we will spring from our underground hiding place and take over the Academy. There will be no more sadness and no more English teachers. Hooray! People will be able to act like humans again. We might even adopt some normal college policies like having fun. If you are interested in joining our subversive group, send no money, but write to Box 483 with your application. We have been watching you and are sure you can fulfill the group's goals. Please read and secure this note from the enemy's hands.

O.T.H.F.A.W.P.

"Well, I'm not sure if this is exciting or creepy," Jan said handing the paper to Angel. Before her roommate finished reading, Jan had already decided to reply. It was out of her comfort zone, given that rule breaking and risk taking were not her strong suits. *But hell, this is the most exciting thing to happen since cornbread.*

Dear O.T.H.F.A.W.P.

It seems a little unfair that you know my name but did not give me yours. I am intrigued, somewhat, by your organization. But I would have to know more. Do you have meetings? When and where? Who is the leader of this esteemed enterprise? How many are in this secret society? Is this a co-ed group? Do you allow persons of color, differing religions and cultures? How does one get selected or qualify to be in this group? Is there some kind of secret signal to identify "brothers and sisters?" What are the dues? Does allegiance to this group supersede allegiances to duty, honor, country?

As you can see, I have a number of questions and concerns about whom and what you represent. I am not one to just dive into something without knowing what I'm getting into. I am cautious like that. Also, Plebe English is the ONLY course I like.

Regards,

Esmeralda (thought I'd use a code name, too)

Jan and her classmates settled into the routine of plebe life: delivering laundry and newspapers to the upperclassmen at zero dark thirty each morning, rushing to and from classes, athletics and formations, and memorizing the ever growing list of poop. Plebes had to memorize The Code of Conduct, General Orders, insignia for all non-commissioned and commissioned officers of the US Army, the location and significance of every monument at West Point, the colors of all service medals, the words to various songs, including: "The Star Spangled Banner," "The Alma Mater," "Benny Haven's, Oh!" "The Corps," and much other West Point or Army trivia. Knowing the menu for each meal and familiarity with any article in the New York Times was also expected.

Testing plebes on poop seemed to be the single, most enjoyable task for upper-class cadets. Any wrong answers usually resulted in demerits. Too many demerits led to a cadet's worst nightmare—walking tours. This punishment was a most effective deterrent because it took away the only enjoyment at West Point—free time. Those with too many demerits spent Saturdays in full uniform with an M-14 over their shoulder, walking back and forth in Central Area. Therefore, every plebe worked very hard at memorizing poop.

"SIR, THERE ARE TEN MINUTES UNTIL DINNER FORMATION. THE MENU FOR DINNER TONIGHT IS ROAST PORK, SWEET POTATOES, TURNIP GREENS, APPLE CIDER, AND BLUEBERRY PIE. THE UNIFORM FOR DINNER IS DRESS GREY OVER GREY. TEN MINUTES, SIR!" Jan stood directly below the wall clock in the hallway and performed her duty as minute caller. It was more like "minute screaming" she thought as she returned to her room to wait five minutes. All other plebes had already left the building to be at formation by the ten-minute bell, giving the upperclassmen plenty of time to haze them.

She returned to the hallway clock. "SIR, THERE ARE FIVE MINUTES UNTIL DINNER FORMATION. THE MENU FOR DINNER TONIGHT IS ROAST PORK, SWEET POTATOES, TURNIP GREENS, APPLE CIDER, AND BLUEBERRY PIE. THE UNIFORM FOR DINNER IS DRESS GREY OVER GREY. FIVE MINUTES, SIR!" She stayed standing at attention under the clock waiting to call the four, three and two minute bells.

Cadet Dogety stuck his head outside his door, "Wishart, tell me the Code of Conduct." When she hesitated, he barked, "I'm waiting Wishart!"

"Sir, I am an American fighting man. I serve in the forces which guard my country and our way of life. I...I am prepared to give my life in their defense. I will... I will never surrender of my own free will. If in command, I will... never surrender... my men while they still have the means to resist. If I escape...I will...I mean, if I am captured...I will... escape...I mean,"

"Which is it, Wishart?"

"Sir, may I make a statement."

"What?"

"Sir, I do not know the third statement of the Code of Conduct yet!"

"Well, you better know it by breakfast, Wishart."

"Yes, Sir!" She would know it cold by then.

Jan found her table and stood at attention behind the end chair. From the Poop Deck, the two story stone structure that stood in the middle of the Mess Hall, a booming voice announced, "TAKE SEATS!" She sat at the end chair next to Cadet Davidson and began filling glasses with ice.

"Sir, the dessert for tonight's meal is blueberry pie. Would anyone not care for blueberry pie, Sir?" Rick Davidson announced from the dessert corporal's chair.

The drink corporal on her other side made a similar announcement. "Sir, the drink for tonight's meal is apple cider. Would anyone not care for apple cider, Sir?"

Jan held the glasses while her classmate poured the cider. Davidson proceeded to cut the dessert. Crust usually made it impossible to cut straight lines in a pie. He also managed to spread blueberry goop everywhere with each cut.

This is not good.

Davidson smirked at Jan before announcing, "Sir, the dessert has been cut and is ready for your inspection, Sir!" Handing the pie to the left, it made its way from cadet to cadet, all the way to the table Commander, Dogety. On its way up the table, Jan heard comments from the yearlings and cows: "uh-oh," "oh-no," and "geez."

When it reached Dogety, he winced and shouted, "You blundering idiot, Davidson! You totally screwed this pie!"

"Yes Sir!" Davidson answered with a grin.

"This is disgusting! All of you give me a 4-C!" Dogety ordered. Each plebe at the table passed a small, green paper, the Fourth Class Demerit Report, up the table. Dogety would fill it out later, stating that the plebes at Table 112 were "grossly negligent" or something to that effect.

After receiving the three slips of paper, Dogety passed the pie back down the other side of the table so that everyone on that side could make their own disparaging remark. One of the cows, a junior year cadet, became enraged. "This pie is gross! No one wants to eat it now!" He threw the pie, like a Frisbee, to the plebe end of the table.

He probably intended it to land on a plate or somewhere on the table, but the pie hit a serving dish, took a bounce, and landed face down in Jan's lap. In a flash, blueberry goop covered the front of her Dress Gray. Her wool trousers began soaking up pie filling.

Everything kicked into slow motion. Jan stood up slowly, exposing the damaged uniform for everyone to see. She stared straight ahead at Dogety, expecting him to shout at her for the mess. Then she looked at Davidson, expecting his usual smirk. Yet both men appeared stunned. No one spoke; the entire table stared at Jan in silence. She felt the familiar lump rising in her throat and the tears that were close behind, but she would never cry in front of them. Without permission and forgetting her hat stowed under her seat, she executed a right face and marched out of the Mess Hall.

As she crossed Central Area, someone yelled out a fourth floor window, "Hey, Beanhead! Where's your headgear?" Jan kept going, knowing that cadet could neither see nor catch her from the fourth floor. She pinged back to her room, tears threatening from the corners of her eyes.

Once inside, the dam burst forth, unrestrained and unrelenting. She unzipped her gray coat, placed it in the sink and began rinsing off the blueberry goop. Her weeping mixed with the tap water as she spoke out loud. "What the fuck am I doing here? This is insane. I hate this place! I hate these assholes! I hate, hate, HATE everything about this hell hole!"

She scrubbed the blueberry spots with soap until they looked black, not exactly the best way to clean wool. She hung the Dress Gray coat in her closet, stripped off her wool trousers and began to work on them in the same way. These pants had to be salvaged at all costs. With only one other pair, she would be forced to wear the wool skirt when her trousers went out for cleaning. Jan loathed the skirt. The skirt screamed: "I AM FEMALE!" No sane, female cadet wanted that much attention. Her classmates could not help either because they needed both pairs of pants, too.

She turned off the water. Her trousers were almost entirely soaked. The blueberry goop was gone, but Jan wondered if they would ever fit the same. Just as she hung them up to dry on the closet door, an upperclassman pounded two loud knocks on the door. "Shit," she mumbled. "Shit, shit, shit." Tired of playing this silly game, sick of all the bullshit, she almost yelled, "GO THE FUCK AWAY, SIR!"

Instead, she took a deep breath and jumped into her PT shorts. "Enter, Sir."

One of only two female cows in Company H-3 stood at the door. "I heard about the blueberry pie," Cadet Rallins said. "I'm so sorry that happened. It should not have. There's nothing that can be done about it now."

Jan stared blankly. *So what's your point, woman?*

"I thought you might be able to use this." She held up a clothes iron that Jan had not noticed. "It might help smooth out any wrinkles."

Jan was so moved by this small gesture she almost started crying all over again. Instead, she cleared her throat. "Thank you, Ma'am." She took the iron from Cadet Rallins.

"If there's anything else you need, please let me know. These guys can be assholes sometimes, but most of them really don't mean to hurt anyone."

"Yes, Ma'am." *Please go away before I start crying again.*

"I talked to the guy who threw the pie. He feels terrible. But he probably won't apologize. So I'm here to apologize for him."

Shit, did you have to say that? Jan eyes welled up again. *Just go away, please!*

"Of course, some guys really are assholes."

Enough already!

"And it's best to just steer clear of them if you can."

"Yes, Ma'am," Jan concurred. *Now please go.* Her prayer was finally answered and Cadet Rallins walked away.

Company H-3's highest-ranking women were two cows. Thankfully, the term "cow" started many years before women were admitted to West Point.

Jan wondered how this stunningly beautiful woman survived so long at the academy. Cadet Rallins seemed to generate controversy every year. She entered a beauty pageant during leave after her plebe year which some considered tasteless. As a yearling (sophomore), she dated the Superintendent's son while he was still a plebe. That infraction made her the first "Century Woman"—with one hundred hours of walking tours. Rallins seemed almost mythical to Jan who rarely saw her in person.

By handing the iron to Jan, Cadet Rallins broke a seemingly, unwritten rule among upperclass women—the "No Helping Plebes" rule. The women in the classes of 1982, 1983 and 1984, probably like the women in the classes before them, seemed to take a hands-off approach to female plebes. It was a mystery to Jan why these trailblazers didn't do more to help the fourth-class women. They could have offered advice or shared wisdom—perhaps only in the latrines away from male ears and eyes—but they seemed content to let plebe women fend for themselves.

Maybe they're just trying to survive too, Jan thought that night. *Well, I can forgive them for that.*

13

Friday, May 7, 1982
0930 Hours

Conrad dismissed Jackson, telling him he might be called back to testify again. Jackson said something like, "Sure thing," before leaving the room. Jan felt most of her energy go out with him. She suddenly felt so tired, so damn tired.

After a latrine and water break, the board reconvened at 0945 hours. Everyone settled into their seats and Conrad asked the plebe runner to get the next witness. At least this one would be a friendly face.

Kristi McCarron walked into the room and stood in the same seat to Jan's right where Jackson had been. Conrad commanded her to raise her right hand and repeat the oath of honor and then motioned for her to take a seat. She winked at Jan as she sat down. "Cadet McCarron, you are here to testify about the events of May second and third. Are you prepared to explain what you witnessed without any bias toward Cadet Wishart or against Cadets Dogety and Jackson?"

"I am, Sir," Kristi said without blinking. Born an Army brat, and later having an ambassador as a stepfather, gave her an edge with these kinds of things. She never seemed intimidated or undone by the military hierarchy. Kristi shrugged off a lot of things that got under Jan's skin. They balanced each other well. Jan provided the seriousness and Kristi provided the screw-it attitude, both necessary for survival at West Point.

"Okay, Miss McCarron, please tell us in your own words what you witnessed on the night of May second," Conrad said.

Kristi took a deep breath, gave Jan another slight smile and said, "Well, Cadet Dogety came to our room about 1900 hours and demanded Jan deliver the routing envelope to Cadet Jackson's room in B-1. It really pissed me off because Dogety knows that Jackson has a reputation of harassing, and even molesting, plebe women."

Wow! She got that in before anyone saw it coming!

"What do you mean, Miss McCarron?" Tourney asked.

"Wait a minute, Cadet McCarron, before you say one more word, do you have any evidence to support that claim?" Conrad asked.

"Well, *Sir,*" she said with the tiniest bit of sass, "Cadet Wishart told me about two incidents during Beast, when Jackass, I mean Jackson…"

"Stop right there, Miss McCarron," Conrad interrupted. "First, this isn't some joke. You will address your superiors with respect. Second, anything Miss Wishart told you about Cadet Jackson is not valid evidence of anything. If you do not have any *PROOF* that Cadet Jackson has molested females, or that Cadet Dogety would have known about his supposed reputation, then you need to reconsider your words before you say something you cannot substantiate."

"Yes, Sir. I will re-word it then. If you ask any *female* plebe who has been under Jackson's authority, you will learn that they all steer clear of him. There's a reason for that. Secondly, Cadet Dogety was present when Jackson practically attacked Cadet Wishart during Lake Frederick week. Dogety told her then that she could have been in big trouble if he hadn't been there to stop Jackson. That tells me Dogety knows exactly what Jackson is capable of doing."

Conrad shook his head. "A complaint was never made. Therefore, it's only hearsay as far as this Honor Board is concerned. I insist you stop making claims you cannot support."

Kristi rolled her eyes and sighed, "Sir, with all due respect, hearsay is all we have as plebes, especially as new cadets in Beast. But there were also a few witnesses to that event at Lake Frederick. It seems to me that a few witnesses to something makes it more than just hearsay."

Oh, Kissy, please be careful.

Conrad began fuming, his neck and cheeks turned bright pink. "Cadet Jackson is not on trial here and nothing has ever been brought to our attention about these alleged misdeeds. Furthermore, none of this has any bearing on the events of May second!" Conrad shouted.

Kristi stared back at Conrad without flinching. Jan loved her for that. "Sir, you did tell me to explain what happened, *in my own words,* and in my opinion, these things DO have a very important bearing on what happened on May second. Sir."

Tourney interrupted again, "Casey, I agree with Miss McCarron. The history of the relationship between Cadets Dogety, Jackson and Wishart *IS* relevant to the events of May second. If there were prior incidents of inappropriate behavior on Cadet Jackson's part, then it casts doubt on his behavior and statement concerning this honor allegation."

Cadet Leavitt agreed with Tourney and Jan noticed a few other cadets nodding their heads. *Maybe we're on to something here.*

"Miss McCarron," he had regained his composure, "do you have any first-hand experience with Cadet Jackson crossing a line with you?"

Kristi hesitated. "No, Sir."

"Well, then, you may provide a list of names of those who would testify against Cadet Jackson's character. Otherwise we will not allow rumors and hearsay to color our opinion of him." He paused to shuffle some papers. "I will allow you to share your personal experiences of Cadet Jackson if you have witnessed something concerning his character. However, you must remain professional and respectful when speaking about ANYONE. Am I clear?" Conrad asked.

"Yes, Sir." Kristi didn't seem the least bit unnerved. "As I was saying, Cadet Dogety tasked Jan to deliver a routing envelope to Cadet Jackson. Dogety had been harassing her all year, ever since he was her Beast Squad Leader. So it didn't surprise me that he would send her on another wild goose chase for his own enjoyment. Cadet Dogety seemed to enjoy messing with Jan, too. She was his little pet project."

"Miss McCarron! What did I just tell you?" Conrad shouted again.

"Oh, sorry, Sir. I forgot to mention that I was in the same platoon in Beast with Jackson, Dogety and Cadet Wishart. So I personally observed and witnessed several incidents which can substantiate my previous claim."

She is so damn cool.

Just as Kristi began getting into the specifics of Sunday night's events, Cadet Conrad announced it was time for lunch. "Miss McCarron's testimony will resume when we come back. I want to remind everyone of the confidential nature of these proceedings. At no time is anyone, ever, allowed to discuss the contents of this Honor Board with ANYONE outside this room. I cannot be any clearer than that. I will see every one back here at 1300 hours. Dismissed."

Everyone stood to leave. "McCarron, stay here a minute with us," Cadet Trane said motioning to Jan and Major Hastings. "I want to have a defense strategy session."

Jan had not even considered a "defense strategy." She first heard about the accusations against her only two days ago. The Honor Board began the next day which was yesterday. They didn't waste any time with this stuff. The accused wasn't allowed to gather information or any other evidence nor obtain legal counsel. If accused of an honor violation at West Point, you were left to fend for yourself for the most part. In other words, you had to find a way to prove your innocence and do it fast. Otherwise, BAM! You were history, gone, done, kicked out for honor—the worst way to leave West Point.

"Sir, what do you mean? Are you saying we should plan out how to argue my case?"

"Yes, Miss Wishart, there should always be a plan—even a bad plan is better than no plan. Well, in this case anyway," Trane said. "Major, I'd like to hear your thoughts as well. What can Miss Wishart do to prove her innocence?"

Please say that again, Sir! The "prove her innocence" part!

"Well," Major Hastings began, "I've already told Miss Wishart, there's not a whole lot she can do except state the truth, ask appropriate questions from each witness, and then try to appear as innocent as possible."

He's useless.

"Okay, Sir, thank you. We don't want to keep you from your lunch." Cadet Trane said, giving Major Hastings his out.

"See you at 1300 hours, then." Hastings stood up and walked out of the room.

"He's about as helpful as a pile of dung," Kristi stated the obvious again.

"Well, let's concentrate on what we can do," Trane said. "Look, this is a classic case of he said/she said, right? Wishart, you have to convince the board that you are AS likely to be telling the truth as Jackson. In other words, you don't have to show he's lying; you only need to show you are NOT lying. Does that make sense?"

"Not really, Sir. How can I show that I am not lying if he is not lying?" Jan asked.

"You just need for them to see things from your perspective. In other words, don't try to make Jackson a badass, though he probably is. Instead, just show them what you experienced that night and the next morning," Trane said.

"Sir, everything I experienced is in my written statement," Jan replied.

"I understand that. But the statements are so far apart that these guys on the Honor Board probably think they have to find one person to be lying and one to be telling the truth. Without any evidence or other witness to the events, by default, they will pick Jackson's version as the truth. After all, he is the firstie about to graduate. If they pick your version, then they have to ruin this guy...they have to kick him out for an honor violation, kill his career and basically end his life. You, on the other hand, are just a plebe. And a female. So you don't count."

"What? Sir, you don't mean that," Kristi insisted.

"Yes, I do mean that. These guys are NOT gonna kick out one of their own just because Wishart says he assaulted her. They have to have proof. They DON'T, however, need proof to find you guilty."

"Then I'm screwed no matter what I do," Jan said.

"Pretty much. UNLESS...." Trane said.

Jan looked at her firstie Knight in Shining Amour, "Unless what, Sir?"

"Unless you can somehow convince them that you are ALSO telling the truth. In other words, you both are right in your perception of the events."

"What the hell...are you talking about?" Kristi asked. "Sir?"

Trane turned to Jan. "I'm saying that you were exhausted from running back and forth between Third and First Regiments, right?"

"Yes, Sir," Jan admitted.

"And when they got you in the CQ room, you were scared shitless, right?"

"Yes, Sir."

"Because they screamed and yelled in your face and accused you of doing something you didn't do, right?"

"Right, Sir."

"Then the next morning, you were exhausted again, having only slept a few hours...when you went to Jackson's room at 0500 hours.

"Well, about 0515, but yes, Sir," she agreed.

"And you were scared—scared shitless because he has a history of hazing you—so in your exhausted, frightened state, you entered his room. Then your version of events may not be considered so unreasonable if they can put themselves in your shoes for a moment. If you went to his room, tired and scared, maybe they will see why things seemed very different to you," Cadet Trane argued.

"But Sir, I'd have to be delusional to have made such a differing account from Jackson. I wasn't out of my mind, Sir," Jan insisted.

"I know, Wishart, I know. I'm just trying to get them to consider that there might be two versions of the same event. Maybe all of it happened—what he says happened and what you say happened. That way, they can have an out. Don't you see?"

"Yes, Sir, I see. I just don't know that it's enough." Jan thought a moment, "Sir," she wasn't sure how to bring this up, "if I can convince Debra Plowden to write a statement about what happened over Army/Navy weekend, would...."

"What? Why?" Trane looked confused.

"Sir, I may be able to raise enough doubt in their minds if they hear about something that happened to her in our hotel room. We all feel fairly certain that Jackson…."

"What the hell are you talking about?"

"Sir, I know it sounds crazy, but I have a very good reason for this…do you…"

"NO!" he shouted.

Jan flinched. She had never heard him sound so angry.

"That's stupid, Wishart! Whatever happened to Plowden has absolutely nothing to do with what's gong on here. If you try a ridiculous stunt like that, they will find you guilty for sure."

Jan felt like an idiot. Of course it was stupid. "Sorry, Sir. I just thought …"

"Well don't do anymore thinking like that! It's not helpful and not relevant to your case. Just focus on the events of last weekend, not on something that may or may not have happened to someone else months ago!"

"Yes, Sir." A long pause ensued as Jan contemplated how she could use Trane's advice. She had accused Jackson of hitting her in the face during their altercation in his room Monday morning which he flatly denied doing. That's why he brought the honor charges against her. He also claimed that she threw a shoe at him, which she readily admitted. *No one is going to believe we are both telling the truth.*

"Jackson's a friggin' asshole!" Kristi said, plainly as always.

The roommates pinged back to lunch formation and fell in their squad lines. Dogety seemed to ping straight over to Jan.

"Miss Wishart, how are things looking with the Honor Board? I know you cannot give me specifics, but can you tell me if things are going well?" he asked.

"No, Sir. Things will not likely go well for me, unless someone validates my side of the story."

"And you're sure there are no other witnesses from Monday morning? Anyone who heard you or saw you in Cadet Jackson's room?"

He almost seemed to be hoping.

"Not that I know of, Sir. I didn't see anyone else that morning."

"But what about one of your roommates—Cadet McCarron or Cadet Trane? Did either of them see anything that could substantiate your version?"

"No, Sir. I told them what happened later, but they didn't notice anything unusual about me that morning."

Dogety lowered his voice, "Miss Wishart, you know I want to help you, don't you?" This was the first time Jan heard him admit anything like this. His eyes held a sadness she had not seen before.

"Sir, I don't know that." She answered truthfully.

"Well, I do," he looked straight into her eyes. Then lowering his voice even more, he added, "I'm trying to figure it out." He walked back to the front of the platoon.

After lunch, Jan raced back to her room to brush her teeth. She found a folded piece of paper lying on her bed.

Jan,

I know you are not supposed to say anything but you have to tell me a little more. I might be able to help..? First, I have to know what are the specific charges against you. Can you just write them down? That way you can honestly say that you didn't talk to anyone...

PLEASE, don't delay!!

SKIP

Jan quickly wrote a note and taped it to her door.

SKIP,

I am under strict orders not to talk about the Honor Board. No one mentioned anything about writing though. Still, I trust that you will destroy this note as soon as you read it. Jackson says I opened his routing envelope, took his notes and replaced them with another note. He's also charging that I lied about what happened Monday morning. He flatly denies hitting me. So, it's likely that he will get me one way or the other.

You've been a good friend to me this year.
Jan

14

Q: What is the definition of leather?

A: If the fresh skin of an animal, cleaned and divested of all hair, fat and other extraneous matter, be immersed in a dilute solution of tannic acid, a chemical combination ensues; the gelatinous tissue of the skin is converted into a non-putrescible substance, impervious to and insoluble in water; this Sir, is leather.

Heritage, Bugle Notes, 81, p. 242

Saturdays were parade days. Even when the football team played away games, the cadets still had to march for visiting dignitaries or reunion weekends or just because it was Saturday.

Jan looped the white starched belt around her waist and pulled tightly so that it held the bayonet firmly in place over her right hip. She lifted the other white straps over her head and across her chest, securing them between her breasts with the small brass shield. She donned the patent leather, pluming hat, which never actually fit on anyone's head, and placed the chinstrap just under her bottom lip. *Whoever thought this hat design was a good idea?* After sliding on the white gloves, she turned to Angel.

"Need help?"

"Check my breastplate, please." Jan adjusted Angel's gold centerpiece, making sure it canted forty-five degrees from vertical.

"How's mine?" Jan asked.

"Looks good," Angel replied. They both grabbed their M-14's from the wooden rack by the door, gave each other one last glance, then shot out of their room to parade formation.

Free time supposedly began when the parade ended. So the roommates frowned at each other when they heard two loud knocks on their door just after they returned to their room.

Do they really have to put a fist through the door every damn time?

"Enter, Sir!" Jan and Angel yelled at once.

Cadet Dogety stood at the entrance to their room holding out a package. "Wishart, this needs to go to Cadet Jackson in Company B-1. You don't mind delivering it for me, do you?"

"No, Sir." As if she had any other options. She couldn't say, "Sorry, I'm busy right now. Why don't you deliver it yourself, Sir?"

"Good!" He tossed the package at Jan. He was close to six feet and probably weighed less than one hundred sixty with not one ounce of fat. His arms extended almost to his knees when standing at attention. Jan noticed his disproportional body during Beast, which seemed like another lifetime ago.

"I'm sure you'll have no problem finding Cadet Jackson's room in First Regiment," Dogety added with a smirk before turning and walking down the hall.

Jan closed the door and turned to Angel. "Shit." Angel didn't like to hear cussing, but Jan felt justified this time. Going to First Regiment would be difficult; going to Jackson's room could be downright dangerous. "Why doesn't he get a male plebe to deliver this?"

Dogety and Jackson both seemed to enjoy harassing plebes. But Cadet Dogety never physically touched anyone without permission. Jackson was a whole different animal. He gained a reputation in Beast for harassing the new cadet women. Jan had first hand experience with that. He didn't hide his verbal assaults either. "Move those fat cheeks, new cadet," Jan heard him say once to a classmate. Another time, she saw him slap a new cadet's butt and say, "You better get that spare tire moving!"

"He's disgusting," Jan muttered to herself, recalling the time he took her for the late night run. But she also smiled, remembering when she hit him with a piece of cornbread at Lake Frederick.

"Maybe he won't be in the room when you get there," Angel said.

"Well, I will just have to cross that river when I get to it or however the saying goes."

"Okay, well, just worry about getting in and out of First Regiment safely," Angel said. Plebes avoided other regimental areas if at all possible because each one had its own rules. No one wanted to "spazz-off" in the wrong side of town.

A small tapping on the door indicated a friendly visitor, another plebe most likely. "Come in," the two roommates said.

Drew entered the room. "I heard our favorite Squad Leader's voice at your door. What did he want?"

"He gave me this package to deliver to Jackson in B-1."

"Oh." And then Drew seemed to realize her double jeopardy, "Oh, shit!"

"Tell me about it," Jan replied. Drew once had to deliver something to Fourth Regiment. Although that trip went smoothly, they heard rumors from other plebes. Crossing over to another regiment felt like crossing into enemy lines, sort of. No one would die, no one would get wounded, and no one would be captured as a POW. But for a West Point plebe, it still felt like walking into the lions' den.

"I'll go with you," Drew said.

It's just like him to offer. Jan knew Drew had her back more than anyone else. He always seemed to be willing to sacrifice his own safety for hers. *He's going to be a great officer one day.*

"No thanks, Drew. It's going to be difficult enough for me to find his room without spazzing off. One lost plebe might go undetected. Two confused looking plebes will definitely stand out." Jan didn't want to get anyone else in trouble for her sake.

"Why don't I just go then?" Drew asked. "Jackson won't mess with me."

"Then they will give me shit for passing off my duty to you. No, Drew, Dogety purposely wanted me to deliver this. He's best friends with Jackson, and if I don't bring the package myself, I will never hear the bottom of it."

"End of it," Drew said.

"Whatever. You know what I mean."

"Well, Jan, I know you can handle this. You've dealt with much worse already," Angel said. And she was right. Jan, Angel, Drew and all their classmates had survived Beast. They were now solidly in plebe year at West Point. They were managing the tremendous demands of the "Fourth Class System" and they were going to survive this. "I'll be praying for you," Angel added. Jan didn't know if Angel was Baptist or Catholic or Mormon; she only knew she was extremely religious.

"Thanks, right now I just need a dress-off." Jan turned her back to Drew who helped execute a perfectly tight dress-off.

"Okay, how do I look?" Jan asked.

"Maavelous, daaling!!" he said.

"You got this, Jan," Angel added.

"Well, here goes!" She opened the door and stepped out into the wild, wild jungle that was West Point.

Hugging the walls all the way down the hall and moving at three times the normal walking speed, Jan made her way to the stairwell. Descending the steps, she lifted her forearms, parallel to the floor. She turned at every corner of the stairwell until she came to the next set of steps. She called it the "plebe shuffle."

Exiting one set of double doors, she pinged across Central Area, the large paved quadrangle separating the Second and Third Regimental barracks. She passed through a sally port, one of many at West Point, which allowed access through a building without going inside. Then she entered the new and strange land.

First Regiment was divided into two sections: New South and Old South. The dilapidated barracks of Old South housed Companies A, B and C. Companies D, E, F, G, H and I were located in two facing buildings called New South. Jan wondered how long these would be called New South—since they were built in 1962, a year before she was born. And now that Old South was being renovated, with scaffolding stretching across the entire front of the u-shaped, gothic stone structure, Jan thought it should be called "New, Old South."

Crossing Old South area, Jan looked for the entrance to B Company. Each leg of the U-shaped building had a set of double doors but nothing to indicate which wing held which Company. She chose quickly. *Better to act like you know what you're doing and be wrong than to act unsure and be right.* Jan learned this lesson early. At West Point, appearing "squared away" was more than half the battle.

A and C companies are probably the end ones. B should be in the middle. She headed up the flight of stairs to the third floor. *Best start there and work my way down.*

As she squared the corner of the last stairwell, an upperclassman screamed, "BEANHEAD, HALT! What the hell are you doing, Smack?"

"Sir, may I make a statement?"

"It better be good!"

"Sir, I'm delivering this package to Cadet Jackson in B-1."

"So? I'll ask again, what the hell are you doing, Beanhead?"

"Sir, I believe B-1 is on the third floor of this building."

"You aren't from around here, are you, Smack?"

"No, Sir."

"Next time you come to this part of the woods, you better get your shit together first."

"Yes, Sir."

"Now get outta here."

"Yes, Sir." Jan executed an about face and began descending the stairs.

"What the hell are you doing now?"

"I'm leaving, Sir."

"Not on my stairwell, you're not. Get off my stairwell and go find your own stairwell."

"Yes, Sir." Jan ran back up to the third floor and began pinging down the corridor. Given that she had made it this far, she decided to look for "Jackson" on the doors. After two complete rotations, she spotted the name. She approached the door and knocked.

"Come in." Jan pushed open the door.

Every cadet room looked the same. A sink counter with laundry bins below and a mirrored cabinet above stood just inside the door on one wall. Usually two beds flanked either side of the room with two desks located just behind the beds facing the door. Cadet Jackson sat behind his desk. Before entering the room, she said, "Sir, I have a package from Cadet Dogety for you."

"Bring it here." He lifted his left hand and waved his fingers, motioning her to come toward him. Jan walked the length of the room coming to Jackson's desk. She set the package down and turned to leave. "Stand fast, Wishart."

Jan faced him again about three feet from his desk. "How's it going over in H-3, Miss Wishart?"

"It's going fine, Sir."

"They're probably way too easy on you over there. Here in B-1, things are different for our beanheads, female beanheads in particular."

Jackson stood up and walked to his door, closing it. *Oh no, here we go.* "Sir, I'm going to report you if you even come near me. I'm leaving now, Sir." She headed toward the door.

Jackson folded his arms across his chest and stood in her way, blocking the exit. Jan narrowed her eyes and tightened her lips in a line. She looked straight at Jackson and said, "Sir, if you don't let me pass, I will scream, and then I will kick you in the balls."

"No need to get all worked up, Miss Wishart, I just want to have a private conversation with you. Since you sauntered over here to Boys-1, I'm going to inform you about our policies regarding females."

For Christ's sake, asshole!

"First of all, no one here cares if you scream. No one here is going to come to your rescue. Besides, you cannot scream your way out of combat, can you, Miss Wishart?" His brown eyes bored into her and she remembered where she had seen them before. They looked just like the eyes on the German Shepherd that bit her in eighth grade. "Just exactly why are you here, Miss Wishart?"

"Sir, I delivered your package." She decided to try to end this peaceably.

"No, I mean, why are you *HERE*? Is it to prove something? Is it for notoriety? Is it to find a husband?"

With his arms still folded across his chest, Jan felt some measure of safety. "I'm here for the same reasons you are, Sir."

"Do you think you can go to war with me, Wishart? Do you think I can count on you in combat to fulfill the mission?" His lower lip tightened. "I'm here to be an Army officer and to fight for my country. I might even die for my country. Do you really think I want to worry about whether or not you need a shower or sanitary napkins or birth control on the battlefield?"

Jan didn't answer.

Jackson lowered his voice, "You should think about that, Wishart. You should think about the fact that you took a spot away from some guy who can fight and die along side me. You should think about what it means to be an officer in the United States Army." He unfolded his arms. Jan immediately took a step backwards. Surprisingly, he turned and opened his door, "Now get the hell out of my Company."

When Jan brushed past him, he slammed his door shut.

She still had to find the plebe stairwell. *Move with a purpose.* Moving quickly was critical to avoiding attention, so she pinged along the corridors, making one more rotation on the third floor before ducking into the women's latrine. Another plebe was washing her hands in the sink. Jan whispered to her classmate, "Where's the plebe stairwell?" Her classmate wisely kept the water running while whispering the directions to Jan. "Thanks," Jan said, "and stay far, far away from Jackson." She pinged out of that building as fast as she could.

Safely back in Central Area, she sighed a breath of relief. *Okay, so why AM I here again?* She often asked herself why she came and why she stayed. Jackson's confrontation only caused her to renew the questioning in her own mind. She didn't agree with him, of course. She knew the Army had plenty of roles for women and should probably have more. She knew, fundamentally, that a government-funded college should be open to everyone. She knew women had as much a right to be at West Point as men. But the debate that raged inside her was if *SHE* should be there. Should she stick it out, miserable as she was, or was it time to *throw in the blanket?*

Then she remembered that all plebes are miserable at West Point.

15

Friday, May 7, 1982
1300 hours

"Jan came back to the room at least twice, in-between trips to Jackson's room." Kristi continued her testimony. "Cadet Trane and I were both there. Every time we saw Jan, she was sweating from pinging back and forth. She was also getting sick and tired of the nonsense." Kristi looked empathetically at Jan. "I told her she should report the whole thing to the CO, but she wouldn't do it. She always felt it was better to just suck it up. That's what Dogety always told her."

"Cadet McCarron," Gaskins, from Second Regiment, spoke up, "did you see Cadet Wishart leave the routing envelope in your room at any point while she went to the latrine or anywhere else?"

"No, Sir. She did use the latrine, but she took the envelope with her. She even said something like, 'I can't let this out of my sight.'"

"So no one in your room that night could have possibly changed the contents of the routing envelope?" Conrad asked.

"No, nobody in our room touched it and Jan never opened the envelope either," Kristi stated.

"How can you know that, Miss McCarron?" Cadet Seymour asked.

"Because we asked her what was inside. And she said she didn't have any idea. If Jan had even peeked inside, she would have said so.

She would have said, 'It's some drunken love notes between Jackson and Dogety,' or something like that."

"Miss McCarron, I have warned you once already. I won't say it again or you will face a regimental disciplinary board. You will use respectful language when speaking about your superiors. Do I make myself perfectly clear?" Conrad laid down the law.

"Yes, Sir." Kristi glanced at Jan.

Oh Kissy, don't be too sassy—or they will definitely find me guilty by association!

"Good. Now tell us what you witnessed after she came back the third time from Cadet Jackson's room." Conrad pushed on, still trying to wrap everything up before the weekend if possible.

"Well, Jan seemed relieved to have found a way out of the courier business. When she came back to the room, about 2030 hours, she said that Jackson wasn't in his room, so she left the routing envelope leaning against his door. She felt happy that the exercise was over. But about twenty minutes later, both Dogety and Jackson showed up at our door demanding to see Jan in the CQ room right away."

"And how long was she gone? About?" Cadet Tourney asked.

"She came back to the room at almost 2200 hours. I remember looking at the clock," Kristi said. "She was sweating again and looked exhausted. She said they accused her of taking their notes and writing another one. She said Jackson was 'in her face,' screaming and yelling at her."

"Did she say what was written on the new note?" Conrad asked.

"She didn't have any idea what was written on anything. She hadn't looked in the envelope at any time. She even thought they were screwing with her again, because they were both drunk, she figured they were just messing with her."

"Did she tell you that Cadet Jackson wanted her to report to his room the next morning?" Cadet Leavitt asked.

"Yes, Sir. She was pissed about it. She felt like she had made enough trips to his room already. And she was pissed at Dogety for allowing this whole thing to go on so long."

Go easy on the "pissed" part, Kissy!

"Anyway, she got up at o'dark thirty the next morning and went to Jackson's room."

"When did she return?" Cadet Tourney asked.

"Well, she was not back when Angel and I left the room to deliver newspapers, about 0545 hours. But I saw she made it to breakfast formation," Kristi said, confirming Jan's statement.

"Did you see Miss Wishart at any other time that morning?" Cadet Conrad asked.

"We both had classes right after breakfast until lunch. I saw her briefly before lunch formation. Then I didn't see her again until we went back to the room after classes to change for athletics," Kristi said.

"And when you saw her, did you notice anything different about her appearance?" Conrad asked again.

"No, Sir, I didn't notice anything. But I wasn't looking for anything either."

"The point is, you didn't see anything unusual about Cadet Wishart's appearance that morning or afternoon, correct?" Conrad clarified.

"No, Sir, I didn't," Kristi said softly.

It's okay, Kissy. It wasn't that obvious.

16

"Upon the fields of friendly strife are sown the seeds that upon other fields, on other days, will bear the fruits of victory...."
General Douglas MacArthur

The gym converted into an obstacle course with low bars, vault horses, flat and hanging tires, an eight-foot shelf, three levels of balance beams, an eight-foot horizontal wall, monkey bars and dangling, thick ropes. This perennial torture chamber, known as the Indoor Obstacle Course Test (IOCT) became the new nemesis for plebes.

"Okay, everyone will run through once for practice. Then you'll do it again for time." Captain Miller announced to the G, H and I companies' fourth-class cadets. He and all the Department of Physical Education (DPE) instructors were in phenomenal shape.

He's a stud muffin! For an old guy.

"The men will go first, then the women," Captain Miller said.

She watched as the guys low crawled under the bars, vaulted over the horses, hoisted themselves onto the shelf, leapt onto bars leading to the upper track, jumped back down to floor mats and through the hanging tires, ran over three levels of balance beams, scaled the eight foot wall, hand-walked the monkey bars, climbed the hanging ropes back up to the track, picked up a medicine ball and ran three laps before crossing the finish line. A big metal bucket waited at the exit for anyone needing to puke.

Most guys negotiated the obstacles with seemingly little effort although quite a few struggled with the balance beams. Some fell off and had to start again. Drew Hambin floated across the tri-level beams. Jan marveled at his agility and strength as he handled all the obstacles with ease.

After finishing the practice IOCT, the men sat down around the edge of the gym where the women had been waiting. "Okay, women, your turn!" Captain Miller shouted.

Jan tried to put on a good face but she knew this wasn't going to be pretty. "Let the faster ones go ahead of us," she whispered to Angel and Kristi while nodding toward Leslie Wright and Debra Plowden. She thought it was best not to get in their way.

"First, Cadet Wright will demonstrate how to negotiate each obstacle," Captain Miller said.

What? The guys didn't get a demonstration! Most female cadets didn't like when the faculty made a distinction between the genders. Having a demonstration for the IOCT, when there wasn't one for the men, was just the kind of "special treatment" they wanted to avoid.

Captain Miller must have sensed the women's concerns. "The reason for this demonstration is due to the fact that women have to negotiate the obstacles differently than men."

Leslie crawled under the low bars, ran through the flat tire station and then vaulted easily over the horse.

Not sure what's different yet.

As she ran up to the six-foot shelf, Captain Miller said, "Notice how Cadet Wright throws her leg up first. Women usually have to use this method to climb onto the shelf. The leg gives you leverage to hoist yourself up."

Okay, I wouldn't have known that.

Leslie continued through the next few obstacles coming to the eight-foot vertical wall. "Notice that Cadet Wright uses her legs to partially climb the wall while grabbing the top of the wall with her hands. This way, she is able to go over using most of her lower body strength."

Okay, didn't know that either.

"Now, see how Cadet Wright moves her legs while traversing the monkey bars. Her legs act as a pendulum for the upper body giving her momentum to grab each successive bar."

There seems to be a pattern here.

"Cadet Wright loops her foot around the rope and secures it with her other foot. Then she lifts her body up the rope using her legs like an inch worm." Jan had no doubt that Leslie could have negotiated every obstacle like the men, using mostly upper body strength.

But the rest of us mortals...well...

They lined up at the start of the course. Jan strategically stood behind several women she knew would breeze through the obstacles. Yet, she chose to go in front of Kristi and Angel, thinking they might be slower. She heard Drew's voice from the line of men along the wall. "You got this girls!" Jan didn't mind when Drew used that word, "girls," because she knew he meant well.

They started in 15-second intervals. Jan saw Leslie take off and negotiate each obstacle much faster than the demonstration. *God, she's a marvel.*

Captain Miller gave Jan the signal to start and she began low crawling. She learned this skill in Beast and it wasn't too difficult for short stretches. Then she skipped through the tires and over the vault; no problem. Jan ran up to the eight-foot shelf, threw her leg onto it and tried to hoist herself up. But her leg fell off quickly, taking away her leverage. Captain Miller said, "Go back and run up to it again, Miss Wishart."

Jan backed up about ten feet and charged the shelf again but still no luck getting the leg to stay. "Miss Wishart, throw your head and upper body to the left while throwing your leg to the right onto the shelf. Become almost parallel to the shelf and use it to help you up."

Easier to say than do or something like that... Jan ran up to the shelf a third time, doing as Captain Miller explained. This time, she managed to get her knee on the shelf. *Wow.* That made all the difference. Jan pulled the rest of her five-feet, ten-inches onto the shelf. She jumped onto the bars above, then onto the track before circling back down to the bars and jumping to the floor mats below. She hopped through the hanging tire and ran over the three levels of balance beams with no trouble. At the eight-foot vertical wall, her long legs came in handy. She used them to step up the wall and grab the top with both hands. Then, she folded her body over the top and flopped onto mats on the other side.

The monkey bars were harder. Jan didn't have an ounce of rhythm in her bones, hence swaying and swinging didn't come naturally.

"Use your momentum to grab the next bar," another DPE instructor said.

What momentum? Jan couldn't seem to get the swinging thing to work. She fell off the third bar.

"Try it again, Miss Wishart." Jan started again, this time making it to the fifth bar. "Once more, Miss Wishart."

I hope the guys aren't watching. Yet, they were. Most of them cheered for the women, but a few shook their heads or looked down. She dreaded what they were thinking—*that we are the weak links in the Long Gray Line.*

Every so often she heard Drew say something like, "C'mon Jan, you can do it!" or "Keep trying, Kristi!" or "Way to go Angel!"

God, I love that boy!

On the third attempt she made it to the seventh bar and the DPE instructor told her to move onto the ropes. It took longer to figure out the rope climb than any other obstacle. After what seemed like an hour, Jan managed to get onto the upper track. She picked up the medicine ball, ran three laps and finally finished the torture chamber.

Down on the gym floor Kristi and Angel were still dealing with the vertical wall. Jan felt sorry for them, yet she mostly felt relieved to see others having more problems than she did. Then she felt guilty for feeling better because they were worse. *God, I'm a mess!*

Women like Leslie and Debra didn't need to practice the IOCT. Women like Jan, Kristi and Angel practiced for several weeks before the official test. The three women arrived at the gym every day before sunrise. Drew volunteered as their coach. *He really is wonderful.* They practiced the shelf, the wall, the monkey bars and the ropes. Then they ran through the whole thing once more for time.

On the day of the test Jan was so nervous she could barely breathe. She lined up behind Debra and in front of Angel and Kristi. The men were either puking upstairs or seated against the wall watching the women. She could hear Drew shouting encouragement.

She hooked her leg onto the shelf the first time. "Way to go, Jan!" Drew yelled. She climbed the wall with relative ease. "Awesome job, Jan!" She monkeyed the bars better than ever and shimmied up the ropes with little difficulty. "You're almost there, Jan!" When she finished, she looked down as Kristi and Angel inched up the ropes. Drew cheered them on, too.

The practicing paid off. When Kristi came over the finish line, Jan hugged and lifted her off the floor. She did the same with Angel. Drew almost scared them to death when he grabbed all three women in a big bear hug.

"We did it, bitches, we did it!" Kristi proclaimed.

Their IOCT scores meant diddlysquat if they didn't also pass the monthly weigh-in. So at lunch, Jan ate half an egg salad sandwich. She feigned sickness at dinner, nibbling only on the roll. She and Kristi hoped they would do well enough at the weigh-in that evening to keep the weight hounds away for another month. They were wrong. Jan weighed-in at five pounds under her maximum weight limit and Kristi, three pounds under hers. Apparently they were considered too close to the line. They were both assigned to the battalion's diet tables starting the next day.

The cavernous, cathedral building with four wings, housed all four thousand cadets for breakfast, lunch and dinner every weekday. The entire Corps of Cadets, by companies, by battalions, by regiments, entered the four wings at exactly the same time. Third Regiment entered Washington Hall by the huge mural depicting twenty great battles and their generals in world history.

Jan and Kristi found their way to their battalion's diet tables, clearly marked with large red "DIET" signs. They stood at attention behind their chairs waiting for the OZ-like voice to announce, "TAKE SEATS!"

Jan felt Dogety approach and stand almost touching her left side. "Wishart," he said quietly, "I see you have the notorious distinction of being on diet tables." She stood at attention and since he didn't ask a question, there was no need to respond. "Do you realize how bad this looks?"

Shit, that's a question. "Yes, Sir," she replied.

"Really, Wishart, a little self control would go a long way." No question, no comment, Jan decided. "Besides," he continued, "you need to sit with our Company, not with a bunch of losers from the rest of the battalion. Get your act together and get off these tables ASAP. Understand, Wishart?"

"Yes, Sir!" Jan wondered why he never said anything to Kristi. *Maybe he misses me!*

"Take Seats!" En mass, the entire Mess Hall erupted in a cacophony of noise as chairs slid back, as plebes carried out their duties, and as everyone began talking, laughing and shouting at the plebes.

After dinner, Jan and Kristi stopped by the mailroom before heading back to their rooms. Another folded piece of paper had been placed in her mailbox.

Dear Esmeralda,

We are a small, inclusive, multi-cultural, co-ed group whose whole purpose is to instill a little fun at West Point. We know our goals are lofty and seem out of reach at times, but we dream big. No, there are no dues and no secret handshakes. We do occasionally have secret meetings however, again, for the purpose of having fun.

Don't let this place get you down. There is hope. Someone does care. We can't give you too much help without being a member. To be a member, all you have to do is make a pledge to have fun at West Point. There is a little more involved, but those details can only be divulged to fellow members.

I understand your caution. And I hope you understand mine. We are a secret organization and I am taking a risk letting you in on some of our priceless values. For if we were discovered, the killjoys would wipe us out. We are gaining strength and soon we will be able to take over. As for now, we must stay underground. I am sure my trust in you will not be detrimental to our cause.

But if it helps, you can call me SKIP.

P.S. Don't forget to secure this letter. You never know where the enemy is. Also, I will not be here from Thursday until Sunday for I have a meeting with other brothers and sisters from our adjoining groups: O.T.H.F.A.N.A. and O.T.H.F.A.A.F.A.

Dear SKIP,

I see that even your code name connotes some kind of lightheartedness. That's very nice. I don't think I can take your pledge. You see, I cannot believe in having fun here. I certainly have not been able to have any fun since arriving. I would like to think that it CAN happen, but I am a pessimist about that. I find it very hard to smile, let alone laugh, at anything here. Maybe you have more skill than I do in this area. Anyway, I am sorry to disappoint you, but I'm probably not a good candidate for your group.

Esmeralda

They endured the diet tables for another fortnight. On the following Sunday, Jan's Squad Leader came to her room. "Wishart, you and McCarron need to report to DPE for a body fat test this Tuesday at 1600 hours."

Jan never knew who made these decisions. Kristi came by a few moments later. "Did you hear we have to get a BFT?" she asked.

"Yeah, Cadet Meyer just told me. I suppose we're not making enough progress on the diet tables...." Jan assumed this was one more way to pressure them to lose weight.

In black, Speedo swimsuits, the two women reported to the Olympic-sized pool. A body harness had been attached to the end of the diving board. Naively, Jan thought the BFT would be done with calipers. *I should have known better.* The DPE officer instructed Jan to step into the contraption first.

"Blow out all the air in your lungs, Miss Wishart. Then we will lower you under the water. Keep holding your breath while we get a reading."

Okay, just so I understand...I'm not supposed to take a breath underwater?? Jan's sarcasm increased under duress. *And exactly how do I hold my breath when I've let it all out beforehand?*

In spite of her doubts, she did as instructed. One officer lowered her into the pool, and while she held her non-breath, the other officer read the scale attached to the harness. They repeated the exercise twice more and averaged the three readings.

Kristi's face reflected sheer terror when she stepped into the harness. "Kissy, it's gonna be fine," Jan said encouragingly. "Think of it as a big bath."

Kristi blew out the air in her lungs before being lowered into the water. When her mouth was almost submerged, she panicked and took a deep breath. They raised her coughing and spitting. It happened again on the second attempt. "Kissy, just relax. Don't try to fight it," Jan said realizing the irony of her own advice. They could never relax because they were always fighting something at West Point.

After three false starts, Kristi finally managed to breathe out long enough for a good reading. The officers decided one time would suffice, and Kristi didn't have to do it again. *How is she ever going to pass survival swimming?*

Cadet Meyer came to Jan's door Thursday evening. "Congratulations, Wishart. You're off diet tables. Starting Monday you'll be back on company tables."

"Sir, may I ask..."

"Your Body Fat Test came back. You and McCarron are well within the limits. Both of you are released from diet tables, unless of course you want to stay on them."

"No, Sir!"

"Good. Those tables are only for fat cadets. You shouldn't have been assigned to them in the first place."

Did he just give me a compliment? "Thank you, Sir!" *And I think I love you.*

She never knew who required them to be on the diet tables, nor who ordered the BFT. It seemed that someone thought they were overweight, and someone else must have thought they weren't. *Dogety probably had something to do with the diet table assignment.*

In a funny way, she was grateful for both directives. The diet tables led to the BFT, and the BFT validated her weight. That all led to the first real compliment she received from an upperclassman. *That made it all worth it.*

17

Friday, May 7, 1982
1430 hours

After a brief break, Jan was allowed to question her roommate. "Cadet McCarron, you stated that I returned to the room about 2200 hours on Sunday night."

"Yes, I recall checking the time," Kristi replied.

"Okay, but you also mentioned that I complained about Cadet Jackson screaming at me in the CQ room. Is that right?"

"Yes, that's what you said."

"Did I complain about Dogety yelling at me also? Do you recall what I said about Dogety's behavior in the CQ room?"

"You said he was kind of quiet and trying to get Jackson to calm down," Kristi said, confirming Jan's previous statement.

"Do you remember what else I said?" Jan asked. They had not rehearsed this, but Jan just assumed Kristi would recall everything the way it happened.

"I remember you said you were surprised by Dogety's demeanor...he seemed more upset with Jackson than with you. You said he stepped in front of Jackson a couple times putting himself between you and him. At one point, you thought he even grabbed Jackson by the arms trying to restrain him."

"Did I tell you about Cadet Dogety's comment when Cadet Jackson demanded that I report to his room the next morning?" Jan hoped Kristi remembered this part.

"Yes, you said that Dogety told Jackson you had had enough punishment and it was time to just let this thing go. But Jackson would have none of it and they got into a shouting match over it."

Good girl, Kissy. "Yes, and did I tell you how the argument ended?"

"Yes, Jackson abruptly pointed his finger at you and said, 'You better be in my room at 0500, Wishart.' Then he just walked out of the room. Dogety told you not to report to Jackson's room, no matter what."

"What else did I say about that, Kristi?" Jan asked.

"You said you had to report to his room or else he might make you do something even worse. You said you were more afraid of Jackson than Dogety, so you would go. I tried to convince you not to, but you wouldn't listen."

Did you have to throw that in?

Trane slid another piece of paper in front of Jan. "This would be a good time to stop. Save some questions for later."

Conrad interjected, "Miss McCarron, how many times have you and Miss Wishart talked about this since Sunday night?"

"Quite a few times, Sir," she answered.

"Since you are roommates, would you say you've talked about it every day since Sunday night?"

"Yes, Sir, we have."

"So, could you be remembering more conversations than what actually took place on Sunday night? Could you be recalling conversations that took place on Monday or Tuesday as well?"

"I still recall what she told me that night, even though we've talked since then," Kristi insisted.

"Well, you mentioned a few extra details here that were not in your initial statement. For instance, you never said anything before about Cadet Dogety trying to restrain Jackson in the CQ room. You didn't write that Cadet Jackson pointed a finger at Wishart demanding she report to his room. And there's no mention of Miss Wishart being afraid of Cadet Jackson. These details are missing from your original statement, Miss McCarron."

What is he, Perry Mason?

"Sir, I may not have..."

"Could it be that the story has grown or changed from its original version?" Conrad continued to push Kristi.

"No, Sir, it's just that I didn't..."

"I just wonder, that's all, Miss McCarron. I'm sure it's nothing intentional. When roommates talk again and again about something, it sometimes becomes more than what it started out to be," Conrad said.

Kristi stared at him. Jan tried to think of something to say. Finally Cadet Tourney, Third Regimental Honor Captain spoke up. "Yes, that's probably true, Casey, but not only for roommates. It could apply to best friends, classmates, or anyone else who might have talked things over after the fact."

Conrad turned a shade of pink. "Well, I think it's time for a fifteen minute recess unless you have a burning question for Miss McCarron that cannot wait, Miss Wishart."

"No, Sir. In fact, I was wondering if Cadet McCarron could leave now and come back later for more questioning."

"Why not continue the questioning after our break?" Conrad asked.

"I would like to question everyone about Sunday night first before questioning them about Monday morning." Jan decided to take Trane's advice on this.

"Normally we would question each witness thoroughly and then move on to the next one. That way we aren't playing musical chairs with the witnesses, so to speak." A few board members chuckled. "Besides, I'm sure the witnesses don't want to keep coming and going. They probably prefer to testify once and be done with it." Conrad obviously didn't like Jan's plan of staggering the witnesses.

"I don't mind coming back," Kristi blurted out.

"And Sir," Jan argued, "the Honor Board guidelines state that I may question the witnesses in any order I choose."

"Yes, any order, but not multiple times," Conrad persisted.

Trane slid another piece of paper in front of Jan. "Keep arguing," she thought that's what it said in his chicken-scratch.

"Sir, if I can choose any order, it seems I can jump from one witness to another and back again. They will spend the same amount of time here, just not all at once, which they might prefer anyway."

"Miss Wishart," Conrad raised his voice, "we are not going…"

"Casey," Cadet Leavitt, from First Regiment interrupted, "may I interject here for a moment?"

"Go ahead, Brian." Conrad seemed happy to let someone else make the argument.

"There's a precedent for allowing the witnesses to come back. I recall an Honor Board last year where a witness was called back two or three times," Leavitt said.

Conrad didn't like Leavitt bringing *that* up. "Brian, we only did that when we discovered there were more questions of that particular witness that had not been asked earlier."

"Yes, I was also there, Casey, but we did allow a witness to return several times."

Conrad sighed, "Okay, listen, this is not a big deal either way, but it's also not the best use of our time, nor the witnesses' time." He looked at Jan, "If you want Miss McCarron to come back later, fine."

Jan nodded her head slightly in acknowledgement, "Thank you, Sir."

Conrad dismissed Kristi until "some time later" and said, "Lets take a fifteen minute break, now while Cadet Sayers goes to collect the next witness." Everyone stood up to use the latrine or go to the Coke machine.

Jan turned to Cadet Trane and whispered, "Sir, the next witness is Dogety. He refused to make a written statement. Can he "plead the fifth" as a witness?"

Trane thought a moment before saying, "He is supposed to answer all questions, but he may try to deflect them. Keep him from going on tangents. Ask direct 'yes' or 'no' questions if you can."

"Sir, I'm not sure I can do this. What happens if I have to throw up?" Jan said, suddenly feeling nauseous.

"Just lean to your left toward Major Hastings. Do not, I repeat, do not, lean to the right. Understand?" he said with a smile.

"Yes, Sir." *Gawd, I love you.*

18

Q: How many lights are in Cullum Hall?
A: There are 340 lights in Cullum Hall, Sir.
Heritage, Bugle Notes, 81, p. 242

"RALLY! RALLY! RALLY!"

Jan, Angel and Drew jumped up, knocking books from their laps and began donning various, non-uniform uniforms. Jan chose the gray pajama top over gray skirt with go-go boots and black beret. The last three female only items were never worn seriously. Even if she wanted to wear them, her calf muscles had doubled in size since R-Day making it impossible to zip the boots.

Angel wore the Full Dress Gray coat with its big brass buttons, tails and cut at the waist in front, over gray pajama bottoms. She wrapped another women-only-never-worn item, the black and yellow polyester scarf, around her head. Jan thought she looked adorable. *All 99 pounds of her!*

The roommates tied Angel's white skirt around Drew's waist using a white parade chest strap as a belt. Jan convinced him to wear her black pumps, which she would never wear anyway, and finished his outfit off with Angel's black beret. Without a shirt, he looked a bit like a Scottish, French cross-dresser who had a few too many drinks.

"You look the prettiest, Drew!" Jan said as all three stared in the mirror at their fashions. They laughed while scurrying to the rally. Once in Central Area, they ran around screaming, shouting and jumping like all the other pent-up plebes.

Many of the guys wore only underwear. Jan wondered whether they were lazy, unimaginative, or, she later considered, trying to make a point like her.

I would never go out in my skivvies though.

The rally ran its course and the three plebes reluctantly returned to the barracks. They entered the room to find Dogety sitting in Jan's desk chair. "What the hell kind of outfit is that, Hambin?" He stood up while the three friends stood at attention. "Answer me, dammit!"

"Sir, may I make a statement?" Jan asked.

"No, you may not! Hambin, answer me. What the hell are you doing in a skirt and high heels?"

"Sir, we went to the rally..."

"What?"

"Sir, we went..."

"I heard that, Hambin, but what about the freakin' skirt?"

"Sir, we dressed him for the rally," Jan blurted.

"I wasn't talking to you, Wishart!"

Drew's face turned red. He hadn't been reprimanded like this since Beast. Jan tried again, "Sir, may I make a statement?"

"What?" Dogety yelled.

"It's my fault, Sir. I told Cadet Hambin to use our clothes rather than waste time going back to his room before the rally. It's my fault, Sir."

Dogety continued staring at Drew. "Hambin, it's not like your room is across Post; it's next door for shitsakes! What kind of sorry ass man wears girls' clothes? You some kind of fairy?"

"No, Sir!"

Dogety continued, "That's the most ridiculous thing I've ever seen in my life. I don't ever want to see that on you or any man again, you understand me, Hambin?"

"Yes, Sir!" Drew said, with a slight shake of his head.

"And as for you, Wishart, you don't TELL anyone what to do. He's a big boy; he can make his own decisions."

No question. No comment.

Then he stepped right into her face and screamed, "YOU HEAR ME, WISHART?"

"Yes, Sir!" she yelled back.

Dogety stormed out of their room. Jan, Angel and Drew let out a collective sigh of relief. "He always finds a way to siphon the fun out of everything," Jan said.

"Yeah," Drew added, "I was just thinking how much I didn't miss him."

Dear Jan,

Sorry, code name doesn't quite fit you. Hope you don't mind if I go back to Jan. I like your name. It's strong and neither common, nor weird. And Wishart? What nationality is that?

You do not disappoint. But I, for one, would like to see you have some fun. And I really would love to see you smile. I know it's hard to do here, but I am living proof that it can happen.

I understand your cautious approach to us, but we are very patient. Just continue to send your questions and concerns to Box 483 (or leave taped to your door), and I will do my best to address your concerns. I still want you to join our organization, but you are proving to be a tougher case than I thought. I won't push you on that issue anymore. Let's just try to get you smiling first.

Congratulations on making the team-handball team. And what happened at the parade last weekend? Your platoon probably got a lot of attention for that.

Hope to hear from you soon,
SKIP

SKIP,

I can't decide whether I like your letters or not. I am a little unnerved that you know so much about my life while I don't even know your name. I might consider you a stalker.

On the other hand, I look forward to your notes. So, while it may be crazy to keep encouraging you, I am going to play along for a while.

Yes, team-handball is proving to be a big help to me. Mainly it gets me out of intra-murder. But I feel bad about leaving Kissy on the H-3 soccer team. I suppose you know her, too?

A couple of guys fell over while standing at attention in the parade. Rumor has it they were hung over. I don't think anyone got in trouble over it, though. If it had been us lowly Beanheads, we'd all be walking the area by now.

Why don't you just tell me your name? I promise to keep it between us.

Jan

A deuce and a half pulled up carrying fifteen fashionably dressed young women seated in opposing benches in the back. Two male plebes opened the tailgate, set a low bench next to it and helped the gaggle of females step down from the Army truck. The women giggled together in groups before walking into Cullum Hall.

"What *IS* that?" Jan asked.

"Fuck Truck," Kristi replied.

"What?"

"Fuck Truck. Also known as Cattle Call."

Jan didn't know about West Point's long tradition of importing young women from nearby Mount St. Martha's College to cadet dances. These ladies wore tight pants, low cut tops, form fitting dresses, high heels, off-the-shoulder jerseys, jewelry and makeup.

In dreary contrast, the Dress Gray uniforms completely covered female cadets—their arms, chest and back—with a clasp closure two inches up their necks. The coat hung down over their buttocks, hiding all signs of femininity. Female cadets could not wear jewelry, nor grow their hair below their collars. Modest makeup was allowed, as long as the eye shadow, blush and lipstick were not noticeable. Jan felt sure they came across like radishes in a basket full of ripe strawberries. "I don't want to go in," she confessed.

"Why not?" Drew asked.

"Look at us, Drew. We look like boys in these things. There are real women in there, with real clothes on, who are a whole lot more appealing," Jan said.

"So what?"

"So, our hopes of getting asked to dance just got run over by the Fuck Trucks," Kristi said it best again.

"I'll dance with you," Drew offered.

"Of course you will, but it would be nice to dance with someone else, too." She knew he was doing the big brother thing, but she wanted to meet a non-relative for once.

"Well, we may as well go in and see what we're missing," Kristi said.

"That's the spirit!" Drew really didn't get it.

They walked upstairs to the big ballroom and stood together observing their male classmates co-mingling with the female civilians. Several H-3 guys: Jones, McGuire, Winnans and Davidson, stood near the snack tables. Jan looked at Davidson, noticing his casual, relaxed body language. He caught her glance and lifted his beer in a toasting jest. She looked away quickly.

Jan and Kristi sighed simultaneously. They felt like distant relatives who had been invited, but not really wanted, at the celebration.

Drew's voice bumped them from their trance. "Let's dance!" His bright eyes beamed as "Twist and Shout" began to play. Jan knew this would be the only offer she would get. She turned to Kristi who was already shouting the words to the song. Then all three plebes pinged to the dance floor. For a few shining moments, they danced and sang like real college co-eds.

Well, shake it up, baby, now, (shake it up, baby)
Twist and shout. (Twist and shout)
C'mon, c'mon, c'mon, baby, now, (come on baby)
Come on and work it on out. (Work it on out)
Well, work it on out, honey. (Work it on out)
You know you look so good. (Look so good)
You know you got me goin, now, (got me goin)
Just like I knew you would. (Like I knew you would, oooh!)

Well, shake it up, baby, now, (shake it up, baby)
Twist and shout. (Twist and shout)

Jan swore off going to any more plebe dances. Her oath lasted until the following weekend when Army played VMI in a home football game. Kristi thought they should try the Cullum Hall dance again.

"Jan, the rats will be there tonight," Kristi said. Rats were VMI's equivalent to plebes.

"Oh goodie! The Mount St. Mattress girls will have even more men from which to choose."

"But there's only enough fuck-truckers to go around for our plebes."

"That's their problem." Jan didn't see the point.

"Jan, while our cadet brethren are cattle calling, the rats will be left without any dance partners," Kristi argued.

"And your point is…."

"My point is VMI doesn't have female cadets. These guys might actually be interested in us. They might be happy to just talk to women—even ones in Dress Gray."

"Are you saying you want to go to the dance?"

"Yes. Let's go and flirt with the VMI rats. Maybe some of our guys will sit up and take notice."

"I doubt it. I'll go only if Drew goes with us. That way we can at least walk in with a guy."

"Oh Drew will definitely go."

They arrived at Cullum Hall to find the same scene: civilian women socializing with male plebes. This time, however, the VMI rats also looked out of place in their similar but not quite identical uniforms. They dared not infringe on the civilian women, who were monopolized by the plebe men anyway. So the rats migrated closer and closer to the female cadets, realizing the plebe women were not spoken for.

"So, how are things going at VMI?" Drew asked one of them when they came within striking range. And that's all it took before Jan, Kristi and Drew began casually conversing with the larger group. Six rats formed a small semi-circle around Jan.

"Would you like to dance?" one finally asked Jan.

"Sure, but I'm out of practice."

"Don't worry about that," he said as they headed to the dance floor. When the fast song ended, he pulled her close and they kept dancing to a slow song. She felt womanly and wanted for the first time in over four months. The VMI rat didn't seem to care that she wore a gray straightjacket. She wondered how hard it would be to transfer to VMI.

When the slow song ended, he offered to buy her a beer. *Oh, wow, it's a real date if he buys me a drink, right?* Jan never actually went on a date with her high school boyfriend. He had asked her to go out with him, but they never did go out. They *hung out* all the time at her house, at his house, at friends' houses, at school and in cars. That's what *going out* meant—*hanging out*. But she always wanted to go on a real date.

They got their drinks and went downstairs to the outside balcony. "Where are you from?" she asked him.

"Virginia," he said.

"No surprise there," she said nervously. "So, do you like VMI?"

"It sucks."

"No surprise there either."

"I really miss being around girls," he said.

"Me, too," she blurted out before thinking. He laughed out loud.

"Bill," he said, when she asked his name.

Same name as Cadet Trane. They talked for two hours on the balcony overlooking the Hudson River, occasionally going back for more beer which Jan offered to buy, but he wouldn't allow. It was cold outside, but she didn't care.

When the pre-Taps alarm sounded at 2330 hours warning all cadets they had thirty minutes to get to their rooms, Jan considered asking Bill to spend the night in her room. But three reasons convinced her against it. One: it was against the rules, big time; two: Angel would not like it; and three: he might expect sex which was still not on her to-do list. Instead, the gentleman rat walked Jan to the walkway leading to her barracks.

"Thanks for dancing and talking," he said.

"It was my pleasure," she replied.

"Wish we could do it again sometime."

"Yeah, me, too."

"Well, goodnight then."

"Goodnight." Bill went with his fellow rats to wherever they went and she entered her barracks alone.

She rounded the corner out of the stairwell and heard a familiar bark, "Wishart!"

"Yes, Sir!" She stopped halfway down the hallway to her room and turned around.

"Were you just fraternizing with that *rat* from VMI?" Dogety asked loudly.

"Sir?"

"You know what I mean." Dogety walked closer to her.

"Sir, I do NOT know what you mean." It seemed Dogety had been drinking. But so had she. *Then again, he could just be his usual asshole self.*

"You were cavorting with that RAT, weren't you?"

"Sir, we were at the dance at Cullum together. As far as I know, that's not against the rules."

"Don't get smart with me, Wishart. I saw you two making out near Grant Hall."

"Sir, I certainly did NOT make out with anyone."

"Wishart, we have an Honor Code here you know."

"Sir, I wish I had made out with him, but I'm sorry, you must have seen someone else." The beers made her bolder than usual.

"Well, who the hell was that I just saw making out with a rat?"

"I have no idea, Sir. Why didn't you just go up and ask them who they were?" She knew she was pushing it.

He stepped right up to her, so his face was only a few inches from hers. "Wishart, I saw them from my window." She smelled the alcohol on his breath.

Peeping Tom? She remained silent and stared back at Dogety, not wanting to say what she was thinking.

"Hey, Sam, call for you," Jan's Squad Leader, Cadet Meyer, interrupted. "Miss Wishart, shouldn't you be getting to your room now?"

"Yes, Sir." She turned and sped away along the wall while Dogety walked in the opposite direction to the third floor pay phone.

Those damn bells.

From its perch above West Point, the Cadet Chapel is considered a stunning exclamation point to an already breathtaking campus. But to Jan, the Cadet Chapel had one huge flaw: its bells. Annoyingly, they woke her up every Sunday at 0800. *God, I hate those bells.* They rang out on the only day plebes could sleep in which caused Jan to wonder if they were part of the fourth-class system. Because sleeping was the ultimate escape from West Point, even better than getting drunk and second only to leave, the bells had to be a form of institutional hazing.

If she managed to go back to sleep after the bells, which was always her preference, she ended up missing Sunday brunch. The Mess Hall opened from ten o'clock to noon for brunch which was another problem with Sundays. *Isn't brunch supposed to be breakfast and lunch? What part of lunch ENDS at noon?*

Plebes were not allowed to go to the snack bar in Grant Hall, nor to *Tony's*, the underground pizza shop right in the middle of Central Area, nor to the Ike Hall cafeteria. And Boodlers, the cadet junk food store, was closed on Sundays. So missing brunch meant no meal until dinner. Jan would have to forage for food.

She pinged along the wall to Kristi and Debra's room. "Hey guys, sorry to ask again, but you got any food I can borrow?" Jan asked as she opened their door. Usually one of them had something in their footlocker. Jan kept meaning to store provisions in her footlocker for Sundays...she just never thought about it until Sunday.

"No, you can't borrow, but you may have something," Kristi said.

"I promise to stock up soon and then you can borrow from me all you want." Jan said halfheartedly, knowing she might never actually do that.

"No you won't Jan, but it's okay," Kristi stated the obvious once again.

"Okay, you're right. May I have something to eat anyway?"

"Only if you tell us what happened last night after we started dancing," Kristi demanded.

"Oh, not much. We got a few beers, sat out on the balcony and talked. He was really nice. He walked me to the barracks just before taps." She turned to Debra, still lying in her bed, "Hey, what did you do last night?"

Debra responded, "I don't dance."

"Well, what did you do then?" Jan asked.

"We had a swim team practice and dinner," Debra said.

"Jan, you didn't ask *me* what happened last night," Kristi interrupted, with a slight smile on her face.

"Well, do tell, my dear."

"Well, Dan, the Rat, and I danced a bit and also had a few beers. Then we went down to Flirtation Walk." Flirtation Walk, off-limits to plebes, was a trail where cadets and their dates could be alone. Jan thought most went to "Flirty" to make out, and probably some had had sex on the mysterious path. It held a certain mystical or mythical appeal to Jan, given that plebes were forbidden on it. Kristi, however, never let rules get in her way.

"Are you kidding? And you didn't get caught?" Jan asked.

"Nope. It was cold, but we kept pretty warm." Kristi giggled.

"Kissy, you amaze me," Jan said.

"We couldn't keep our hands off each other, even after we got back. We kept necking right up until taps. Then we both started running to our rooms, without even saying goodbye." Kristi described it like she was recalling a playful childhood memory.

"Wait, Kissy, were you making out by Grant Hall?" Jan wondered if maybe….

"He had my back right up against the wall," Kristi confirmed.

"Oh man, Dogety saw you!" Jan said. "He thought *I* was making out with the rat."

"No shit! What did he say?"

"He said," Jan lowered her voice to mimic Dogety's, "'Wishart, I saw you making out with that rat by Grant Hall' or something like that."

"Damn! What did you say?" Kristi's eyes widened.

"I said it wasn't me. He didn't believe me at first, so I told him I wished I had made out with someone, but unfortunately I hadn't. You should have seen his face. He looked like he was going to burst a blood vessel."

"Do you think he knew it was me?" Kristi asked.

"Hell no. He obviously didn't get a good look. I'm only about a foot taller than you, Kissy."

"It's a good thing he's blind as well as stupid!" Kristi laughed.

Debra sighed, "Are you two done talking about your sexual escapades? I'd like to go back to sleep."

"Hey, I just came for the food." Jan grabbed a package of cheese crackers from Kristi before heading back to her room.

The other problem with Sundays was what to do with the rest of the day. Nothing else absolutely had to be done, so the afternoon always led to brooding, ruminating and contemplating.

I wish I had the guts to do what Kissy did last night. I might have ventured further with Bill at a normal college. At a real university, I could wear whatever I wanted. I could eat whatever I wanted. No one would care how much I weigh or how fast I run. I could have a boy in my bed and sleep in every day if I wanted.

So why am I still here?

This debate raged on every Sunday afternoon. The only way to escape the argument in her brain was to curl up on her bed with her "Gray Girl." Issued to all new cadets on R-day, this warm, gray, comfy comforter became every cadet's best friend. Plebe Gray Girls were crispy and bright gray, *if there is such a thing as bright gray.* Firstie Gray Girls were the best—dull gray, soft and worn like the Velveteen Rabbit. These comforters were called Gray Girls long before the advent of women at West Point. Jan didn't mind the name; she certainly didn't want to share her bed with a Gray *Boy* every night.

135

"Angel, hope it's okay if I put on my Sunday afternoon uniform," Jan said as she rolled on her bed pulling the comforter over her body.

"What uniform is that?" Angel asked.

"Gray Girl over Gray Girl," she said before drifting off to sleep.

Dear Jan,

Please don't be too unnerved by my letters. I am not stalking you, and I am not dangerous in any way. I just happen to be in the general vicinity and notice things about you.

For instance, I have yet to see you smile. I know it's a tough thing to do here, but that's part of how we can be subversive. Smiling is good for us and it totally messes with the enemy. Killjoys don't know what to do with smiling. Try smiling and see what happens. Besides, I bet you have a really great smile. I bet you have an even better laugh (but one step at a time).

I'm sure "Kissy" understands you had to choose team handball over "intra-murder." (Great term.)

I'm sorry to keep you in the dark about me, but if you think back about 2 weeks, we met in the mailroom. And this past weekend, we met under some less than desirable conditions. Soon you will figure it out.

I hope you enjoy your Thanksgiving leave.

SKIP

SKIP,

Okay, I assume you are a cadet. And since cadets cannot lie, cheat or steal, I will take your word that you are not dangerous.

But I still have no idea who you are. I assume you are male and given you are in the "general vicinity" that narrows it down to about 1,000 guys.

I don't recall meeting anyone in the mailroom, and I have no idea when we met under less than desirable conditions.

OH GOD, PLEASE TELL ME YOU'RE NOT DOGETY!

IF you are, this correspondence is over!

Jan

19

Sam Dogety entered the room and walked behind Jan's chair to the witness table. His six-foot frame seemed smaller than usual as he raised his right hand and repeated the Honor Board oath. Jan felt her cheeks redden when he sat down and glanced at her. She took a deep breath trying to quell the queasiness in her stomach. Dogety could either make this whole thing go away or make sure *she* went away. It all came down to the this man who had made her life mostly miserable all year.

"Sam, you declined to submit a written statement which is your prerogative. However, we need to hear what you witnessed last Sunday night. So please, whenever you're ready," Conrad said waving his hand. Dogety fidgeted in his chair. He picked up his gray saucer hat which he had laid down on the table in front of him. He started twirling it in his hands, staring intently down at the activity. When he didn't speak or look up for a few more seconds, Conrad cleared his throat. "Um, Sam, are you ready to start?"

"I...ah...I would.... rather answer questions, if that's okay," he said finally.

Conrad seemed confused. "Well, normally you would tell us what happened, then we would ask questions if we have any."

"But if it's not against the rules, I'd rather just answer your questions." He stopped twirling the hat, but kept holding it between his knees.

"All right, then," Conrad continued, "What happened on the night of May second, with regard to Cadet Wishart, Cadet Jackson and yourself?"

Dogety leaned forward in his chair, "I mean, specific questions. You have the basic statements from both Wishart and Jackson, so just ask me specific questions about the gray areas."

Dogety, what are you trying to do here?

"The first major gray area," Seymuor interjected, "seems to be what happened in the CQ room. Tell us what you witnessed there on Sunday night."

"Could you be more specific?" Dogety asked.

Jesus, Dogety, just tell them what you know!

"Well," Seymour continued, "how did you question Cadet Wishart?"

"We asked her what she did with the original correspondence between myself and Cadet Jackson," Dogety said.

"No, I mean, *how* did you question her? Did you scream at her? Was she in the Smack position?"

"I raised my voice but not sure if you'd call it screaming. And yes, she was at attention against the wall."

Tourney jumped in, "Would you say Cadet Jackson screamed at her?"

"Yes."

"Did he scream in her face?" Tourney asked.

"Yes."

"And did you try to stop him or get him to calm down?" Gaskins asked this time.

"I asked him to lower his voice. But he was pretty agitated."

"Did you," Tourney again, "at any time, try to restrain Cadet Jackson?"

"I did," Dogety looked back down at his hat.

"Why? Why did you try to restrain Cadet Jackson?" Leavitt asked.

"I was a little worried Markus might...might make too much of the incident." The room silenced.

"What do you mean?" Leavitt asked in almost a whisper.

"I mean I have seen Markus lose his temper before and I thought he might... well, I didn't want him to do anything he might regret," Dogety said without looking up.

Again the room became quiet. "Did you think he might hurt Miss Wishart?"

"I...I don't, no, I didn't think he'd hurt her," he paused, "but I didn't want to find out."

Conrad interrupted, "Sam, we all know it's acceptable practice for upperclassmen to question plebes in the manner described by both Markus and Miss Wishart. We've all done it; it's not anything unusual. So I am perplexed as to why you might think this was troubling."

"That's true, Casey. But we had been drinking, as you know," Dogety admitted.

"Could that have also altered your perception of the events?" Conrad asked.

"Maybe," he said, "but I don't think so."

Conrad had heard enough, "It's seventeen hundred hours, so let's stop here until after dinner. I expect everyone to be back in this room by nineteen-thirty. Remember everything said in this room stays in this room." He stood up and closed his folder.

Jan watched Dogety get up from his chair like an old man. He looked at Jan but quickly dropped his eyes when he saw her staring back. She felt a strange sensation, something like sadness. She never expected to feel sorry for Dogety, but as he walked out the door, with his shoulders drooping, she suddenly wanted to run over and hug him.

20

(Whistle)—BOOM! –AHHH
U.S.M.A. Rah! Rah!
U.S.M.A. Rah! Rah!
Hoo—Rah! Hoo—Rah!
AR—MAY! Rah!
Team! Team! Team!
Rocket Yell, Bugle Notes, 81, p.285

Plebes continued to mark time by counting down the days until the
next opportunity to leave West Point—Thanksgiving, the Army/Navy
game, Christmas, Spring Break, and the ultimate opportunity to leave
for good: graduation. Each milestone was so highly anticipated,
because cadets lived for when they could leave, and no one ever
wanted to come back. The common joke went,

"Hey, what's that loud noise you hear when returning to West
Point?"

"Oh, that's the giant sucking sound!"

Her parents drove the four plus hours to pick her up for
Thanksgiving leave. When she slid in the backseat, she realized she had
been holding her breath. As they drove away, she turned to watch
West Point's massive stone buildings fade from view. As a plebe, she
didn't have many opportunities to look around. From the safety of her

parents' car, she saw why cadets sometimes called West Point their "Rockbound Highland Home." Yet, she thought it looked nothing like a home. "Fortress" was the word that came to mind. The square, cold, gray, gothic structures seemingly lined up "dress-right-dress." Even the Cadet Chapel, considered the queen of all the buildings, appeared to Jan like a stone giant commanding the Army of buildings from her mountaintop.

A few miles past the West Point gates, Jan peeled off her Dress Gray uniform. She put on "civvies:" jeans and a t-shirt, and for the first time in five months, she felt almost normal. Tears welled up in her eyes when she walked through the door to her childhood home.

Mrs. Wishart prepared a big Thanksgiving dinner with the usual fare—turkey, mashed potatoes, stuffing, gravy, green bean casserole, squash casserole, cranberry sauce and rolls. Jan assumed the diet tables would be in her near future.

The whole family sat at the dining room table in their usual spots. The three brothers sat on one side, the three sisters on the other. Mom and Dad, sat at each end of the table like bookends. Jan always sat closest to her father. She had been sitting in that spot for as long as she could remember. *Why don't I ever sit next to mom?*

The noise level in the Wishart dining room was proportional to the Mess Hall with plenty of talking, laughing, joking and story telling. If anyone fell silent, it meant they had the flu or something.

"So Jan, tell us about West Point," Samuel, the middle brother asked.

"What do you want to know?" Jan wasn't about to say any more than was necessary.

"What's it like? What do you do everyday?"

"Well, we get up early. Depending on our assigned duties that week, we deliver newspapers or laundry to the upperclassmen rooms. Then, we read the paper, memorize the menus, go over any other stuff we need to know while cleaning our room, making the beds and getting dressed for breakfast formation."

"What time is that?" her mother asked.

"Breakfast formation is at six-twenty. We get up by five-thirty."

"So you have all that done before then?" brother Peter asked this time.

"Yes, and when we practice the indoor obstacle course test, we get up at four-thirty."

"But you get to sleep in on the weekends right?" This question came from her older sister, Maryanne, who had already graduated from college.

"No, we have one or two Saturday classes and then room inspections, and then we usually have to march for a parade. And if there's a home football game, then we have to go to that, too." Jan resented the football attendance requirement. *No one is required to go to any other sport.*

"Do you like it?" Peter asked. The room suddenly became quiet.

"No, not really," Jan replied softly.

"Just quit then," Peter said.

"I can't...yet."

"You can, right now if you want," he insisted again.

"That's enough, Pete," Mr. Wishart intruded. "Anything worth something is going to take hard work."

Jan didn't share all the details of her life at West Point. When she did talk about it, she made it seem humorous or silly, never mentioning the times she cried herself to sleep under her Gray Girl. It was one of those things, like *The Depression*, which could not be adequately described, only something you endured.

Her friends couldn't understand either. They lived in the normal world, going to normal colleges. They were having sex, smoking pot, drinking, and having sex. But her best friend, Regan, had always understood her. Ever since Jan called her a stuck up snob in the fifth grade, they had been best friends. They played the same sports, shared most of the same classes, and spent many nights partying in high school. So it came as a bit of a shock when Regan told Jan she had slept with Jan's only boyfriend in high school, Tim.

They met at their favorite hangout, Mel's, a local hole in the wall place. *God, it's good to see her.* After ordering beers and burgers, the two friends fell into their familiar conversation. Each one shared the highlights of their first semester at college. Both had a few funny stories. Jan didn't tell any of the bad ones.

After an hour or so, Regan said, "I have to tell you something, Jan." She said it so seriously Jan could only imagine she was either pregnant or had cancer.

"Is everything okay?"

"Yes...and no. I have a confession to make."

"You don't need to confess anything to me, Regan."

"Yes, I do." Jan could not imagine what she had done.

"Tim and I were together."

A long pause followed as Jan absorbed the meaning of "together."

"Oh."

"It was a one night thing. You know how it can be in college. A bunch of us got drunk, and he stayed over in my room."

"Oh."

"Tim didn't want to tell you, but I told him I could not keep secrets from you."

"Oh." She started to sound like a seal.

"I don't blame you if you hate me. I hate myself for doing it. It was just that once, and it won't ever happen again, I promise."

"Okay."

Just then, Tim showed up. Regan turned to look up at him and said, "Tim, we just finished talking about you."

"Oh really," he said. "I hope it was good."

"Well, I told Jan what happened," Regan admitted. Silence. "I told her we didn't mean to hurt her and that we were both drunk." Tim wouldn't look at Jan. Jan wouldn't look at Tim. Regan just looked away.

It occurred to Jan that she had two options. *I can fly off the handle bars, hit the glass ceiling, and never speak to either of them again. Or, I can let them off the hanger and hope we can all just be friends.* She only knew she didn't want her best friend to keep apologizing while her now ex-boyfriend acted deaf.

"Guys," she said, "look, it's college. Things happen. I wish it hadn't happened, but I understand. It's been a crazy semester for me as well.

Things got out of control a couple of times for me, too. I get it." Jan wasn't lying. Everything she said was technically true. They could interpret it however they wanted.

Tim pulled out a chair and sat down. He turned to Jan and said, "I'm sorry."

"No worries, Tim. Besides, I thought we had broken up when we left for college." *Okay, not exactly true, but given the situation, I can assume this should have happened.*

Tim looked like a dagger pierced his stomach. "Oh," he said.

It was a double betrayal. Not only because her best friend had sex with her boyfriend, but the added insult was that *she* hadn't even had sex with her boyfriend. *Hell, we didn't even get to third base!* As she lay in bed that night, she felt a heaviness in her chest, as if someone had dropped a large stone on her lungs.

She thought about what Dogety would say to her. "Suck it up, Wishart! What are you whining about now? Did you think they were just going to play checkers while you were away? No one is going to wait on you. So get your head out of your ass and move on."

Having been under Dogety's tutelage for so long did have its advantages. *Dogety, sometimes I really do like you.* Jan couldn't believe that thought just crossed her mind. When she awoke the next morning, she decided to take Dogety's advice. *It's no big deal. No worries, move on, it's over, no problemo.* And even though she didn't feel that way, she would, by God, act that way.

Upon her return to West Point, she swore she heard that giant sucking sound. But she could also hear the echo of sucking, and fucking, back home. It was as though she could never go back, and yet, she dreaded going forward.

The most anticipated non-leave event, other than graduation, was the Army/Navy game. One week after returning from Thanksgiving leave the Academy bused all four thousand cadets to Veterans Memorial Stadium in Philadelphia. The cadets marched onto the field for the pre-game ceremony. All went as practiced many times before.

Then it was game time. If Army beat Navy, plebes would be allowed to come off the walls upon their return to West Point. They would still be required to ping, but without squaring corners, they could literally cut their travel time across Post in half. Therefore, the Army/Navy game meant more to plebes than the Super Bowl, The World Series and the Stanley Cup Playoffs combined.

Prior to 1981, there had been seven tied games in its almost one hundred year history, the last one in 1965. This time, the old rivals tied again, 3-3. And although it was better than losing, a tie was still not a win.

Jan had been getting used to disappointment. *Close but no cigarette. Oh well, what's another six months of wall hugging?*

Once back at the hotel, Jan changed into her new jeans, bought at the Cadet Store just for this occasion, paired them with her favorite *Jethro Tull* t-shirt and her old *LL Bean* rubber shoes. She hoped to meet a few nice young men. *Okay, even just one will do.*

Drew came to their room looking like a GQ model. Jan marveled at his attire. Most cadets wore Levi's or Wranglers with t-shirts, cowboy boots and/or cowboy hats. But Drew wore an expensive brand of black jeans, with an untucked, button-down, white shirt, the sleeves rolled up to mid forearm. He wore dark, cordovan loafers without socks. His hair, short like all cadets, had been slightly gelled, giving him the look of a professional model. No other cadets dressed like him. *His taste is impeccable,* Jan thought, *in clothing and friends.*

They went down to the hotel bar where many of the cadet lodgers partied. Jan saw Jackson standing next to Dogety. "What's he doing here?"

"Those two do everything together," Kristi said. "I bet they even sleep together."

"Let's not go there," Drew said.

"Right, don't want that picture in my head," Jan replied. They found a small round table near the bar and ordered drinks. Jan asked for a Long Island Iced Tea, the most alcohol bang for your buck she figured. Kristi ordered a beer on tap and Drew asked for a coke.

"Do you drink, Drew?" Kristi asked.

"No, not really."

"Good God, how can you not?" Jan asked.

"I don't know, I just never got started. I prefer to keep my wits about me at all times," he said.

"Well that's good, cuz I prefer to lose mine as often as possible," Kristi said. And Jan agreed.

The bar was brimming with cadets, from plebes to firsties. Their little table soon became adjoined to three more tables. Angel and Debra joined the group and even Dogety and Jackson took a spot with the enlarging group of drinking cadets. Trane and his girlfriend showed up, too. Jan and Kristi never had to buy another drink; new ones just appeared in front of them. Their chairs remained open whenever they left to go to the bathroom, but if a guy left his seat, someone else sat down in his place. Drew lost his seat when he went to order another coke.

After about an hour, Jan noticed Bill Trane and his girlfriend facing each other and leaning against one wall. They seemed to be arguing. Cadet Williams looked like she had been crying and Trane seemed to be pleading with her. At one point, he began holding her wrists, but she shook them loose from his grip. Then she shouted something at him and stormed off. Jan watched as he rotated from a side lean to facing outward toward the table of partying cadets. Jan waited for him to look up and when he did, she nodded at him, almost to say, "If she doesn't work out, I'm available." But Trane just turned and walked out of the bar.

Jan looked back down at her drink in front of her, embarrassed for nodding at Cadet Trane. *What am I thinking?* After reprimanding herself for letting her guard down and being an idiot, she regrouped, put on a smile and looked back up at the table of cadets.

She immediately noticed something wrong with Debra. Her eyes were closed and her head looked like it was about to drop off her neck. Jan motioned to Angel who was sitting closer to Debra, *Is she all right?* Angel shrugged her shoulders. Jan turned to Kristi, "Hey, look at Debra. Does she appear okay to you?"

Kristi looked down the table. "She looks like she's about to pass out."

"I think we better get her back to the room." Jan figured Debra wasn't used to drinking the way she and Kristi were. *Sure she can swim, but she can't drink worth a damn.*

Jan and Kristi lifted Debra out of her chair. Angel gathered up her sweater and purse. The three, plebe women of H-3 dragged the fourth to the elevator. Debra could hardly walk. Her speech was incoherent.

"Geez, Debra, have you ever even drank before?" Kristi asked.

"Da…."

"I think that's a 'yes,'" Jan said.

Angel held the elevator door, "She only had about three drinks, I think. She ordered one, someone bought her another and I gave her mine which someone bought for me." Angel didn't believe in drinking. It was against her religion or something like that.

The elevator stopped at the sixth floor. Jan and Kristi dragged Debra down the long hallway until they reached their room. Angel used her key to open the door. They heaved Debra onto one of the two queen beds.

"God, I wonder how she's going to feel in the morning," Kristi said.

Jan was a little worried. "Do you think she might puke all over our stuff while we're gone?" Then because that sounded selfish, "I mean, should we stay with her in case she gets sick?"

"She'll be fine. We can check on her in a couple hours," Kristi said.

No one wanted to spend the rest of Army/Navy night in their room. So they left Debra lying drunk and alone in the hotel room. They would later regret that decision.

At almost four in the morning, Jan and Kristi went with a group of cadets to get something to eat. They walked to the Seven-Eleven across the street. Angel decided to call it a night, so she was the first to return to the room.

She knew something was wrong as soon as she opened the door. Clothes were strewn everywhere; sheets and pillows were ripped off both beds. The bathroom door was closed, and she could hear Debra throwing up.

"Debra, Debra, are you alright?" Angel pounded on the locked door.

"Nooooo..."

"Open the door and I'll help you."

"Noooo..."

"Debra, it's me, Angel. I can help you."

"Noooo..."

"Okay, I'll be right back, Debra, I'm going to get Jan and Kristi."

"Noooo...."

Angel tore down the hallway, then jumped up and down while waiting for the slowest elevator on earth. She finally reached the empty lobby and ran out the main doors and across the parking lot. She looked both ways on the usually busy street before darting across to the store with the big, green and red seven sign.

Jan and Kristi, Slushies in hand, walked out of the convenience store and bumped into a frenzied Angel. "Jan, Kristi," she barely breathed, "come quick, something's wrong with Debra." It took a second to sink in. Then Jan and Kristi looked at each other, threw their Slushies on the ground and took off running back to the hotel.

They found the room just as Angel had with Debra still locked in the bathroom. Jan tapped quietly on the door. "Debra, it's just us— Kristi, Angel and me. We're here to help you. Please open the door."

"Noooo.... go away." She still sounded somewhat drunk but also like she had been crying.

"Debra, no one is going away until you open this door." They waited another long minute. Then they heard Debra slide across the floor as if she was low crawling. The door unlocked and Jan opened it gently.

Debra was curled up in a fetal position in front of the bathtub. She wore only a bra. The room smelled of vomit, pee and something else. Towels were everywhere; some were bloody.

"Debra, are you cut?" Jan crouched down to examine where she might have been injured.

"Noooo...." Debra coiled even further into herself. Jan looked up at Kristi and Angel, still standing in the doorway.

"Should we get help?" Kristi asked.

"NO!" Debra shouted from inside her cocoon.

"Debra, what do you want us to do?" Jan asked.

"Just clean up and help me back to bed."

"Okay, sure. We'll take care of everything…" She nodded to Angel and Kristi who turned into the room and began re-ordering things. Jan leaned down closer to Debra. "They're picking up the room now, Debra." She thought about what to say next. "Debra, why are you undressed?" Jan didn't think Debra would have had the energy or the desire to disrobe.

"Someone came in," she said so quietly Jan almost missed it.

"Someone came in the room?" Jan asked back softly.

"Yes."

"Who? Who came in the room?"

"I don't know."

Jan was beginning to put things together. *No, please tell me I'm wrong.* "Debra, what did this person do…when they came in the room?" Jan held her breath.

"I don't know," Debra's voice grew even quieter.

"What do you remember?" Jan asked.

"I remember…. I remember someone coming in and taking my clothes off. I could feel him and hear him but I could not move. I was so drunk and so scared. I just pretended to be asleep, which I was really. I mean, I felt like I was asleep, but I also knew what was happening."

Oh shit!

"Then I don't remember what happened until I woke up puking in the toilet and heard Angel knocking on the door. I don't remember walking to the bathroom, I don't remember locking the door, and I don't remember anything after…" she trailed off.

"Was it only one person?" *Please say yes.*

"I think so…I didn't hear anyone talking."

Jan unfurled her crouch and sat down on the tile floor with her back against the bathtub and her legs jutting out in front. She let out a deep breath. "Debra, we should report this to the Officer in Charge."

"NO!" Debra sat up. "If you say anything, I will never speak to you again!" Angel and Kristi appeared in the doorway. "That goes for you two, too! No one says anything about this! I mean it!"

They were silent for a long moment. Finally Kristi said, "we'll do whatever you want, Debra. But don't you think we should at least try to find out who did this?"

"NO, I DON'T!" Debra was shouting again. "DO YOU THINK I WANT EVERYONE KNOWING WHAT HAPPENED HERE?"

Angel chimed in, "But Debra, it's not your fault."

"LIKE HELL IT ISN'T!" Then she started laughing, sort of. "What will everyone think? Huh? Everyone saw me drunk! Everyone will think it was my fault whether it is or not!" She took a deep breath. "And everyone will blame you guys for leaving me here alone and drunk! Did you think about that?"

Jan had not thought about that. Debra was right; they were at least partially to blame. They had left their classmate, their company mate, in a vulnerable situation. One of them should have stayed with her.

"Besides, nothing actually happened," Debra said. "Someone came in here and took off my clothes. Big deal." But Jan looked again at the bloodied towels and she knew something *had* happened. Something *really bad* happened. Debra seemed to know what Jan was thinking. "I got a bloody nose from falling on the toilet."

Everyone knew she was lying. And Debra knew they knew. So she looked away from them. Technically, they could have brought honor charges against her. Winnans would have insisted on it. But it never even crossed their minds.

After breakfast the next morning, the four women packed and loaded their bags on one of six busses parked in front of the hotel. They were the first ones on the bus, except for Dogety who sat in the very last seat. Just as they sat down, Dogety said, "I'd like a word with you four." They stood up and walked to the back of the bus. "Miss Plowden, do you realize these three classmates saved your butt last night?"

Jan's eyes widened. *Oh no, no, Sir...don't...*

"If not for these three, you might have been in really deep trouble."

Dogety, please...stop.

"Your may not remember what happened because your condition was very unbecoming an officer. But your friends made sure you didn't do anything even more stupid. They looked out for you. They kept you safe."

For Christ's sake man, enough...

"McCarron, Trane and Wishart, you did the right thing when you saw your classmate was inebriated. You took decisive action and prevented any further harm. I commend your actions."

They stood silently, stunned at his speech.

"I hope this experience gives you all a better appreciation for 'Cooperate and Graduate.' And if the shoe is ever on the other foot, Miss Plowden, I hope you would do the same for one of them."

He finished his lecture, but the four women didn't move.

"Dismissed."

That word shook them out of their trance. They walked silently to the front of the bus.

21

Friday, May 7
1730 Hours

Jan heard Angel calling the two-minute bell and decided to skip both formation and dinner. She wasn't hungry and couldn't eat even if she tried. *What are they gonna do, give me demerits?* An Honor Board tends to make all other punishments seem lame.

She lay back on her bed and closed her eyes. She wouldn't sleep even though she felt like sleeping for a hundred years. She just wanted to be alone and quiet, but the sounds of slamming doors, yelling and marching always permeated the air at West Point. One could never find real silence. She placed her palm over her eyes and tried to think of something, anything, other than reality.

Two knocks at the door interrupted her brief moment of semi-peace. "Come in." She assumed it was another plebe as the knocks were not particularly loud. Sam Dogety pushed open the door, stepped inside her room and closed the door. She didn't even get up from her prone position. *What's he gonna do, give me demerits?*

"What do you want, Dogety?" Jan decided she didn't give a rat's ass at this point. He sat down on Kristi's bed, directly across from her.

"Who's SKIP?" he asked.

"What?"

"I need to talk to SKIP," he said. "It's urgent."

"How do you know about SKIP?"

"That's not important. Just tell me who he is." He seemed to be more energized than the last time she saw him.

"Why do you need to know?" she said still lying with her palm over her eyes.

Dogety took a deep breath. "Jan."

She turned her head to look at him. Then she sat up slowly, sitting on her bed facing him.

"Jan, I need your help," he said gravely.

"*You* need...? What's wrong with you? I'm the one in big trouble here, remember?"

"Yes, but just hear me out. We don't have long before someone hears or finds us. I know you are innocent and I will tell the truth, don't worry. But you have to remember that I will forever be known as a rat when I do. My Army career will be over before it even begins once I give testimony that betrays my classmate and best friend. Can you understand what I'm saying Jan?"

She felt the room swirl around her as she contemplated what he said. *He admitted my innocence. He will tell the truth. I won't get kicked out for honor.* "I understand that you have just admitted that I'm innocent and that you can testify to that."

"Yes, I can, and I will, if necessary. I'm trying to save both of us here, Jan. Don't you see?"

"No, not exactly, *Sam.* You're not charged with an honor violation." How dare he even compare his situation to hers?

Dogety took a deep breath. "I'm so sorry for this whole mess. It's my fault you're in this position, and I am truly sorry. I won't let you go down. But I don't want to go down either. That's why I need SKIP."

He wasn't making any sense. What the hell did SKIP have to do with anything? "How can SKIP possibly help?"

"I have it on good authority that SKIP can prove you're telling the truth."

"YOU can prove I'm telling the truth!" She practically shouted.

"All I can do is testify to what I saw on Monday morning. And that's probably not enough to clear you of both charges. But I hear SKIP knows more than that, and if he can testify, it works for both of us. Jan, please help me here. My classmates will never forget if I am to blame for Markus Jackson, lacrosse team captain, being kicked out a week before graduation. You do realize that he will have to serve four years in the Army as a Specialist? This will ruin him, and I cannot be the one to do it."

Jan looked down at the floor. "Well, I can't help you anyway. I don't know who SKIP is; he's never told me."

"Can you get him to testify? Explain to him that he needs to come forward for your sake," Dogety pleaded.

"And for yours?" she asked.

"Yes, and for mine."

22

"The Code requires complete integrity in both word and deed of all members of the Corps and permits no deviation from these standards....These standards are rigidly enforced, and any intentional act in violation of the Code by a cadet is cause for separation from the Military Academy."
Honor, Bugle Notes, 81, p.35

The entire Corps of Cadets survived the Army/Navy weekend and returned to the gray walls of West Point by late Sunday afternoon. All was *normal* again by Monday morning. Term-end exams (TEEs) were rapidly approaching, and everyone hunkered down for intense studying. Exam week was the last obstacle before Christmas leave, the biggest break for plebes to date. Jan could hardly breathe thinking about this extended time off, never mind study. Another letter from SKIP helped to further divert her attention.

Dear Jan,
No, I am not Dogety. I can assure you of that. But good guess on my being a male cadet. I had a hard time figuring out how you found out, but every organization has its leaks. I guess this proves I am hiding in plain sight.
We bumped into each other several times during Army/Navy

weekend, once quite literally. I don't think you noticed. But I hope you enjoyed the festivities.

Well, we just have to get through TEE week. Then it's finally Christmas leave. I hope you have a great time at home and I look forward to hearing from you when we get back in January.

Take care,

SKIP

Classes, athletics, minute calling, formations, inspections, poop, laundry sorting, paper deliveries and term end exams (TEEs) made it almost impossible for plebes to do anything else. Yet in the middle of exam week, Jan and Drew found time to go running, still the only way to be alone and talk freely. They set off from Mahan Hall with Jan setting the pace. Drew didn't try to outrun her or pick up the speed. She deeply appreciated his lack of needing to show off.

"Did I tell you who I think did it?"

"Did what?"

She gave him an exasperated look, "Drew! C'mon! The one who raped Debra at Army/Navy?" She hadn't told another living soul about that night, except Drew. She knew he could be trusted with their secret.

"Oh, that." It seemed Drew didn't want to talk about it.

"Jackson," she said and waited for Drew's response. Their Etonic sneakers slapped against the pavement making the only sound on the cold, December afternoon.

"I could see that," Drew said after a pause. "But why do you think it was him?"

"He was with our group in the hotel. He and Dogety are like fleas on sticky paper."

"Jan, a lot of guys were in our hotel. It could have been anyone."

Jan had already given it a lot of thought. "Kissy and I talked about it. We have zero physical proof. But we both feel sure he did it."

"How could he have entered the room? Didn't the doors lock automatically anytime you left."

"I don't know. I know we didn't think about locking the door when we left her in the room. But even if the door was locked, how hard would it be for him to get another key? If he went to the front desk and asked for a room key because he had misplaced his, they would give him one. Who would think a West Point Cadet would lie about that? It was probably very easy for him to get a key."

They ran a few more yards in silence. Jan wanted more than anything to find a way to prove Jackson raped Debra. But Debra did not want to pursue it further. How could she accuse him without a witness or some other tangible evidence? "Drew, we can't do anything about it without Debra's involvement. We don't have any other evidence. But I swear, on my life, if I ever find a way to nail his ass, I will."

They continued jogging down Thayer Road, to Thayer Hotel and Thayer Gate, all named for Sylvanus Thayer, the father of the military academy. *Why didn't they name the gate 'Sylvanus' just to add some variety?* The two friends turned around and headed back along the same route. They ran in step to a subliminal cadence, a residual effect of their training.

"Do you ever feel like this place will wear you down so much that you won't even be the same person you once were?" Drew asked, breaking the silence.

"It already has," Jan admitted. "But maybe I needed to be another person altogether. Maybe I needed to change."

They heard the distant sound of a bugle playing and abruptly stopped running. They stood at attention until a cannon fired. Then they saluted toward the vicinity of The Plain where the US flag was being lowered. Stopping and saluting was required of anyone in earshot of Retreat every evening at 1730 hours.

Once jogging again, they talked of brighter topics like their exam schedule, SAMI, laundry duties, and Dogety. Always they talked about Dogety.

Dear SKIP,

If I don't come back after Christmas leave, you'll know I've decided to quit. I probably failed my history exam anyway. And you wanted me to smile?

Sorry, still having trouble with all that fun stuff. Maybe you can clue me in as to how I might see the humor in all of this? Seriously, I know you mean well, but I am so sick of it all. I just don't think I can stand to come back and face all these gray walls for another semester.

So, maybe I will see you in January, maybe not. I guess it will be a surprise for both of us.

Good luck and thanks for trying to cheer me up. You really did try.

Jan

She packed her things, which fit nicely into a small bag, and waited for her parents. They were meeting at General Patton, the statue facing the library. Supposedly, he faced the library because he never went there as a cadet. While Jan waited under his watchful eye, she realized that she also had rarely visited the library that whole semester. In fact, she never went to "Boodlers" (the cadet junk food mart) either. She never snuck out to Flirtation Walk. She never spun the "lucky spurs" on the Sedgwick Monument. She never counted the lights in Cullum Hall. She never saw the inside of the Old Cadet Chapel where Benedict Arnold's name is gouged from a plaque. She never looked at the "Foundation Eagle" or noticed the evolution of the full dress hat in the stone carvings above Grant Hall. She never looked for the mistakes on the French Monument and she never really appreciated the huge mural in Washington Hall. There were so many things Jan didn't see, didn't do and didn't know. Would she want to live her whole life thinking, "I never even finished plebe year?"

Before her parents pulled up to the curb, she knew she would come back after Christmas. Despite what she wrote to SKIP, she was not going to leave West Point without finishing plebe year.

Besides, after six months in a sea of men, I've only made two male friends. And one of them is anonymous. I have to come back, if only to find out who the hell he is.

Jan's period showed up the day after she arrived home. Maybe it was "perfectly normal" to stop menstruating at West Point, but it only fueled her fear that she might be turning into a man. So, when it returned after six months, it felt like an early Christmas gift. *Okay, I haven't grown a Y chromosome yet.*

She spent several days hanging out with Regan and some of those times included Tim. He had a new girlfriend at college; Jan pretended to be happy for him. While she wore a "leave me alone" face at West Point, she wore a "hey, it's all good" face at home. When her parents and siblings asked how things were going at Woo Poo U, she shrugged and said something like "Oh, it's going" or "fine." She wanted to say, "It sucks, I hate it and I wish I never applied." But no one really understood, and they couldn't help even if they did. So when Kristi's letter arrived two days before Christmas, Jan felt elated.

> *Jan,*
>
> *I'm going out of my mind. My mother and stepfather want me to wear my uniform every time we step out the door. My older brother sleeps all day, my younger brother watches TV all day, and my sister whines all day. Because I graduated high school in the states, I don't even have any friends here in Bonn. I AM GOING CRAZY!*
>
> *Then I remembered that you have the all American, white, suburban family life that I desperately need. So, can I come stay with you? I will call soon and make sure it's okay. We can go back to Woo Poo U together. I hope you don't mind because I HAVE to get out of here!!!*
>
> *I promise I won't eat much, and I can sleep on the floor.*
> *YOUR BEST FRIEND,*
> *Kissy*

Jan's family never had a problem with friends coming over or staying for extended periods of time. It was one of the great things about a big family. No one noticed a few extra bodies hanging around.

Kristi called on Christmas day and asked if she could arrive in three days. She planned to spend two thirds of Christmas leave at Jan's house. "Kissy, do you really want to spend the last two weeks of leave away from home?" Jan asked.

"Absolutely," Kristi said emphatically. "If I have to go to one more function in my uniform, I am going to kill someone."

Jan met Kristi at Logan Airport three days after Christmas. Snow started falling as they loaded her bags into the car. It continued to come down, heavier and heavier, as Jan drove the car back to New Hampshire with Kristi. What should have been a one hour drive turned into two and a half, allowing them plenty of time to catch up. After the usual banter about their families and what they got for Christmas, Jan asked, "Kissy, do you think you will stay at West Point?"

"Unless I fail out, yes. Why?"

"Don't you ever want to quit, go to college somewhere else and live a normal life?"

Kristi said, "Sometimes, but I have always wanted to go to West Point. Even as a little girl, I dreamed of going."

"You're kidding, right?"

"Seriously. When my dad died, I vowed that I would go to West Point, as he did. I just always knew it was my destiny to go to the military academy."

Jan looked at Kristi. "How did you figure that when West Point didn't allow women until five years ago?"

"Oh, I just knew. I knew my dad would help make it happen," Kristi said.

"Okay, wait. Did you just say that you believe that your *dead dad* helped make sure West Point opened it's doors to women and to you in particular?"

"Yes, something like that," Kristi replied.

"Well, that's certainly...a...leap of faith."

"I guess I never worried about it. I always knew he was watching out for me and that I would go to West Point." They rode in silence for a few moments as Jan tried to process what it meant to know, to really know something. Without proof, without facts, without prior knowledge nor without inside information, how could anyone possibly be sure of anything? Kristi seemed to believe, with full confidence, in something that could not have been foreseen at the time. She had a dream, a vision for her life, and somehow, the death of her father gave birth to it.

Jan wondered what she would be like if her own father had died. She couldn't imagine that event inspiring her outlook or destiny. The last thing she could imagine coming from it was a vision, a plan, or a dream for anything. Her father's death, any death in the family, could only be a bad, bad thing. Something so awful could not possibly produce an assurance, a confidence in something else. It just made zero sense. *And honestly, if finding answers comes only after a death, then I prefer to just stay in the dark, thank you very much.*

"What about you, Jan?" Kristi asked. "Will you stay at West Point?"

"Probably not."

"Why? You seem to be doing really well."

"Well, for one, I hate it. I hate the way we're treated, yelled at and made fun of all the time. Two, I hate math, science and history. I practically failed history. The only course I like is English which everyone else seems to hate—so that tells me there's a disconnect somewhere."

"And three," Jan said, as she hunched over the steering wheel, "I hate the outfits. They don't do anything for my figure."

Kristi looked at her friend negotiating the car through the snowfall and started laughing.

"What's so funny?" Then Jan began giggling, too, which slowly grew into one of those rare, gut busting, tear producing, uncontrollable laughing fits. She pulled the car onto the shoulder of the road with squinting eyes full of laughing tears.

The roadside ruckus finally subsided, and for the rest of the snowy drive, they talked about SKIP's possible identity, Drew's virtues, Dogety's vices and Jan's boyfriend/best friend event.

When Jan explained the Tim and Regan "incident," Kristi's reaction was nothing less than visceral. "How could they do that to you? And why would Regan even tell you? WHAT did that bitch hope to gain by telling you, JAN? Think about it! What was the point in telling you?" Jan hadn't thought about that. "If I did something like that, and I really cared about you, I would never tell you. I mean, what good would it do? The deed was done, it couldn't be undone. But it could have been left in the closet where it belongs!"

They decided to go to the biggest New Year's Eve party in town. Tim's parents, with four notorious, party-animal sons, allowed alcohol and loud music every year at their home. The local teen band played from the large back porch overlooking a field. A huge bonfire had been lit in the center of the field. Smaller fires in fifty-five gallon drums stood at various intervals between the house and the bonfire along with a couple fire pits on the porch. It was party heaven—New Hampshire style. An unwritten rule of small towns applied: as long as nothing got out of hand, the police and fire department would keep a professional distance.

Maybe Kissy's right about Regan. Jan stood next to Kristi by the bonfire drinking beer wondering if she would ever know anything for certain. But this was not a night for contemplation, she decided. *You shouldn't think too much on New Year's Eve.* In that effort, she mindlessly chatted with a few high school acquaintances before Regan arrived at the bonfire, standing beside Jan. The old best friends hugged. "Regan, this is Kristi, my friend from West Point."

"Oh, hey, nice to meet you!" Regan turned to Kristi.

"What's your name again?" Kristi asked.

"Regan. I'm Jan's best friend."

"Not anymore," Kristi said with a chuckle. Jan elbowed her.

"Actually, Jan and I go back a long way, don't we Jan?" Regan looked at Jan, seemingly for reassurance.

"Yes, we do. We've had a lot of fun over the years!" Jan admitted.

"Until recently," Kristi said under her breath.

Jan changed the subject and hoped Kristi would not make any more cutting comments. Tonight was not the time to bring it all back up. *Better let those sleeping dogs lie under the porch or however the saying goes.*

Three port-a-potties lined the perimeter of the field, seeming to hold the line of woods from advancing. At least four people waited to use each one.

"Dang, I can't hold it much longer," Kristi announced loudly.

"Well, get in line like the rest of us," a waiting woman said.

"Kissy," whispered Jan, "We don't need pot-a parties."

"Oh, right," said Kristi, "We have quads of iron!"

"Ab-so-shits-a-lutely." Drinking brought out more swearing than normal. They walked past the port-a-potties and into the woods until they couldn't see the line of people. They unbuckled, unzipped and pulled down their pants. Only when their asses were hanging out in sub-freezing temperatures did they discover the flaw in their plan.

"Shit! It's cold!" Kristi exclaimed.

"And we don't have any TP!" This realization set off another round of laughter. They finished peeing but couldn't stand up. From a squat, with their asses in the wind, they continued to howl. Jan fell over sideways. Then Kristi followed. Both in fetal positions, laughing so hard they could barely breathe.

They should have stayed at Tim's house all night, but they were young and stupid, so Jan drove home. Fortunately, they made it back without incident and went to bed sometime after three in the morning.

Jan heard the ringing Cadet Chapel bells. *Damn bells.* Somewhere in the transition from asleep to awake, she realized the West Point bells, though loud, could not possibly be heard in New Hampshire. But something kept ringing.

Her clock said it was two-thirty in the afternoon. Jan rolled over, hoping to go back to sleep, when her mother softly knocked on the bedroom door.

"Jan, it's for you," she whispered.

"Who is it?" asked Jan.

"I don't know. Do you want me to ask them to call back?"

"No, it's fine; I'll take it." Jan mumbled as she dragged herself to the receiver. The only phone in the house was mounted on the wall separating her bedroom from the kitchen, its long cord stretching into Jan's room. While Kristi kept sleeping, Jan took the phone from her mom, closed the door and slid down to the floor. She took a deep breath, trying to stop the spinning in her head.

"Hello," she said groggily.

"Jan?"

"Yeah."

"Jan, it's Debra Plowden."

"Oh...oh, hey, Debra." She tried to sound awake, alert, alive.

"Are you okay? You sound a little sick."

Jan cleared her throat, "No, no, I just..." *THINK!* "I just had a big New Year's Eve."

"Oh, you're hung over then."

Well, yes actually.... "Um, I probably had a little too much," Jan admitted.

"Okay, well, I can call back later..." Debra offered.

"No, it's fine, Debra, really. Why are you calling? Everything okay?" Jan and Debra were not exactly close.

"Well, I wanted to tell you personally that I am not returning to West Point."

That woke Jan up. "What? Why not?"

"I think you know why, Jan." Debra paused. "I haven't been the same since Army/Navy. You've probably noticed."

Jan felt a little guilty for not noticing. "I thought you were doing well."

"Well, I'm not. And I can't go back there and live in fear anymore."

It occurred to Jan that while they all lived in some fear of getting in trouble or failing a course, Debra had been dealing with a much deeper level of fear. "Oh Debra, I'm so sorry this happened. But I still think if we talked to Captain Spanner..." Captain Spanner was H-3's Tactical Officer (TAC). TACs were assigned to each company for supervising, disciplining and mentoring the cadets.

"No, Jan, I don't want to involve the TAC or anyone else."

What else can we do, then? Jan paused before speaking again. "Debra, do you remember anything else about that night? *Anything* that might help us know who did this?"

"I've tried to," Debra sighed. "It was such a...a...I don't know. I didn't see his face, I didn't hear him speak. I really couldn't tell you anything about him."

They both fell silent for a moment. Then Debra spoke again, softly, "You might think this is really weird but the only thing I remember is a giant bird. A huge condor or something, with its wings spread out, as if it was going to devour me. I've even had a couple of nightmares about Pterodactyls."

Jan couldn't think of anything to say to that. The thing that popped into her mind would not have been appropriate. *You were raped by Big Bird?*

Debra went on, "I know you must think I'm crazy. Maybe I am. But that's all I remember. A giant bird with its wings spread as if it was in flight."

Jan didn't know anything about trauma but she thought the bird image might be less scary than the real thing. Maybe the brain makes up something to protect itself if the actual thing is worse. "You're not crazy, Debra. Who knows how your mind processes something like that? And you were drugged or drunk or something. I guess we'll never really know."

"Yeah," Debra said, "it could just be my way of coping with something I couldn't control. I guess I'll be wondering what really happened for the rest of my life."

Jan hoped she might remember something before then. "Debra, if you *do* remember anything, I hope you'll let us know. We need to get this guy before he strikes again."

"If I remember something, I will tell you. But I'm done with everything and anything to do with West Point."

Jan fell silent again. She had moments when she hated the place, too, but probably nothing like the way Debra did.

"Jan, I just wanted you to know that I won't be coming back. Not ever."

Jan wished Debra would be more willing to find out who did this to her. But there was no way she could or would drag her into something she clearly opposed. "Okay, Debra, I understand. I can't blame you for wanting to leave. Hell, I want to leave most times and I didn't..." Jan realized she was about to step in it.

"Exactly," Debra let her off the hook.

"Well, is there anything I can do to help you? Is there anything you need me to do when I get back?"

"No, thanks. I've already notified the official channels of my decision. They will send my personal stuff which isn't much. I'm applying to our local college. I hope to move on to a normal, happy life."

Jan suddenly felt very sad for Debra. "I know you will."

"Thanks, Jan. Say hello to Kristi and Angel. I really hope you guys make it."

"Thanks, Debra. We hope we can also, but it's still a long road ahead. Send us your address so we can keep you posted."

"I might do that in a few months. First I just need time to be away from all the reminders."

"Okay. Well," Jan wasn't sure what else to say, "we'll miss you."

"Thanks. Good luck, Jan."

"Good luck to you, too, Debra."

23

Friday, May 7, 1982
1915 Hours

Dear SKIP,

I hear you might be able to testify on my behalf. Is this true? If so, I need to know ASAP, so I can request you as a witness. I HAVE to know your name, however. I don't think they will just allow me to call "my anonymous pen pal, SKIP" to the witness chair. I don't know how you might be able to help, but I'm hoping it's true. Please respond tonight!!
Jan

She wrote SKIP in large letters on the note and taped it to her door before walking to the windowless room in Mahan Hall. At exactly 1930 hours, Conrad called the Honor Board to order again.

"Let's get right back to business," he said. "Does anyone have any more questions for Cadet Dogety?"

"Yes, I do," Tourney said. "Sam, what happened after you tried to calm Markus down?"

"We yelled at each other for a bit, then Markus demanded that Miss Wishart report to his room at 0500 the next morning. When he left, I told her NOT to obey his order. But obviously, she did anyway," Dogety said while looking at Jan.

"Did you think Miss Wishart had written the note in the routing envelope?"

"No, I have seen her handwriting and it didn't look anything like hers. Also, I don't believe Miss Wishart would lie to us. If she had done it, she would have admitted it."

"Did you explain that to Markus?"

"Yes, that's what we were arguing about. He was convinced that she had *something* to do with it," Dogety said.

"Did you see Miss Wishart the next morning, Sam?" Gaskins asked, jumping ahead.

"Briefly, yes."

"When was that?"

Dogety cleared his throat, fidgeted in his chair, and then said, "I saw her between first and second class periods, about 0845 hours. She reported to my room saying she had something to tell me."

"Please explain what happened next," Gaskins said.

Dogety appeared ill. He looked over at Jan, then at Bill Trane, then back to Casey Conrad. He opened his mouth, like he was going to speak, then he closed it and dropped his eyes to the floor. Jan thought she saw his lips moving as if he was talking to himself or praying.

"Sir, may I ask a question?" Jan looked to Conrad for the answer.

"What is it, Miss Wishart?"

"Sir, I would like to call a recess," she stated rather than asked.

"Why, Miss Wishart, do you need a recess?"

"I believe there's a new witness, Sir."

"What are you talking about?" Conrad almost shouted.

"Sir, I have information that someone saw something pertaining to my case, but I need some time to ...to...secure his information." She hoped they wouldn't ask for a name.

"Miss Wishart, we cannot stop the proceedings just because you want to chase down a new witness."

"Well, Sir, I just found out about this witness tonight at dinner time."

"Miss Wishart, we are running a highly irregular Honor Board as it is. We are running out of time. TEE week starts Monday, and some of us need to study. If I adjourn now, we will lose precious time that will have to be made up tomorrow," Conrad said. "Besides, you had a full day to submit your witness list."

"Sir, the Honor Board guidelines stipulate that new witnesses can be called if and when they are determined to have information pertinent to the case. I believe this witness has information pertinent to my case, and I need some time to get his statement."

"I am well aware of the Honor Board guidelines, thank you." Conrad stood up. "I need the Regimental Honor Captains to step outside with me for a moment. Everyone else remain here." He walked out the door followed by Cadets Tourney, Leavitt, Gaskins and Seymour.

When they were gone, Trane turned to Jan, "What are you doing?"

"I'm trying to get a witness...."

"I understand that much, but why now? Why not wait till we adjourn?" Trane asked.

Because I don't even know his name, and I have to write notes back and forth to communicate with him. She needed as much time as possible to convince SKIP to come out of hiding. That's what she told herself anyway. But she also wondered why she didn't ask for the recess at the beginning of this session. Why did she wait until Dogety was about to answer a critical question? Was she trying to protect him? Or was she afraid of his answer?

Conrad and his cabinet returned to the room. While standing, he said, "Miss Wishart, as much as we'd like to finish questioning Cadet Dogety tonight, we realize that you can call as many witnesses and in whatever order as you want. We want to afford you every opportunity to do so. Therefore, we will adjourn for the night and reconvene at 0830 hours tomorrow morning." He closed his folder before walking back out of the room.

"I hope winning this battle doesn't cost you the war..." Trane said.

"I hope not either, Sir."

24

Q: How is the cow?

A: Sir, she walks, she talks, she's full of chalk, the lacteal fluid extracted from the female of the bovine species is highly prolific to the nth degree.

Heritage, Bugle Notes, 81, p. 242

Jan's parents drove them back to West Point on January 10, 1982. Her dad attempted a few jokes and small talk. When he didn't get any response from the young women, he gave up and turned on the radio. They were not in the mood for conversation, laughter or anything other than staring out the windows and trying to enjoy the last few moments of peace.

West Point was not a war zone. They knew that. There were many people in the world living with real suffering. Sometimes Jan felt guilty for being so miserable at one of the best institutions in the country. Complaining about it felt a little like not eating her peas at dinner. Her mother would rightly say, "There are starving children in Africa who would love to eat those peas!" And no matter what she said, it always came out sounding like whining.

Besides, some female cadets seemed just fine. Wright always appeared happy, confident, and totally in her element at West Point.

She and other well-adjusted women caused Jan to think that her own skin just wasn't thick enough. Or perhaps those women didn't hear the comments and chuckles from clusters of men. She didn't know how they could have avoided it, though. The sexual and bodily comments, some from cadets and some from officers, were constant. Every day, sometimes several times a day, Jan heard something about her body, another woman's body or the female body in general.

As she stared at the passing white lines on the highway, she resolved to put on a kind of body armor—a mental and emotional shell—for the coming semester. She would keep vigil and stay on guard, so that when she heard snide remarks, sarcastic jokes or sexual comments, they would not penetrate her skin. They would simply bounce off her from now on, she told herself.

By fifteen hundred hours, Jan and Kristi arrived at the gray walls, the gray halls, the gray gloom and doom of West Point to fight another day.

The first order of business was to change rooms again. Because Debra did not return, Jan, Angel and Kristi moved to a three-person room. Inspection scheduled at twenty hundred hours meant they were ready by eighteen hundred hours. They used the extra time to memorize the menus for the week, the number of days left for every major event, and other necessary "poop," all while polishing their shoes.

KNOCK, KNOCK! Popping to attention, the three roommates shouted in unison, "Enter, Sir!" The door violently swung open. Dogety stood in the hallway in civilian clothes. Jan thought he seemed uncomfortable out of uniform.

He was born wearing Dress Gray.

"Is this room ready for inspection?" he asked.

"Yes, Sir!" They replied simultaneously.

"Good." Dogety walked into the room. He looked around, at the bookshelves, the beds and the closets. He opened the medicine cabinet and the laundry bins. Then he started to walk out the door. "Guess what, ladies?"

One of the five responses didn't quite work, so Jan said, "What,

Sir?"

"There's a new chain of command in H-3, and I'm now your Executive Officer."

Damn.

"What do you think of that?" he asked.

The three plebes looked at each other. Kristi and Angel kept quiet, but Jan said, "Sir, I think...." She wanted to say something semi-congratulatory—without being too over the top. "Sir, congratulations on your promotion."

Dogety did get a promotion, but everyone knew he aspired to be the Company Commander. Executive Officer fell one rung short of his goal. It's like Vice-President. You have a title but not any real power...unless, of course, the head honcho quits or dies.

He said, "I suggest you three get this room squared away before the next inspection. You know my standards, Miss Wishart."

He walked away and Kristi closed the door. "His mother must have dropped him when he was a baby."

"That's just Dogety, Kissy. He's wired to be an asshole." Jan resigned herself to another semester under his thumb. "You guys will get to see what I dealt with all during Beast."

Kristi seethed, "Well, he's a dick head! And if he brings that Jackass dude around here, I'm going to kick them both in the balls!"

They set out on a reconnaissance mission to find Drew's new room. Hugging the inner walls of the barracks and pinging at three times the normal walking speed, they read the nametags on the doors without moving their heads. Looking two or three doors ahead, Jan spotted "Hambin" on the last door, second floor, west side. She made the sharp left turn to Drew's room. Kristi followed, and Jan knocked softly three times. "Come in."

Jan and Kristi walked all the way to the middle of the room before realizing they had the wrong one. The male cadet, lying on his bed in his underwear said, "Can I help you, ladies?"

"Uh, Sir...we, uh, we..." Jan stuttered, flummoxed by his bright pink boxer shorts with something written in black all over them.

"Yes, you were saying.." he said.

"Sir, we thought…" She tried to read the words on his boxers. Something like *love me, kiss me, baby, hot, cute* and other amorous terms. "We..uh…we thought this was Cadet Hambin's room." She finally managed to get it out.

"Well, I'm afraid you are mistaken, my dears." He didn't seem at all angry that they interrupted his bedtime in his favorite, sexy boxers.

"Sorry to bother you, Sir," Jan said, executing an about face and striding past Kristi to the hallway.

"Nice underwear, Sir," Kristi said as she followed Jan out the door.

"The pleasure was all mine, ladies!" they heard him say as they shut the door.

The nametag read "Hanlin" instead of "Hambin." *Rookie mistake.* They set off again and found Drew's room on the East side, center hallway, second floor. "Come in," he said.

"Oh thank God it's you!" Kristi said.

"Who else would it be?"

"Oh, some guy named Hanlin." Jan told him what happened.

"Hanlin has some pretty fancy underwear," Kristi added. "Pink with sexy writing all over."

"Well, you went to the right, wrong room," Drew said. "He's one of the coolest firsties in our Company."

"Well, it looked like he was about to get pretty hot." The three friends broke out laughing along with Drew's cute new roommate.

Plebe English continued, as did History of Modern Europe, foreign language (Arabic for Jan), Calculus and Military Science (MS). Psychology replaced the computer class and the PE courses changed, from Self-defense for Women and Boxing for men, to Survival Swimming for both. To ensure attention to detail, the academic schedule included alternating days, numbered one and two respectively. On one days, half the plebes attended foreign language, computers or psychology, and history. The other half took math, PE, English and Military Science, sometimes called "mandatory sleep." On two days, the schedule reversed. Twice a week, a STAR day was added—once on day one and once on day two—where plebes had to attend all of their classes. Then, the classes were shortened to one hour, except for computers, math, language or Chemistry, which became one hour, one and a half hours, and two hours long, respectively. This method, along with Saturday classes, ensured pinging continued to be necessary to the fourth-class lifestyle.

The male cadets lined the pool deck, many with their hands folded in front of their genitals. Some guys, braver ones, folded their arms across their chest or just dangled them at their sides. The women exited their locker room with arms folded across their chests or clasped together in front of their crotch.

Jan tugged at her black, one-piece, non-lined, non-cupped, Speedo swimsuit. *Obviously no one asked what we thought about these god-awful things.* But the men had it worse. They wore tiny, black, one-piece, non-lined, non-cupped Speedos. No sane American male would wear such a thing in real life.

Jan and Kristi looked like kindergarteners on the first day of school, each trying to hide behind the other women in the class. They came together with their male counterparts by the pool, where three DPE instructors awaited. *We should get a passing grade just for walking out here in these god-awful suits.*

The men stared at the women without even trying to be discreet. The women, on the other hand, kept looking away from the scantily clad men. But Jan stole glances when she thought they weren't looking. She had never seen practically naked men before. Jan's cheeks flushed when she noticed Drew, his new roommate everyone called Jenk, and Rick Davidson in the group of exposed men.

Captain Janes, in the standard black shorts with black and white referee shirt, explained a new swimming method called "The Bob and Travel." Captain Forrest, in a swimsuit, jumped off the diving board to demonstrate this technique. Then it was the cadets' turn.

Jan jumped into one end of the Olympic-size pool, keeping her body completely straight, arms overhead. Under water, she let out all the air in her lungs, which she had already practiced with the body fat test, and allowed herself to fall completely to the bottom of the pool. Once her feet touched, she pushed off the bottom with her legs, simultaneously arching her arms in a wide circle down to either side of her body, thrusting herself back up to the surface, a small distance beyond the first spot. She took a deep breath at the top, then repeated the process until she arrived at the far end of the pool.

Jan's swimming classes at Camp Alexander during the summers of her childhood had paid off. She finished "The Bob and Travel" across the pool in adequate time, climbed out, crossed her arms in front of her chest, and waited for Kristi. Jan unconsciously began praying for her roommate.

Kristi jumped into the pool, went down to the bottom, pushed off and came back up. *So far, so good.* She did it once more before panicking on the third attempt. Jan saw flailing arms in slow motion under water. Kristi came up choking and spluttering water then went under again. The DPE instructors at each side of the pool, along with Captain Janes next to Jan, saw it all.

"Sir, should someone help her?" Jan asked.

"Let's give her a minute, Miss Wishart," he said. "She may self-correct." But Jan knew Kristi would not "self-correct." After what seemed like minutes but was probably only seconds, all three DPE instructors dove into the pool simultaneously. Like dolphins, they swam over to Kristi and lifted her to the surface in one swift motion and then onto the pool deck. Captain Janes coached Kristi as she choked, gagged and spit up water. "Lean forward," he said. "Relax your breathing, Miss McCarron."

"Take it slowly," Captain Forrest added. "You're okay, Miss McCarron."

That little blunder resulted in Kristi's demotion from "Drowning 101" to "Dog Paddling 101," the class for mostly inner-city kids who never learned to swim. It also ended Jan and Kristi's one and only class together.

Dear Jan,
I'm glad you decided to come back to our Rockbound Highland

Home. I'm also pleasantly surprised to see we have a class together. Oh, I probably shouldn't tell you that. You might start being suspicious of everyone in all your classes. Okay, I will narrow it down for you. Let's just say I REALLY look forward to seeing you in class.

I am saying too much to someone who has not yet joined our organization. I have to stop now as it would be dangerous for both of us.

Just know I am glad you came back and I hope to hear from you soon. It's been a while since we last corresponded and even just writing to each other is a subversive way to have fun, isn't it? I think I even saw you smiling recently.

SKIP

Dear SKIP,

You might be REALLY happy to see me in class uniform, but my guess is that you are one of the leering guys in my Drowning class. Although it seems to me that there are a few other women more worthy of your attention, I will take it as a compliment that you REALLY look forward to seeing me. I REALLY look forward to knowing who you are!

In fact, this is REALLY starting to drive me crazy. I am REALLY getting unnerved by your spying!

Jan

She scoured the pool deck at the beginning of the next survival swimming class but only recognized Drew, his roommate and Rick Davidson. A couple others looked familiar, perhaps from another class or her battalion. With all of them, she tried to keep her eyes above their chest level.

They conquered "The Bob and Travel" across the pool in Speedos and then again, wearing fatigues and boots. This entire sequence, jumping into the pool wearing fatigues and boots, then removing them while "Bobbing and Traveling" to the other end of the pool, is how Drowning 101 got its name.

As grueling as the course was, it was the god-awful Speedo that motivated Jan to pass Drowning 101. Even if it killed her.

A familiar voice called the ten-minute bell. "Sir, there are ten minutes until dinner formation. The menu for dinner is—oh shit, I don't know. And who cares anyway? But get your asses outside in Dress Gray over gray. Ten minutes, Sir!"

Dogety stood under the hall clock wearing the full-dress hat, tennis shoes, and the dress-gray coat, on backwards. He turned to go back to his room. That's when Jan pounced.

"BEANHEAD, HALT!"

Role reversal, a long-standing tradition on the one-hundredth night before graduation, allowed plebes their only chance to haze firsties. The first classmen dressed in rally-type attire and spazzed off in every possible way, knowing they were not really going to get in trouble.

"Yes, Sir." Dogety turned to face Jan.

"Do you know how ridiculous you look, Beanhead?"

"Yes, Sir!"

I should have known he would not play fair. "Your coat is on backwards. Take it off and turn it around."

"Yes, Sir." He removed the coat, revealing only the white t-shirt underneath.

"Dogety, you have a scrawny chest. Have you been eating? Do you do any push-ups or sit-ups? Your arms look like spaghetti for God's sake." None of it was true. He had a very nice chest with strong arms, but this wasn't about reality, Jan decided.

"Sir, at least...."

"Is that one of your five responses, Dogety?"

"Well..."

"No excuse, Dogety! Your body looks like a limp noodle. You obviously don't work out enough, nor are you eating enough! Otherwise, you would be more filled out, stronger and more attractive to women."

"Sir, I..."

"Quit callin' me 'Sir,' Bitch!" The words flew out of her mouth and she regretted it immediately. But this would be her only chance to give the shit back to him, even if she had to pay for it later.

She walked to him, putting her face only inches from his. In a voice barely above a whisper, she said, "You're not just spazzing off in my hallway, Dogety. You're an embarrassment to the entire Long Gray Line. Grant, Lee, Pershing, Patton, MacArthur and Eisenhower—all of them are turning in their graves now because of you. These great ones who came before us—their honor, their sacrifice and their spirit—are still here but you are tarnishing that legacy. You will NOT make a mockery of this great institution. Now get the hell out of my hallway!"

Silence.

Even Jan could not believe she had repeated, practically verbatim, the words Jackson had fumed at her in Beast. She had not realized how much she had internalized. "Do you understand me, Dogety?"

He turned and walked away.

Jan and Kristi moseyed into the Mess Hall as all firsties were known to do. They sat on either side of Angel, the table Commander. The cows and yearlings took their usual spots. Dogety, Trane and Wincowski sat in the plebe seats.

"Ma'am, the drink for tonight is lemonade. Would anyone not care for lemonade, Ma'am?" Wincowski yelled.

"Sir, the dessert for tonight is chocolate pie. Would anyone not care for chocolate pie, Sir?" Dogety continued to show disrespect toward the plebe women.

Jan decided not to say any more to Dogety. But Kristi said, "Dogety, do we look like SIRs to you?"

"Yes, Sir."

"Leave it alone, Kissy," Jan whispered.

"Dogety, the reason you can't tell the difference is because you don't have any experience with women," Kristi shouted down the table.

Oh no...here we go.

"Men who know women don't have a problem recognizing them," Kristi added. "But you always have problems with that...hmmm..."

Kissy, leave it alone.

"Sir, I know one when I see one," Dogety spouted off.

"Shut up, Dogety!" Angel yelled. Jan and Kristi looked at her incredulously. Angel never said anything mean or remotely cross. "You don't have an opinion here."

Wow! Angel! Who would have known?

One minute after the study hour bell sounded, Dogety pounded on her door. Jan had already filled in her roommates about the minute calling incident, and they all knew he would come for her.

"Come with me, Wishart!" He was wearing his Full Dress Gray coat, the coat with brass buttons and tails. Jan followed him to Cadet Holdern's door. "Wait here." Dogety went inside the new Company Commander's room. Jan stood outside, desperately trying to hear through the door.

She was not sorry for saying those things to Dogety, and she would not apologize or whatever else they wanted her to do. But then she began to panic. *What if I have just blown everything? What if they kick me out for insubordination? Or worse, what if they give me a hundred hours of walking tours? Oh damn, why'd I open my big mouth?*

"Cadet Wishart, report to the Company Commander!" Dogety shouted from inside.

She opened the door, stepped into the room and saluted. "Cadet Wishart reporting as ordered, Sir." The room was dark, lit only by candles on the sink, the desks, and the windowsill. Firstie sabers, pulled from their scabbards were displayed across each bed. The Company Commander and his Executive Officer, Dogety, were seated behind their desks, in Full Dress Gray. Cadet Trousdale, Jan's second semester Squad Leader, stood in the middle of the desks facing Jan. *Oh man, this is serious.*

Holdern saluted back from his seat and said, "Cadet Wishart, Cadet Dogety reports that you have been highly disrespectful and insubordinate and have acted in a manner unbecoming an officer tonight. Is that correct?"

"Sir, may I make a statement?"

"Go ahead."

"Sir, tonight was role reversal. I spoke to Cadet Dogety in the same way others have spoken to me in the past."

"Was it disrespectful, insubordinate and unbecoming, Cadet Wishart?"

"Yes, Sir, it probably was." Jan could not say otherwise.

"Probably?"

"Yes, Sir. It was."

"Cadet Wishart, what did you say exactly?" Holdern asked.

"Sir, I told Dogety he had arms like spaghetti and his body looked like a limp noodle."

"Is that all?"

"No, Sir. There was more," Jan admitted.

"Well?"

"Sir, I told him he was unattractive to women, and I called him a bitch and an embarrassment to the Long Gray Line." *Okay, I will be packing my trunk tonight.*

Jan couldn't be sure, but she thought she saw a faint smile on Cadet Holdern's face. Her Squad Leader cleared his throat. Both looked down for a moment. The Commander looked back at Jan and said, "If you felt you were treated in a disrespectful manner, why didn't you report it to your superiors before?"

"Sir, I..." *Since when do plebes demand respect?*

"What, Wishart?"

"Sir, I just...I just didn't know...."

"Ignorance is no excuse, Cadet Wishart. If you had a legitimate grievance, you could have come to any one of the upperclassmen in your chain of command and it could have been dealt with professionally," the Commander stated.

"Yes, Sir." *It's that chain of command thing...*

"Miss Wishart, it is never appropriate to degrade someone. You will never lead people by attacking them personally. Do you understand me, Cadet Wishart?"

"Yes, Sir." *Although that was the whole point.*

"There's never any excuse, even during role reversal, to talk that way to subordinates. You will never garner respect as a leader if you speak to people like that. It's unacceptable and I will not tolerate it in Company H-3. This is a serious offense, Cadet Wishart." Cadet Holdern seemed to have a slight smirk.

"Yes, Sir."

"Please leave the room while we discuss your punishment." Jan executed an about face and walked out closing the door behind her. She waited in the hallway again but didn't try to listen to the conversation this time.

Whatever! If they send me packing, maybe it's for the best anyway. She thought she heard an argument between Dogety and Holdern. But then she heard laughter and thought she must have been mistaken.

Just as she decided to lean her ear to the door, Dogety shouted, "Wishart, report to the Company Commander!"

She reported as before, then Cadet Holdern said, "Cadet Wishart, you have committed a serious offense, you have insulted a superior officer. You have shown disrespect for your chain of command. You have displayed conduct unbecoming an officer. Do you have anything further to say in your defense?"

"No, Sir." *I'm screwed. Do not pass go, do not collect $200...*

"With Cadet Dogety's full support, we have decided to give you another chance, Miss Wishart. We believe you can learn from this incident and use it to become a better officer. Therefore, we have decided not to give you demerits or area tours for this infraction," Holdern said. "Cadet Wishart, you are going to dig a grave instead."

What? "Sir, I don't understand?"

"We've had a death in the H-3 family tonight. Our mascot, Cadet Harold, has met an untimely demise." He said this with a completely straight face. "We were just preparing for the burial with full honors when your situation came to our attention."

Dogety finally spoke, "I will show you the location where you will dig Cadet Harold's grave, which must be the size of a shoebox. You will do this using only your bayonet and a Mess Hall serving spoon. Do you understand your task, Miss Wishart?"

"Yes, Sir." *Cadet Harold?* She didn't even know they had an H-3 mascot.

"Good." Then both the Commander and the Executive Officer stood at attention. Cadet Holdern said, "Present Arms," and they all saluted. Jan didn't quite understand who was saluting whom. Then she noticed the upperclassmen staring at the floor. Between the beds with the unsheathed sabers was a shoebox.

Jan followed Dogety outside across The Apron and onto The Plain. She was never afraid of Dogety; she just hated how much he seemed to disdain her. As they walked, she thought she felt disgust flowing from him. When they arrived at the center of The Plain, Dogety pulled out a large spoon, handed it to Jan and said, "Start digging, Wishart."

Jan knelt down and began to dig the hole. The bayonet proved to be an essential tool in the half-frozen terra firma. She forgot to wear gloves, and her fingers became numb from the cold. Once she loosened the ground with the bayonet, she was able to scoop out the dirt with the spoon. Dogety walked around her in circles like a wolf stalking its prey. For at least twenty minutes, he said nothing. Then he stopped pacing and said, "Wishart, you surprised me tonight. I never thought you had it in you. I thought you were too weak for this place. But tonight, you proved otherwise. You can take it, AND you can dish it out. You made me proud, Wishart." Jan kept digging, ignoring him. "WISHART! I'M TALKING TO YOU!"

"Yes, Sir."

Then Dogety squatted down and put his face right up next to her ear. "I did a pretty good job with you after all. I can graduate knowing my work here is done." Then he stood back up and resumed his circling. She finished the hole in about an hour. Dogety measured it and made her dig another inch deeper.

At 2400 hours, Company H-3 held formation on The Plain. One of the cadets played "Taps" on a flute while another ceremoniously lowered the shoebox casket into the hole. The Commander shouted "Present Arms." All of Company H-3 saluted as Cadet Harold the Hamster was laid to rest.

25

Friday, May 7, 1982
2030 Hours

Dear Jan,
I've been trying to talk to my Honor Rep, but he's been "tied up" all day—that's all his roommate will tell me. You didn't tell me much, but I believe I will be able to help. I have filled out a statement and only need to submit it to the Honor Rep. I want to be sure to follow the chain of command, but I understand that once it's submitted, I will be called to testify.
I guess the jig will be up for me then.
SKIP

She quickly scribbled a reply and taped it back on her door.

SKIP,
This is great news...I don't know what it is you know, but I trust it will be useful to me. Don't delay! Make sure your Honor Rep gets in touch with my Honor Rep, Cadet Trane, ASAP! I'm going to bug him until he tells me he's heard something. I will go by his room every 30 minutes tonight...so get moving. PLEASE!
Thank you so much.

Jan

Jan filled in Angel and Kristi quickly while changing into shower uniform. Then, dressed in only a thin, gray, polyester bathrobe, over flip-flops, with a towel draped over the right arm, she pinged down the hallway to the women's latrine. After showering, she exited the latrine in the same way only with wet hair.

Dogety called to her as she passed his door, "Miss Wishart, come here for a minute, please."

Dang. Haven't we had enough time together today? "Yes, Sir?" She stood at the entrance to his room. His roommate probably had a weekend pass.

"Come in, please," he said. She walked into his room in the bathrobe and flip-flops, towel still draped over one arm. "Please, sit down." Cadet rooms have limited seating choices: a bed, a desk chair, a footlocker or the floor. Jan sat on his roommate's bed. Dogety stood up from his desk, walked to the door and closed it. Then he sat down on the bed, next to Jan, so close that their thighs were touching.

Both stared at her flip-flopped feet. Neither spoke for what seemed like a full minute. Then, he placed his right hand over her left, picking it up gently and moving it onto his thigh. Jan couldn't move. Fraternization was forbidden between plebes and upperclassmen. If anyone opened Dogety's door at that point, they would have been in even more trouble. Holding hands behind closed doors was bad enough. Jan dressed in only a bathrobe made it even worse.

But she wasn't terribly worried about being caught at that moment. For most of the entire year, she wanted Dogety to leave her alone. Now, she felt something different, something strange and hidden but also somewhat familiar. It gnawed at her, but she couldn't think of the word to describe it. Anger maybe, because he wasn't supposed to be tender. He was supposed to play his usual role, and she didn't know quite what to do with this "nice" Dogety. Maybe she felt angry that he waited this long, almost to the end of the year, to be vulnerable with her.

"Jan," he said, "you don't need to help me. I need to help you."

"I know you do. That's what I have been saying all along," she turned to face him.

"Well, you've taught me a valuable lesson. I will make this right," he said turning to her.

An uncomfortable silence stood between them. Sam Dogety dipped his head toward hers. She did not back away. He kissed her lips once, softly and gently. They parted momentarily. Then both came toward each other with a fierce, desperate resolve—kissing so hard it almost hurt.

26

A cadet's busy schedule is not without its lighter moments.
Cadet Activities, Bugle Notes, 81, p.89

West Point turned even grayer in late February. Plebes formed up
for breakfast in morning grayness and again for dinner formation in
evening grayness. A perpetual cycle took hold—gray over gray over
gray over gray.

The fourth classmen continued to count down the days until spring
break, ring weekend and graduation. This part of poop seemed to serve
a greater purpose. *It's a daily reminder that all this shit will eventually
end.*

With drill suspended during these gray months, Jan and Drew
joined the Cadet Ushering Club. In Dress Gray over gray with white
belts and white gloves, they handed out playbills at Eisenhower Hall for
a new Broadway play called, *Fiddler on the Roof.*

Dogety and his date came to their door. "Evening, Wishart," he
said.

"Evening, Sir."

"When did you start ushering?"

"In January, Sir."

"Oh. First time I've seen you here."

First time I've seen you here, too.

"Next time, shine your shoes. Those are unacceptable, Wishart."

"Yes, Sir." Jan gave a thumbs-down signal to Drew. Jan judged male cadets, giving an inconspicuous thumbs-up at her side if one was good looking. Thumbs-down meant "not so much." Drew judged the female companions. They rarely encountered male and female cadets together. And they never saw female cadets with civilian men.

Jan enjoyed this unofficial part of ushering—judging the looks of male upperclassmen. She rated them not only on their facial attraction but also on their body type—tall, short, heavy set, skinny, etc. The cadets had to pass the "whole package test"—good-looking face, nice hair, above-average height, and not too heavy nor too skinny. Most importantly, above all else, the male cadet had to say "thank you" when she handed him the playbill. Even if all the physical attributes were there, a "non-thanking" cadet automatically received a thumbs-down from Jan. She gave the thumbs-down more often than not.

Drew gave Dogety's date a thumbs-up. *Shit, why couldn't she have been butt ugly?*

After the show began, an old woman, who was about fifty, rose from her seat and walked up the aisle to their door. Jan got up from her back row seat, opened the door and waited in the lobby until the woman returned from the restroom. As Jan reached for the door again, the woman whispered, "Excuse me, Miss. I just have to ask you a question."

"Yes, Ma'am?"

"Are you a lesbian?"

What?? "No, Ma'am, I'm not." She held the door as the woman entered the theater again. Then Jan whispered to her, "Are you?"

The woman huffed and snorted back down the aisle to her seat. *Ha! That's what you get for asking a stupid-ass question!!* Jan returned to her seat next to Drew who signaled thumbs-up.

Dear Jan,

No need to be worried. I am not a stalker. But you'll have to excuse guys for staring at you in Drowning. We males tend to stare at females, especially when they have little on.

I heard you had the honor of digging the grave for dearly departed Cadet Harold. It was certainly a better sentence than what they could have given you. I hope you will be more careful. There are a lot of killjoys here who do their best to make sure no one has fun.

I hope to hear from you soon,
SKIP

Dear SKIP,
Ah-ha! So you are in my Drowning class! That narrows it down considerably. I don't think you are in my Company, so you are probably in G or I. It won't be long now until I discover your identity. I hope you're ready!

And while men may like to stare at women with very little on, all that leering makes us rather uncomfortable. A little subtlety would go a long way. Especially since we are practically naked in the Speedos. But I have to admit, you guys have it worse Speedo-wise.

Yes, I dug Harold's grave. Apparently, there are no secrets at West Point. I have tried to stay away from the killjoys. Unfortunately, they seem to find their way to me anyway. There are just so many of them. There is one in particular who takes great pleasure in trying to upset me. Not that he has to try very hard. I am generally unhappy anyway.

I guess most of it is because of this place—the rules, the demands, the stress of being a plebe. But sometimes I wonder if there are other reasons. I come from a really good family. I have parents who love me and have always taken good care of me. I have friends back home and one or two here. I really have no reason to be unhappy—no excuses for being miserable (other than the whole WP thing).

Yet, I am.
Jan

"Take boards!" Captain Ortiz commanded. The entire calculus class popped out of their chairs to stand in front of a section of chalkboard. Jan lifted a piece of chalk and rested her head against the black slate. Captain Ortiz said, "Set up the integral to determine the work to empty a full swimming pool of water that has a rectangular bottom with length twelve feet and width ten feet and a rectangular top with length twenty feet and width ten feet. The pool is eight feet underground. The water has a density of approximately 62.4 pounds per cubic foot. You may work together in pairs."

Oh, gawd. She lifted her head and tried to write something, *anything*, on the board. To her left, Rick Davidson scribbled intensely on his chalkboard section. She wished this prior service, combat veteran, whom everyone seemed to fawn over, would demonstrate a weakness in at least one thing.

She concentrated. *Swimming pool is twelve feet by ten feet at the bottom.* Drawing a rectangle, she wrote "12" on the long side, and "10" on the short side. She drew another one on top and wrote "20" and "10" on the long and short sides. Then, she drew lines between the two rectangles and wrote "8" next to one of the connecting lines. *Water density is what…?*

She put squiggly lines in between the two rectangles to simulate water while she tried to remember the density.

"Sixty-two point four pounds per cubic feet," Rick Davidson said.

"Thanks," she said, thinking he was a bit presumptuous. She wrote the water density on top of the waves. Then she sighed. *I have no freaking idea.*

"Would you like some help?" Rick asked.

Not really. But since I am pretty much lost, I guess any help is better than none. "Um, yes, please. If you don't mind," Jan said.

"I'm pretty sure I can figure it out."

I'm sure you can. You know everything, don't you? "Great, that's just…great."

"It's not that hard really."

Nothing's hard for you, I know…

"Just think about it like this: we are trying to determine the work to empty the pool, right?" Rick moved over to her chalkboard section.

"Uh, okay," she said. *He can be "Mr. Know It All" because I am clearly not.*

"So we say work equals," he wrote "W=" on the board. "The water density or 62.4 pounds has to be lifted from zero to eight feet which is the depth of the pool." He continued writing the equation.

Jan tried to follow him. "Then we multiply the results of that by the volume of water or length times width times height." He moved closer to her and pointed at her trapezoid drawing with simulated water. "See, you have it all drawn out already." Then he wrote the equation again on her board. "Work equals 62.4 integral of zero to eight times ten times Y plus twelve times eight minus Y times DY." He turned to her, only a few inches away.

She looked from the board to him, "Are you speaking English?"

"Did I lose you?"

"Way back at W equals."

"Okay, sorry, Jan."

Maybe he's not such a bad-ass after all. "Oh, it's not your fault. I'm just not the sharpest knife in this calculus drawer."

"Well, I could…"

"Take seats!" Captain Ortiz commanded. Jan sat back down while watching Rick Davidson return to his seat. "Looks like most of you worked through the problem correctly. Cadet Davidson, please explain how you came up with your equation."

Rick walked back to the chalkboard with Jan's pool drawing. "Cadet Wishart has given us a visual depiction of the problem." The class chuckled.

Jan glared at him. *Jerk!*

After he finished explaining, they went through a couple more practice problems at their desks while Captain Ortiz walked around checking their work. She managed to make it look like she had a handle on the situation. But she thought calculus felt more like drowning than "Drowning."

Drew sat on Jan's bed with his back leaning against the wall and his long legs dangling over the side. They wore the winter PT uniform: gray sweatshirt with ARMY in black letters across the chest over gray sweatpants.

"Drew?" Jan asked when Angel and Kristi left the room.

"Yes, dear."

"Do you think I'm pretty?"

"Honey, your very pretty."

"Hmmm."

"Hmmm, what?"

"Well, I don't think most guys consider me attractive."

"Of course they do."

"Well, then why do they all act like jerks?" Jan's voice rose.

"Well, first, they don't ALL act like jerks. Some do, sure, but some women are jerks, too. So, we're even on that score."

"Drew, come on. I'm awash in a sea of men, and you're the only one I can talk to. What does that say?"

"It says I'm an awesome guy." He looked at his nails.

"That's true; you are. But it also says guys avoid me for some reason..."

"Well, it could have a teensy, weensy bit to do with you." Drew held his thumb and forefinger close together in front of his face.

"What do you mean?" Jan didn't like where this was going.

"Well, you are a little intimidating. Guys are afraid of girls, you know?"

"No, I don't know. Enlighten me."

"Women scare men; they always have." Drew seemed to know all about the subject.

"You have got to be kidding me. It's men who are the scary ones! They have all the power, too. Since when have women been in charge of things?"

"Well, okay, you're right of course. Men have always dominated the world. But women have power over men, sexually and otherwise."

"What? How so?"

"Well, men want women. They want to have sex of course, but they also want a woman to love, respect and need them. The great fear of men is that women will reject them. And since women can read emotions better than men, they can detect our fears and weaknesses, and that scares us even more. So women have the real power because men live in fear of losing their attention and affection. Do you see?"

"No, but go on," Jan said, fascinated.

"Also, men compete for women. A man might kill his own brother over a woman. Sometimes, men will act like they don't want a certain woman, either because they don't think they can get her or they are trying to get her to want him first. He will act like he doesn't need or want her, hoping she will want him."

"That's stupid."

"I never said men were the smartest creatures around. But in your case, guys are intimidated because you look pissed off all the time."

"I AM pissed off all the time."

"Maybe if you smiled, or seemed less angry, guys would seem more friendly to you," he said.

"Well, what am I suppose to do? Walk around like this?" Jan made a fake grin. "I'd rather be real. When I smile, it's real."

"All I'm saying is that may be why guys seem to avoid you. *If* they really are avoiding you. It could just be in your imagination."

"No, they definitely avoid me." She paused before asking, "You don't think it's the uniform then?"

"Jan, guys can see beyond the uniform."

"Well, if they can see beyond the uniform, why can't they see beyond my pissed-off face?"

"Now you're asking too much. We aren't *that* deep."

He confirmed what she had long suspected. *Guys are shallow.*

"Okay, but what about you, Drew? Why aren't you attracted to me? Are you playing hard to get with me?" She decided to just come out with it.

"No, Darling. I love you, and you are very attractive. I just prefer a different type."

"Oh, thank goodness. I prefer a different type, too. But I do adore you; I want you to know."

"We make a good pair, don't we?" Drew asked.

"Yes, we do my friend. Yes, we do," she confirmed.

27

"Sir, have you heard anything yet from a possible new witness?"
Jan stood at Cadet Trane's door, hoping he had SKIP's statement already
in hand. She had been to his room three times that night, but he had
been out until now.

"I've just returned from talking to him, in fact. He is finishing up his
statement now," Trane said. "He doesn't want me to tell you who he is.
Apparently he wants to surprise you at the board tomorrow. Won't
that be exciting?" He winked at Jan.

"Sir, I'm willing to let him handle this however he wants given that
he might just save my ass."

"Yeah, you really gotta give him credit, coming forth at the last
minute." Trane walked over to his sink and began washing his hands.
He looked in his mirror while talking to her, "I'd like to know how you
knew he could be a witness when you don't even know who he is?"

"Well, Sir, it's a bit...irregular." She didn't want to explain.

He began drying his hands on a towel. "Wishart, *you* are irregular.
And I mean that in the best possible way."

"Thank you, Sir."

Jan hurried to the latrine for a shower and made it back to her room just as Taps played at 2300 hours. All overhead lights had to go out, but cadets could study in their room or in a common area. Jan had always made it her personal goal to go to bed at Taps, and except for the last week, she had been successful. She hadn't been able to fall asleep or stay asleep in the last five days, and she knew sleep would elude her again. Angel and Kristi were awake, too, both trying to prepare for exam week.

"Hey, guys, I'm going to take a little jaunt around the neighborhood," Jan said. "I figure I can't get in any worse trouble." If these were her last few nights at West Point, she might as well go exploring. She felt a hankering to spin the "lucky spurs" on Sedgwick, stroll down Flirtation Walk, and maybe even navigate the bowels of Washington Hall. "I may never get another chance to see the sights around Post if I don't go now."

"I'm game," Kristi said.

"No, Kissy, you don't need to get in trouble on my account." Jan had caused enough problems for her friend.

"Where we going?" Kristi said without hesitating.

"First stop, Flirtation Walk." Jan knew Kristi would not stay behind. "Angel, don't wait up for us."

"Have fun. I will pray your safe return." No one realized how important Angel's prayer would be.

28

Q: What is the largest piece of granite turned in the Western Hemisphere?

A: The shaft of Battle Monument, Sir.

Heritage, Bugle Notes, 81, p.244

"Beanheads, halt!"

They had gotten lost backstage after attending the post-show party hosted by the Cadet Activities Club. Jan and Drew had had several beers each before trying to find their way out of Eisenhower Hall. They ended up emerging through a side door where a firstie and his date just happened to be located.

Oh, for cryin-out-loud, just leave us alone.

But the firstie would not leave them alone. "You two reek of beer. What are two beanheads doing at Ike Hall?"

"Sir," Drew began, "we were ushing the show."

"You were USHING, were you?"

"Sir, we were USH-ER-ING," Jan corrected.

The firstie looked at Drew. "Where's your hat, Beanhead?" Drew instinctively lifted a hand to his head.

"Sir, may I make a statement?" Jan hoped to change the subject, somehow.

"No, you may not. What are your names and companies?"

"Cadet Hambin, Sir, Company G-3, Sir."

"Cadet Wishart, Company H-3, Sir."

"You're both drunk! You're off limits! You're missing your goddamn hat! What the hell were you two doing in there? Screwing around?"

They both answered simultaneously.

"Yes, Sir!" "No, Sir!"

The plebes looked at each other, wondering who had answered correctly. Drew's mouth twitched at the corners, and Jan could tell he was about to lose it. And if he went over the fence, she would follow. She quickly turned back to the firstie.

"Sir, we are a little drunk, and he's missing his hat, but no Sir, we were not screwing around. Sir."

"Oh, really?" The firstie took a step closer.

"Yes, Sir, I think I would remember that," Drew stated.

Silence.

"I think I would, too, Sir," Jan loved this aspect of drinking. She became bolder and unafraid of repercussions.

The firstie continued to stare at them in silence. *This isn't rocket science, buddy...* When he still didn't say anything, Jan began to wonder what he was thinking. *Is he picturing us screwing? Is he wondering if he could get away with it in Ike Hall, too?*

Drew began to snicker. *Uh-oh.* Jan couldn't contain it either. They were both too tipsy to care about the consequences. Drew made a snorkeling noise. Then Jan snickered through her nose, desperately trying to maintain some decorum. *We're screwed.*

The plebes started laughing in earnest. The firstie's date began laughing, also. He turned to her and said, "Not you, too." Then with a wave of his hand, he said, "Get outta here, you two. And don't let me catch you screwing around here anymore."

Jan and Drew scurried away, continuing to snorkel-snicker until they reached the safety of Trophy Point. On the steps of Battle Monument, facing the Hudson River, they fell out in full-on laughter.

The moonlight floating on the river looked like a white ribbon strung from the banks of the Hudson to some magical destination.

Their laughter echoing off the cannons and granite seemed to follow the ribbon road and then return again like voices from heaven.

They sat down on the sacred steps where 2,230 names of the Civil War dead are inscribed and "Fame" perpetually blows her trumpet atop the massive granite shaft. Jan wished they could stay there till dawn, soaking up the beauty and peace of the moonlit night. She didn't care if they missed TAPS, the signal when all cadets had to be back in their rooms. *I'll risk the demerits for this.*

They both stared at the Hudson River in silence, not as plebes, not even as cadets—but as young college kids, enjoying a moment alone on a beautifully clear evening with the quiet souls of the past.

Dear Jan,

I will admit to being in your battalion. But I will neither confirm, nor deny any other assumptions you have. To do so would be to jeopardize our organization. You know I can't do that.

I am a little afraid of you finding out who I am. In some ways, being anonymous makes it easier to talk to you (Okay, write to you). On the other hand, I can't wait for you to know.

It saddens me to hear that you are unhappy. I know it's hard, especially plebe year. I wish I could say or do something to help you feel better. But all I can do is try to cheer you up with these little notes.

SKIP

SKIP,

Even though I don't know who you are, you have been a real friend—one of only two guys here I actually like. So don't be afraid when I discover your identity. Notice I wrote "when" not "if."

Jan

Jan attended a religious retreat in early March. Getting away from West Point, even if it meant praying and going to church, was always better than staying. So she went with a couple of Team Handball teammates and pretended to be slightly interested in Christianity. The retreat, as it turned out, was a wonderful, peaceful, relaxing, even joyful experience. Jan began to believe that her life might change for the better as a result. But upon her return, as the bus drew closer to West Point, she could feel the lightness from the weekend dimming, dimming and dimming until it turned back to gray.

Jan found Angel studying at her desk when she entered the room late Sunday afternoon. Angel had been issued an academic warning in Calculus which prevented her from going to the retreat. Jan put her bag on the bed and began unpacking. "How was it?" Angel asked.

"Great! We ate at round tables—without any pecking order," Jan replied. "I hope you get to go sometime; it was a lot of fun—I mean as much fun as you can have without drinking!"

"I hope so, too," Angel said.

"Where's Kissy?" Jan asked.

"She had to go home. Her brother died."

"WHAT?" Jan stood in the middle of the room, stunned. "What happened?"

"Her brother was killed in a car accident."

"Oh, GOD! How did she find out? Who told her?" Jan could not even imagine hearing that kind of news—especially during plebe year.

"The TAC came to the room yesterday and told her to come to his office to call her mother. Her mother told her on the phone. She came back to the room then packed and left." Angel seemed to be rattling off a list of supplies.

"Oh, God! Poor Kissy!" Jan sat down on her bed. Losing a brother, losing anyone in her family, was incomprehensible to Jan. She stared at the floor contemplating Kristi's new tragedy—a brother now gone along with her father. Jan's shoulders began to shake; she felt her face crinkle, and then the sobbing came. She put her hands to her face and bent over until her head came down to her lap. She cried for Kristi, for the dead brother, and for Kristi's mom, sisters and stepfather. She cried for the loss of childhood, the loss of innocence, and the loss of all that was once easy.

She cried until she felt a pencil hit her head. Jan lifted her head and said, "What did you do that for?"

"Dammit, Jan! Why can't I cry like that?"

"What do you mean?"

"Nothing, forget it. It's just that I feel sorry for Kristi, too."

Kristi returned the following Sunday. Jan gave her a hug and asked if there was anything she could do. "No, there's nothing anyone can do." After dinner that night, Kristi's Squad Leader came to the room.

"Cadet McCarron, I am sorry to hear what happened," he said.

"Thank you, Sir," she replied.

"It's going to be hard, but you can do it. Just focus on your studies and plebe duties and try not to let this setback keep you from your goals."

Setback? Is that what losing a brother is??? A setback? God! What's wrong with some people?

"Yes, Sir," Kristi said with a sigh.

Her Squad Leader left. Jan closed the door and turned to Kristi, "I think he just offered his condolences, don't you?"

"I think so; it sure sounded like it," Kristi agreed.

"Well, Kissy, I guess it's better than what Dogety would have said." Then mimicking Dogety's voice, Jan said, "McCarron, just because your brother dies, doesn't mean you get to slack off. Now go get my laundry from the dayroom!"

Jan immediately wished she hadn't said it. She was about to apologize profusely for being so insensitive when Kristi grabbed her M-14 rifle from the rack and pointed it at the door.

"If he comes here tonight, I'm going to shoot his balls off!!"

That's how Jan knew Kristi was going to be okay.

They soon fell into their normal, daily routine of classes followed by either parade drill or athletics, along with three meal formations, studying, polishing shoes and memorizing poop every night. Rallies didn't happen nearly as often post football season. That was a good thing as plebes were getting fed up with the whole mandatory fun thing.

Dear Jan,

I am really sorry to hear about your roommate's loss. I hope she will be okay, and that you will be able to help her through this difficult time. I'm sure you are a good friend to her.

Also, I hear you went on the Sabbath Rest retreat! What did you think? I went last semester and loved it. It was so great to get away and spend some quality time with God. Anyway, I hope you enjoyed it as much as I did.

Hope to hear from you soon,
SKIP

SKIP,

My roommate is doing okay, although I cannot imagine what it must be like for her. She not only has to deal with her grief, she has to do it during plebe year at Woo Poo U. That can't be good. Thanks for asking about her. We are doing our best to help her get through it.

I enjoyed the retreat very much, mostly because I got away from here for a few days. But I'm not sure I understand all that Bible stuff. It sounds good. Almost too good. But I don't think God is that involved with us, IF there is a God. I mean, don't you think He/She would have bigger issues to worry about than our little lives? Anyway, everyone was really nice and I loved eating meals at round tables.

Jan

29

Friday, May 7, 1982
2320 Hours

Jan opened the door and looked up and down the hallway before darting out to the nearest stairwell. Kristi followed close behind as they stealthily descended the steps to the main barracks door. This was the tricky part because barracks doors always slammed shut. Jan slowly pushed the handle until the door opened wide enough for the two plebes to escape. She placed a rolled up newspaper between the doors and closed it gently. Then they sped along Central Barracks, ducking under cadet room windows before reaching Thayer Road. General Patton watched holding his binoculars as they skirted the USMA library. After passing Mahan Hall, they made a sharp left down a hundred or so stairs leading to the arched, gated entrance to Flirtation Walk. To Jan, it had always seemed like an enchanted portal, a secret opening to the forbidden, magical forest. But that night, it just looked like a plain gate, an old one at that.

"Does this look like the same Flirty entrance to you?" Jan whispered.

"Yeah, why?"

"It just seems different."

"It is dark out, Jan."

"I know, but it seems...ordinary."

They ran the trail known as Flirtation Walk. It was a bit shorter than Jan imagined and not really all that scenic. But that could have been due to the darkness.

They continued running back up the hundred or so steps and all the way over to Old Sedgwick where they spun the infamous spurs. Again, it felt anticlimactic to Jan. "Well, now we're two for two."

"Yup! Anything else we should do while we're at it?" Kristi asked.

"Let's just explore Washington Hall a bit. Then, we'll call it a night."

Washington Hall housed not only the massive Mess Hall but also dozens of rooms above and below. All the spaces needed to feed four thousand cadets, three times a day, seven days a week, were located in its depths. There were huge kitchens, pantries full of bulk food, and storage rooms for dishes, linens, cutlery and cleaning supplies, to name a few. Jan and Kristi rode a service elevator to the lowest level marked B-3. Relying only on illuminated exit lights, they wandered down several hallways before finding a small elevator. It could only hold two people at the most. They boarded and closed its metal cage. Without pushing a button, the elevator began descending. "Oh, shit," Kristi said.

"Did you hit something?" Jan asked.

"No, it must be possessed."

"Don't say that." Jan tried not to think of *The Shining*.

The personal elevator came to a sudden halt one floor down. Jan and Kristi opened the gate and stepped into what looked like a small office. A desk, a chair, a lamp, a typewriter, and a small trash can were neatly lined against the opposite wall. A loveseat was propped against the right wall.

Jan and Kristi stepped into the office. "Weird place for an office," Jan said.

"Yeah, I wonder who works here." They heard a sound coming from a door located on the left wall, opposite the sofa wall.

"Shhhhh," Jan whispered as she tiptoed to the door. She put her ear against it and Kristi did the same. They heard a woman laughing and then a man's voice, sounding as if he was teasing the woman. "Do you want an adventure, Kissy?"

"Why else are we down here?"

"Okay," Jan quietly turned the doorknob. The door opened to a narrow hallway. She turned to Kristi, still standing behind her. "Do you think there's a flashlight anywhere?" Kristi walked back to the desk and opened a drawer. It squeaked when she pulled the handle.

"Shhh.....it." Then lifting a flashlight out of the drawer, she said, "But lookie here."

"Bring it to me. Quietly. Please." Jan shone the flashlight down the hallway, lighting up two doors, one on each side of the hall. "They must be in one of those rooms," she whispered.

The roommates tiptoed to the first door on the right. Jan leaned her ear against it. No sound. She looked at Kristi before turning the knob slowly. The door opened to darkness and complete quietness. The flashlight lit up a stairwell with steps going only up.

"Must be the other one," Kristi whispered. They tiptoed to the second door.

The woman's voice became audible again, but she wasn't laughing. She seemed to be crying. "Just let me....please...I promise..."

"It doesn't sound like she's very happy," Jan whispered.

"No, she's crying, I think."

They stood silently in the dark hallway for another moment, both wondering what to do. Jan didn't feel right opening the door this time, knowing two people were probably having a lover's quarrel. She didn't want to burst in on that.

But Kristi had a different thought, "Ah hell, what else do we live for?" She lunged for the doorknob and swung open the door.

30

"How are they all?"

"They are all fickle but one, Sir."

"And who is the one?"

"She who stands atop Battle Monument, for she has been on the same shaft since 1897."

(The last two lines were dropped from required plebe knowledge after women were admitted to West Point)

While the upperclassmen went on spring leave, the plebes stayed behind and attended all their usual classes. But roaming the entire campus at leisure is about as good as going to Myrtle Beach in the West Point scale of things. With drill and athletics canceled for the week, the atmosphere was almost euphoric.

Walking across Central Area to and from classes, to the gym, anywhere—without having to ping and square corners—felt strange. West Point is probably the only place where doing normal things feels weird. Spring leave week gave plebes their first glimpse of what it would be like as upperclassmen. Jan noticed right away that it felt much better than being a plebe. *Maybe I could come to love this place, if I can just hang on long enough.* For the first time since R-Day, she felt she could maybe, someday, possibly, sort of, become comfortable as a cadet at West Point. *Hopefully the next three years will be very different.*

Plebe Parent Weekend started on Friday afternoon when families and friends descended upon West Point. Kristi's parents didn't make the trip from Germany, so she joined Jan and her parents for lunch on Saturday in the Mess Hall. Then the plebe women showed Mr. and Mrs. Wishart their rooms, the day room, the CQ office, Cullum, Grant and Eisenhower Halls, and all the major statues and monuments before ending the afternoon with a short walk in the library. Saturday night dinner, a formal affair for cadets and their dates in the Mess Hall, meant that most female plebes made other arrangements that night. Jan's parents treated for dinner at Thayer Hotel, a wonderful excuse to miss the "other thing." After dinner, most classmates attended the plebe ball at Eisenhower Hall while Jan and the plebe women she knew were free to do something else.

Jan and Kristi walked to Cullum Hall after bidding the old people goodnight. With a pitcher of beer, they sat at a table on the large porch overlooking the Hudson River. March is still cold at West Point, but with big, gray, wool coats and beer, it gets downright warm. They drank the whole pitcher and went back for another.

Halfway through the second one, Rick Davidson and six other male plebes stumbled onto the porch. A few burps and farts punctuated their discussion of the places they had "plugged a girl." One bragged about doing it in his parents' bed, another in a teachers' lounge, and yet another managed to do some plugging while on an Amtrak train.

An unspoken agreement passed between Jan and Kristi as they locked eyes. They would wait it out. *Humiliated, yes; leaving, no.* They resolved to stay put no matter how cold or obnoxious things got. *Those jerks will have to leave first.*

Suddenly, one of the guys threw up. He puked on the porch, then ran to the railing and continued to vomit over the side. His friends laughed uproariously, even cheering on his regurgitation efforts.

This nullifies our previous agreement. "Kissy, we need to bail." Jan made sure Rick saw her disgust.

"Yup, agreed."

"As much as I'd like to stay and enjoy the show, we don't want to be left cleaning up this mess."

"Right you are."

"Exit, stage left."

'Yes, Ma'am." They grabbed the pitcher and their cups and relocated to a small table inside.

A short time later Rick Davidson appeared with another full pitcher of beer. He placed it down on the table along with three plastic cups. "I'm atoning for that circus outside," he said. Jan and Kristi stared at each other, not quite trusting his motives. "Oh, come on, ladies, it wasn't that bad, was it?"

"Well, let's see, Kissy, did *you* enjoy hearing where girls get fucked?" Jan looked at Kristi.

"Well, it was enlightening," Kristi said.

"That it was, but would you say it was entertaining, humorous or even remotely interesting?" She wouldn't look at Rick.

"No, certainly not."

Rick pulled up a chair and sat down at the table. "C'mon, you have to admit some of it was funny."

"No, no, I don't think any of it was funny," Jan said.

"Stupid, revolting, disgusting and yes, even enlightening. But funny? No," Kristi added.

"Okay, okay, so that's why I'm here with a fresh pitcher of beer—to make up for the bad behavior," Rick said.

"So you admit it?" Jan asked.

"Well, yes, although, *I* didn't say anything that would have offended you."

"Actually," Jan turned to Rick, "you offended us by *NOT* saying anything—by *NOT* telling them to shut up nor even acknowledging our presence."

Rick looked confused. "So I should have said, 'Guys, shut up, ladies are present?'"

"Yes, exactly."

"But I thought female cadets didn't want to be singled out and didn't want to be treated differently."

"*Male cadets* are clueless," Jan said looking away.

"We're damned if we do and damned if we don't with you guys."

"*You gals*, you mean," Kristi said.

"See what I'm talking about?" Rick looked at Jan. She glared back at him. She thought he might be another Cadet Trane, older and wiser than most guys in their class. But he also might be just another dickhead.

"Okay, well, let's not let good beer go to waste," Kristi said as she lifted the pitcher and poured. She and Rick chatted away while Jan stewed in silence.

Those damn bells. Thirsty and famished, Jan rolled out of bed and rambled to the sink. After downing a quart of tap water, she lumbered back to bed. Kristi stirred and looked down at Jan from atop the bunk beds, "How are you feeling?"

"Fine, just thirsty. And hungry."

"When are we meeting your parents for brunch?"

"Eleven," Jan replied. "Kissy?"

"Yes?"

"What do you think of Rick Davidson?"

"He seems like a nice guy," Kristi said.

"Doesn't he seem a little, too...I don't know...like he has everything going on?"

"Maybe," Kristi agreed.

"And why's he trying to be so nice to us? I mean, what's his agenda?"

"Jan, maybe he's just a nice guy who happens to be good at everything."

"Doesn't that freak you out just a little bit?"

"No, not really." After a long pause, Kristi asked, "Why's that a problem with you?"

"It's just weird, that's all. I mean, most guys have at least one flaw. Something I can see, or tell, that makes a guy just a little more human. But Davidson is like some kind of mutant. All the guys want to be like him. He's tall, good looking, athletic, smart and confident. He's too confident...it unnerves me."

"Jan, you do realize that the same could be said about you."

"Are you kidding me? I'm practically failing three classes, I have to "study up" for every PT test, and I haven't had a real date in my life." *A boyfriend is not the same as a date.*

"I'm sure there are things he's not good at either; you just can't see them. Just like most people don't know how hard you work before PT tests or that you never had a date. They assume you have guys lining up to go out with you."

"Oh c'mon, Kissy. It's obvious that he's in a whole different league than I."

"No, it's not obvious. The only thing that he seems to have that you don't—is confidence. And even that isn't obvious to the casual observer."

"Right. And it's his damn confidence that really pisses me off."

They showered, dressed in Dress Gray, and met Jan's parents for brunch at the front steps of the Mess Hall. This would be their last meal before the upperclassmen returned and the normal routine resumed. They joked and laughed with Mr. and Mrs. Wishart over lunch, never betraying the dread that percolated in their veins.

She hugged her parents, told them she was fine and walked back to the room with Kristi. "Kissy, you're right. I'm going to be more confident from now on."

"There ya go. I knew you'd come around."

"Ya, well, just don't expect me to be good at it."

The bad guys returned Sunday night. Jan, Kristi and Angel stayed in their room hoping to eek out every last minute without harassment. Just before study hours, the Commandant of Cadets came over the Corps-wide PA system. "Attention all Cadets! Attention all Cadets! This is General Mullenbehr, Commandant of Cadets." As if they didn't know. "I want to welcome the upperclassmen back from spring leave. I trust everyone had a safe and restful break. Now it's time to buckle down and get back to the task at hand. I also want to congratulate the fourth classmen for a successful week here. Everyone should be proud of the way you conducted yourselves, especially during plebe-parent weekend."

Yay, we made Daddy proud!

"As a reward and to allow our fourth classmen to take one step closer to recognition, plebes will no longer have to square corners."

A huge roar, louder than any rally, went up throughout the Corps. Jan and Kristi jumped on their desks and started dancing and screaming with joy while Angel jumped up and down on her bed. In every fourth room across the regiments, the celebrating continued for several minutes. "Attention all Cadets! Attention all Cadets!" The Commandant resumed, "Plebes will continue to walk at quick-time. They will continue to ping in all academic and Corps-wide areas. Squaring corners is the only requirement lifted. The Superintendent and I offer our congratulations to the Class of 1985. Beat Navy!"

Jan, Kristi and Angel kept dancing and jumping until they were suddenly cut off by two loud knocks at the door. The three plebes jumped back to the floor, straightened their uniforms, and yelled in unison, "Enter, Sir!"

What a surprise. Dogety stood at the door still in civilian clothes.

"I hope you three don't celebrate too much. Just because you don't have to square corners anymore doesn't mean you get to slack off. I will be expecting even more out of you now. Do you understand, Beanheads?"

"Yes, Sir," the three replied.

"Good! Wishart, report to my room at 1930 hours."

"Sir, may I make a statement?"

"What?"

"Sir, that's study hours, and I am not allowed to enter upperclass rooms." An easy out, she thought.

"I know that, Wishart. Did I say to report IN my room?"

"No, Sir."

"What did I say, Wishart?"

"Sir, you said to report to your room at 1930 hours."

"That's right. Can you handle that, Wishart?"

"Yes, Sir." Then Dogety walked away. Jan turned to Kristi, "What the hell does he want now?"

Kristi replied, "I don't know, but I'll go with you."

"No," Jan said, "It'll only make it worse. He didn't tell you to report, only me."

"Jan, don't let him dick with you. If he tries to do any shit, go right to the CO and report his ass."

"Right. It'll be his word against mine, and who do you think his classmate will believe—him or me?"

"Well, first come back here, tell us what happened, and then we will all go to the CO's room," Kristi offered.

"How does that help anything, Kissy?"

"Then it will be the word of three of us against his."

Jan loved Kristi for trying. *Even though her logic is not always on bar.*

She knocked on Dogety's door at exactly 1930 hours, wearing her PT uniform with sweat pants and sweatshirt, since he hadn't specified one. "Open the door, Wishart, but don't come in." Jan pushed the door open and remained in the hallway. "Glad to see you're on time, Wishart."

Dogety sat on his bed, shining his shoes. Jackson sat at Dogety's desk with his head in a magazine.

"What are your general orders?" Dogety asked.

"Sir, I will guard everything within the limits of my post and quit my post only when properly relieved. I will obey my special orders and perform all of my duties in a military manner." Jackson lifted the magazine so it sat upright on the desk. *Playboy.*

"I will report all violations of my special orders, emergencies, and anything not covered in my instructions to the Commander of the relief." Jackson turned the magazine so that the binding was now horizontal.

"Very good. Now repeat the phonetic alphabet."

"Sir, alpha, beta, charlie, delta, echo...." Jan got about halfway through the alphabet before speaking up. "Sir, I am not going to keep doing this if he's going to keep doing that." She nodded her head at

Jackson who still leered at the magazine.

"What?" Dogety seemed momentarily confused. Then he turned to Jackson. "Dammit, man!" Dogety jumped up and grabbed the magazine out of Jackson's hands. He seemed genuinely embarrassed. "Dismissed, Wishart!"

Jan turned and pinged back to her room. *He's just screwing with me. Because he can't SCREW me!* She smiled all the way back to her room.

Dear Jan,

Yes, God is THAT involved with us. I believe God knows and loves each one of us. And He always wants to have a deeper relationship with us. But we run away, ignore or otherwise keep a distance from God. We are often unhappy because we don't understand His peace and purpose for our lives.

As you can tell, I am a believer. I hope someday, you will become one, too. I have been praying for you…. and Kristi, of course.

SKIP

SKIP,

Okay, I have no idea what planet you come from. But, let me say that I DO believe in God…but not as you do. I believe God exists and maybe even cares a little about us. But he/she has wars, hunger and disease to worry about. And it looks like things aren't going very well in any of those areas. So, either God doesn't care or God cannot change it. It seems to me that if God cared and could change things, there would be a lot less suffering in the world.

I believe, as you probably do, that both faith and happiness are choices we make. So I am going to CHOOSE to be happy and see what happens.

I'll let you know.

Jan

31

Saturday, May 8, 1982
0030 Hours

Jan reactively shined the flashlight in the small room. The woman's hands were tied to old pipes hanging from the wall. She sat on a desk, legs splayed open, shirt torn from her chest, and her breasts exposed. A man stood in front of her, between her legs, thrusting his hips back and forth, back and forth. Gray trousers were crumpled on black cadet shoes; a Dress Gray coat was lying on the floor next to his feet.

Jan's first reaction was to apologize profusely. But the look on the woman's face, a look Jan would never forget, quickly changed her mind.

Kristi, on the other hand, seemed to understand right away. "WHAT THE FUCK ARE YOU DOING?"

The male cadet, whose back had been to them, suddenly pulled away from the table and turned around. A giant eagle tattoo spread across his chest, its wingtips spanning from shoulder to shoulder.

32

Q: "How many days until graduation?"
A: "SIR! There are thirty-five and a butt days until graduation
and graduation leave for the Class of 1982, Sir!"

March gave way to April and the sun began to hang a little longer in the gray skies over West Point. The plebes could smell "Recognition" even if they couldn't quite see it yet. But the firsties had one more milestone to celebrate—ring weekend. The huge, class rings were given out during a special dinner on the first Friday in April. Then a dance on Saturday night gave them an opportunity to show off their bulbous jewelry. The other three classes laid low. It was the firsties' last special event, other than graduation, and everyone else seemed to know their place.

After the festivities on Friday night, firsties across the Corps returned to the barracks and stuck their hands out to plebes who dropped to one knee and feigned unbridled excitement over the rings. The hallways erupted with the shouting of plebes: "OH MY GOD, SIR! WHAT A BEAUTIFUL RING! WHAT A CRASS, MASS OF GLASS AND BRASS! IT MUST HAVE COST A FORTUNE! MAY I TOUCH IT, PLEASE, SIR?"

Jan avoided the hall altogether that night. But the next day, after classes and SAMI, as Jan pinged to the latrine, she saw Jackson walking toward her. *Why doesn't he stay in First Regiment?*

He stuck his ring hand out, fingers extended, like he was the Pope. *Dammit.* Jan dropped to one knee and recited the mantra, not quite as loudly nor as enthusiastically as it should have been.

"Oh my God, Sir, what a beautiful ring. What a crass, mass of glass and brass...." And just before she said the last line, Jackson took a step closer so that his ring hand was just in front of his crotch. "May I touch it, please, Sir?"

"Yes, you may," Jackson said. She was supposed to touch his ring like it was the Hope Diamond, but she stood up instead.

"Don't you want to touch it, Wishart?"

"No, Sir, I do not." Then she added quietly as she pinged away from him, "It's too small for my taste."

They had to climb the ten-meter platform as part of the final hurdle in Drowning 101. Drew had ascended first. Jan was supposed to be next, but she stepped aside and motioned for Rick Davidson to go before her. The last thing she wanted was him staring at her Speedo ass all the way to the top.

"Ladies first," Rick said.

"No, no, age before beauty," she insisted.

"Get on with it you two!" The DPE instructor yelled. Rick jumped on the ladder, climbing like a monkey. Then Jan began the ascent, slowly and cautiously. About halfway up the ladder, her fingers locked on a rung at eye level. Her left foot froze one rung above the right, both legs quivering. Her eyes glazed over with terrifying dizziness as she tried to focus on the pool stretched out in front of her.

"What's wrong, Wishart?" The DPE instructor shouted.

I can't move. I can't....

"Wishart, are you okay?"

"Sir, I...I ....I..."

"Jan, Jan," Rick called from the top of the platform. "Look at me." Jan lifted her face and saw Rick about a mile above her. "Listen to me, Jan. Just keep looking at me and keep climbing. Don't look down and don't look out."

But she still couldn't move. "Jan, you don't want to do this all again. So, just keep your eyes on me and keep climbing. I promise you will not fall."

She decided to trust Rick Davidson. She locked her eyes on his and began to climb again, slowly. Drew also appeared at the top of the platform, encouraging her. "You've got it Jan, almost here, keep climbing."

Taking twice the normal amount of time, she finally reached the top rung. Rick grabbed her right arm, while Drew grabbed her left. Together, they pulled her up the last few rails, until she stood at last on the platform.

"Good job, Jan. You did it!" Drew said.

"Thanks for your help, guys." She blinked the salty water back inside as her eyes began to fill. She might have hugged both of them but she wouldn't consider doing it in the Speedo.

"That was the easy part," Rick said. "Now we have to jump off."

Easy for you, maybe!

"Mr. Hambin, are you ready?" The DPE instructor bellowed from ten meters below.

"Yes, Sir." Drew walked to the edge of the deck. Then he stepped off. With his body erect, knees slightly bent, eyes to the horizon, arms crossed in front of his chest and opposite hands on his shoulders, he held this position until his body cut through the water. Once submerged, he fell to the bottom and pushed off with his legs, beginning the Bob and Travel sequence.

"Miss Wishart, you're next," came the command from below.

Rick looked at Jan. "I was joking before. This is actually easier than climbing up. Only one step."

Great. Thanks. She inched to the edge of the platform. Her legs shook involuntarily. Only the fear of peeing superseded the fear of falling in that moment. She could not and would not look down. Rick stood a few feet behind her, his arms folded across his chest.

The DPE instructor talked her through the steps. "Keep your head up, knees bent, cross your arms in front of your chest, and don't unlock until you hit the water."

"You got this, Jan. It's gonna be fine. No problem," Rick said from behind.

"Cadet Wishart, are you ready?"

"Ah, um....Yes, Sir."

"Step off!"

But she didn't move.

Rick whispered, "Step off, Jan."

And then, just like that, she stepped forward onto air. On the long way down, she thought about a quote she once heard. It was something like, *Courage is not the absence of fear but the willingness to walk into that fear.* In this case, she *jumped into it.*

They would have to jump twice more, once in fatigues and boots, and finally in the full uniform—ruck sack and rifle included. But she knew she could do it again, now that she managed that first one. And Jan wouldn't even mind climbing the ladder in front of Rick because, then, she would have pants on.

Dear Jan,

Okay, you are definitely a tough case. But I love a challenge. I hope you will not mind if I respond to your thoughts about God.

To your point that God doesn't care about us: Millions of people down through the ages have given witness to a loving God, myself included. So if God doesn't care about us, all those people are either delusional or just mistaken. I happen to think they can't all be wrong.

Secondly, God chooses not to "fix" everything in this world. God has chosen to redeem the world by working within the limits of our broken and flawed world. Besides, if everything were perfect here, we would have no desire for our eternal home. God has made a place without evil, sin, sickness, suffering and death. It's called Heaven.

ALL problems will not be solved on earth. And we have to work out some things on our own—including faith—which often only comes through trials. So, I guess even suffering can serve God's purposes.

I'm glad you are choosing to be happy...does that mean I will see you smiling soon?

SKIP

Reverend SKIP,

Methinks you missed your calling. Shouldn't you be in Bible College or something? I did find your explanations rather interesting and I promise to give them some further thought. But I hope you are not expecting a convert.

All this past week, I repeated, "I choose to be happy," over and over again. I also tried to think happy thoughts, memories from my childhood with my friends and family. It was a nice trip down memory lane. But I cannot say that I feel any happier.

I think there must be a "happy" gene which you seem to have. I must have missed that line on R-day. Actually, I was mostly happy before coming to West Point. So, it might have something to do with that whole thing.

Well, it seems we are at an impasse.

By the way, it occurs to me that we always talk about me in these letters. It would be nice to talk about you sometimes. Oh, right, we can't because I don't know who you are.

Jan

Company H-3 marched to the Army Athletic Field House, fronting the Hudson River for the final fitness hurdle of the year. Two minutes of push-ups, two minutes of sit-ups and a timed two-mile run, Jan thought The Army Physical Readiness Test (APRT) should have been called the "2-2-2" test.

Female cadets were keenly aware of the prevailing notion that because they did not have to meet the same physical requirements as men, their arrival only brought down the standards of West Point. Therefore, the pressure for women was not just to pass but also to surpass previous scores. What no one mentioned was that most women met and exceeded previous scores for men. And because most men felt the need to do better than most women, all the standards went up. It was the law of competition or perhaps, simple gender dynamics.

Jan hoped to beat her BEAST APRT of 25 push-ups, 60 sit-ups and

17:30 run time. This time, she wanted 30 push-ups, 70 sit-ups, and a 16-minute run.

"FIRST GROUP, ASSUME THE FRONT LEANING REST POSITION." Jan placed her hands on the mat, with straight arms directly under her shoulders. She stretched her legs out to the other end of the mat, held up only by her toes. "GET SET, BEGIN." Jan started her push-ups. The clock didn't matter, her strength would give out before time. She concentrated on making sure each push-up was executed correctly, otherwise it would not be counted. Slowly and deliberately, Jan made her upper arms come parallel to the ground with each push-up. Kristi knelt beside her head and kept count. Jan heard her say "21," and she knew she had planned it right. With time and energy left, she kept going. Kristi said, "30."

Yes, I did it.

"45 SECONDS REMAINING." Jan knocked out another 10 more before time ran out.

Wow, 40 push-ups! I almost doubled my Beast number!!

They switched roles and Kristi did very well also, making 32 push-ups. Then everyone switched back again for sit-ups. Jan interlaced her fingers behind her head while Kristi held her feet. The feet holders had to be sure those preforming sit-ups did not lift their buttocks off the ground. A good sit-up required the head coming all the way up to the knees or it didn't count. "GET SET, BEGIN!"

Jan could bang out sit-ups all day. Time usually gave out first. So she started pumping, up and down, up and down. She heard Kristi say, "50."

"ONE MORE MINUTE."

Dang! I am smokin'!

She heard, "75," then "80,"...then "85"....

"TIME'S UP! CEASE WORK, CADETS!"

90 friggin sit-ups! Take that Dogety!

The first portion of the APRT finished in less than fifteen minutes. Company H-3 then proceeded outside for the two-mile run. Every thirty seconds, a group of ten cadets began running until they came to the "turn around point." There, they circled around an orange cone and ran back to the starting line.

In the last group of plebes, Jan, Kristi and Angel lined up for the start of the two-mile run. The three women took off together, but soon Jan pulled ahead of Angel and Kristi. Most of the guys started in earlier groups and began returning on their left. "Good job, Jan, you're doing great," Drew shouted as he ran past. Cadet Trane and a couple other upperclassmen cheered her on as well.

"Good running form, Wishart." Dogety said as he passed. That was a compliment, she figured, coming from him.

Just as she was closing in on the "turn around" cone, a male cow shouted, "Move those thunder thighs!"

And then, it just didn't matter anymore. It didn't matter that she knocked out 40 push-ups and 90 sit-ups. It didn't matter that a handful of guys cheered her on. It didn't matter that she finished the two miles in 15:45. The only thing Jan absorbed, the only thing Jan thought about for weeks, was her thighs.

33

Saturday, May 8, 1982
0040 Hours

Jan's breath caught. She was seeing but not believing.

He bent down, fumbling with his pants, trying to pull them up to cover his now limp penis. As he struggled with the trousers, he shouted, "You really fucked up this time, Wishart."

Several paint cans were lined up just inside the door. Kristi grabbed one and threw it into the room knocking him backward onto another desk.

Jan flew out the door, followed by Kristi. They ran across the hallway. Jan flung open the door, and they raced up the steps two at a time, coming to B-3. The rapist shouted from somewhere below, "I'm gonna kill you both! You fucking cunts!"

The roommates reached B-2, B-1, and finally G where Jan flung open another door leading to one of the Mess Hall kitchens. They had no idea where they were in relation to their barracks, but they kept running. Halfway through the kitchen, Kristi spotted a large butcher knife hanging on the wall. She grabbed it and kept running behind Jan. They passed through two double swinging doors into the massive Mess Hall. Only exit lights could be seen in the dark cavernous space. Jan bumped into a table. "Shit!"

"Jan, let's hide under a table. There are about five hundred in here; he'll never find us."

But Jan didn't like the idea of being trapped. What if he did find the one they were under? Then what? "Kristi, you hide under that table," she pointed to one nearby. "I'll keep moving and draw him to another part of the Mess Hall. When you hear him leave this area, take off and go find the Cadet in Charge of the Guard."

Kristi didn't like the idea of splitting. She figured two are better than one. Especially if it came down to hand to hand combat. "Jan, let's stay together."

"Okay, well then, let's head to one of the exits and figure out where to go once we are outside."

"You sure we shouldn't just wait him out in here? He can outrun us."

"I'm sure we can't have a meeting and discuss all the options." Jan seethed between her teeth.

"Okay, you decide then," Kristi said. Jan didn't want to hide, but since Kristi did, she agreed. Their eyes had adjusted to the darkness and Jan crawled under what looked like table 149 while Kristi crept under table 163. They both kept in a crouching position in case they had to make a run for it.

Only a moment later, they heard the attacker lumbering through the kitchen through which they had just passed. He pushed through the double swinging doors and began prowling up and down the rows and rows of tables.

"I know you bitches are in here," he shouted. "I can smell you."

Jan kept quiet under table 149. She heard him come closer and closer. He approached her table. She held her breath. She saw his black cadet shoes as he walked passed. *That's it, bastard, keep going.*

She watched his shoes as he turned at the end of the row and came back down the next row over where Kristi's table was. "You can't fool me, bitches, I'll find you eventually." Jan saw him stop right next to table 163. "Ah, what have we here?" He lifted the tablecloth with the toe of his shoe.

Kristi bolted out the other side and began running wildly, butcher knife in hand. Jan jumped out from her hiding spot and ran after her friend, relying mainly on sound given that she could barely see anything. They ran into tables, chairs and food carts, knocking over dishes, silverware, serving trays, and any number of condiments. Thankfully, their pursuer had the same problem. But he was faster and more nimble at getting back up and was quickly closing the gap.

Kristi ran toward the Poop Deck, the large stone balcony in the middle of the Mess Hall where announcements were made at every meal. Jan ran after the shadow that was her roommate, following it up the steps of the Poop Deck. *No, Kissy, not up. Anywhere but up.*

The man saw the two women enter the stairwell and gave chase. "Now, you're going to pay," he shouted.

"Kristi, what are you doing?" Jan called to her friend.

"Just keep following me, Jan," Kristi called back as she reached the balcony and raced across it. Jan followed, making sure not to look over the sides. They arrived at the other end where another stairway lead back down to the main floor. Kristi turned to Jan, "You know where you are now, go get the CG and come back as quickly as you can."

"What about you?" Jan asked.

"Just go!" Kristi shouted.

Jan didn't think. She just ran down the steps, two at a time. She kept running, out a familiar exit, then all the way to the Command Guard office where she flung open the door, and shouted, "COME QUICKLY! SOMEONE'S TRYING TO KILL MY ROOMMATE!"

34

Accomplishment of the mission
Welfare of his subordinates
Efficient use of resources
Responsibilities of a Commander, Bugle Notes, 81, p. 57

Staying focused on academics became a huge problem for most cadets by the end of April. Everyone began planning and imagining their summer leave. Jan knew she needed a study group to help her focus on term end exams, so she rounded up her small band of friends. Drew and Jan sat on her bed while Kristi and Angel sat on the floor for their first session at 2000 hours.

"Officer in the building!" Someone shouted from the hallway and the four plebes popped to attention. Metal taps from an officer's shoes became louder and louder. *Click, click, click, click.* The tapping stopped when G-3's Tactical Officer, Captain Easmann, arrived at their door. Behind him stood Drew's Squad Leader and Company Commander.

"Cadet Hambin, come with me," Captain Easmann ordered.

Jan and Drew looked at each other. Then he shrugged his shoulders and walked out of the door, following his TAC. Jan tiptoed to the door, peeked around the frame, and watched as Drew disappeared in the stairwell.

The next morning, Jan's history professor ordered the class to pick up their desks and place them a couple feet apart from each other. The "Stagger Desks" command was kind of like "Fallout." Everyone moved their desks to random, disorderly positions. This supposedly diminished the ability and temptation to cheat. She rushed through the pop quiz, not caring about her grade, dropped the paper on her professor's desk and ran out of the door to find Drew.

She couldn't study after Captain Easmann took Drew away. His room had been empty both times she had checked before Taps. She couldn't sleep most of the night either and hadn't seen him all morning. Now she knocked softly again on his door.

"Come in."

Claude Jenkins, Drew's roommate, sat at his desk behind his neatly made bed. The other bed, Drew's bed, had been stripped. No sheets, no blanket, no pillow. Drew's desk sat empty. Papers, books, alarm clock were all missing.

"Where's Drew?" she asked.

"He resigned," Jenkins said.

"WHAT???"

"They made him move all his stuff to Transient Barracks this morning."

"Why?"

"He should tell you."

"Tell me now!"

"I'm not supposed to say anything."

"C'mon Jenk, you know I'm his best friend."

"That's why he should be the one to tell you. I'll go with you to see him if you want."

"Yes, I want to see him. But give me a hint, dammit."

Claude Jenkins stood up. "C'mon, let's go."

The two plebes raced over to "Transient Barracks," which wasn't the name of a building like Thayer Hall or Washington Hall. It was the label given to a set of rooms used to transfer cadets out of the Corps—a holding area for anyone who resigned or was expelled.

They found Drew there alone in a room with all his bags packed.

He seemed smaller somehow. He looked defeated, empty. Transient.

"Drew!" She ran to hug him. He had tears in his eyes, and Jan's started to well up also. "Drew, what happened?"

"I had to resign," he said. "I didn't have a choice."

"Why?" Jan asked as Jenkins stood quietly next to her.

"A couple of my wrestling teammates accused me of being a homosexual. They said I tried to touch them in the locker room."

Jan gasped, "Oh, Drew!"

"I know. It's not fair. It's not right. But it's their word against mine. And there are two of them."

"No!" she cried. *No, No, NO!* "They can't do this, Drew; we can fight it."

"I'm afraid we can't," he said.

Jan stared at him in disbelief. *I lift mine eyes...* "Why not? We've fought plenty of things already. What's one more?"

Drew sighed, "This is too big, Jan. I can't win."

...to the hills, from whence cometh my help. This couldn't be happening. Not now. Not to Drew. Weren't there plenty of other cadets who didn't want, or didn't deserve, to stay at West Point? Shouldn't Jan be the one to leave? She didn't know what to think or how to feel.

"*Are* you a homosexual?"

"No!" he said immediately. "Of course not."

It didn't matter either way to her. Yet homosexuals would never be accepted in the Army. Everyone knew that. Drew continued, "the TAC told me I had two choices: I could resign and leave with dignity or I could try to fight it and get kicked out anyway."

Or was it: From whence cometh my help? Is it a statement or a question? "Drew, there's got to be a way to fight this. I will stand by you. So will Kissy, and you, too, Jenk, right? She turned to Drew's roommate.

"Uh, I...I'll do what I can," Jenkins said.

"Thanks guys, but there's nothing anyone can do. It's over," Drew sighed. His shoulders fell.

I lift mine eyes...to the hills... "Drew! Drew! Drew!" She choked as she said his name "How can I stay without you?"

"Don't say that, Jan. You've done everything on your own and you'll be fine." He put his arms around her.

"No. No, I won't be fine." She hugged him again. The two friends sat down on the bed. Jenkins sat on Drew's footlocker. They talked for close to an hour until there was nothing more to say. Nothing could be done. They were powerless to change the judgment and sentence. There would be no leniency. No appeal. No pardon.

They could only say goodbye and hope that someday, everything would be okay. But Jan knew nothing would be okay. Nothing would ever be okay.

She hugged him one last time. "Drew, I don't want to stay here without you." She felt the tidal wave rising in her bowels. *I will not cry, I will not cry, I will not cry.*

"I *want* you to stay. I want you to finish. Make me proud," Drew said.

"I can't, I can't…"

"Stop that right now, you hear?" He cut her off. "Besides, you have other friends, Jan."

"No one like you!"

"Well, that's true, but still, you have friends here who need you and who will take care of you."

She felt Jenkins' hand on her shoulder. "C'mon Jan. It's time to go."

"Take care of her, Jenk," Drew said, "and let her bitch at you every so often."

Jan slunk toward the door. She heard Jenkins mumble something to Drew. It sounded a little like "she already does."

As soon as they exited the building, Jan took off running. She ran along the Apron fronting The Plain, past George Washington on his high horse and past MacArthur on his pedestal. The tears would not wait until she was safely under her Gray Girl this time. Like Clark Kent in a desperate search for a phone booth, she ran faster and faster. She had to find a spot, anywhere, to hide and transform from one person into another. She kept running away from the barracks toward the road leading up to the Cadet Chapel. She ran so fast, the tears didn't fall down her cheeks. Instead they traced a line from the outside corners of her eyes to her ears, dropping inside her eardrums. It seemed more like her ears were crying. She thought how funny it would be if people cried from their ears instead of their eyes. She thought about all those nights in Beast when she cried herself to sleep. Lying face up, her tears fell in her ears then too.

This isn't really crying. Since the tears go from one orifice to another. Since they never fall down my cheeks. Since they never land on my chest, or my lap, or my arms. Since they start inside and finish inside....they really don't count. And I've never really cried at all.

Dear SKIP,

Drew Hambin, my best friend, resigned today. His teammates accused him of being a homosexual. I do not believe it—but even if it is true—it still does not alter my opinion of him. He is a good, kind and intelligent person. He was a good cadet and he would have been a great officer. They labeled him guilty before he could even speak for himself. We may have overcome some prejudices, but mankind will always carry resentment for a different kind. I'm not saying Drew is a homosexual— I'm saying that even if he is—why should that stop him from being a good Army officer?

Drew's resignation shook my belief in this place even more. If his teammates lied, then that shoots the honor system all to hell. And as to my belief in a good and caring God...well, this situation didn't help that either.

Jan

Dear Jan,

I am very sorry to hear about Drew. I know you must be quite upset. Yet, I'm sure Drew would want you to hang on and finish what you've started. He would want you to succeed.

We are very close now to finishing this year. It's right around the corner. I suppose if you have not guessed my identity by recognition day, I will reveal myself to you. I sort of prefer to stay in hiding, but I know it's not fair to you to keep you guessing. Still, I hope you will not treat me differently once you know who I am.

Keep your head up. Despite this setback, you still have a lot to be happy about.

SKIP

Deep down, Jan believed Drew might be gay. Although, she also wondered if the charges were trumped-up out of jealousy. Drew's good looks, athletic prowess, and total ease around women might have been threatening to guys who wanted to have even one of those qualities. She just could not believe he would try to molest his teammates. *He's just not that incredibly stupid.*

Anyone who made sexual advances on someone else in an inappropriate way ought to be "resigned," she accepted that much. *If that were really enforced, then there might be more cadets in transient barracks than in all of Old South.*

Although Jan didn't know Jenkins very well, he seemed almost as upset about Drew's departure as she was. She stopped by his room on occasions to commiserate with him and because she just wanted to make a new friend if possible.

Claude Jenkins was an average guy. His height, weight and looks were average—not great, not bad either. He seemed to be about average in academics and athletics. That made him just about the ideal friend, she figured. *Just like me, Jan, the middle child, the average girl. Jan, not Jane nor January nor Janiqua. Just Jan.*

They bonded quickly in those last few weeks. On Thursday afternoon in late April, they ran up to the Cadet Chapel. They kept going all the way up to Michie Stadium where their journey as new cadets began. They circled the football field, ran back down to Lusk Reservoir, and stopped at the chapel entrance. The trees, just coming back to life, swayed slightly from the gentle breeze. They sat on the stonewall fronting the massive oak, chapel doors and took in the grand view of West Point.

Sam Dogety parked his car in the firstie parking lot behind Michie Stadium and began walking down the long hill to the barracks. He saw Cadet Wishart running with some plebe guy around the football field. Then he saw them run past Lusk Reservoir, heading back down to Thayer Road.

He wished Wishart had been his classmate. He would have liked to have known her better. She was a sorry new cadet at first, but she had pushed through and won his admiration after all. She persevered when a lot of others had given up. She just hung in there. And sometimes, that's what mattered most.

He had to admit he liked Wishart. He really liked her. He wouldn't mind dating her, but fraternizing was forbidden. And Sam Dogety followed the rules, most of them anyway. Besides, he doubted she would have anything to do with him. She made it very clear how she felt about him, mostly by her facial expressions, but sometimes by the way she said things. She always sounded pissed off when answering his questions. He knew she only spoke to him because she had to, never because she wanted to. He also knew he was partly responsible for that.

He approached the Cadet Chapel and saw the two plebes sitting on the stonewall in front. They seemed to be having a serious conversation. Sam wondered if he was her boyfriend and felt a pang of jealousy.

Graduation was less than two weeks away. His West Point days were finally coming to an end, thank God. Most cadets hated West Point while they were cadets. They only grew to love it in memory. *I will only climb this hill a few more times. I only have five exams left. I only have a few more chances to haze plebes. May as well enjoy all of these things before they're gone forever.* "Wishart!" He shouted as he walked toward the Chapel steps.

"Yes, Sir." Both plebes popped to attention.

Dogety turned to Jenkins and said, "You're dismissed." Jenkins shot a glance at Jan before jogging down the steps leading to the back of the Mess Hall.

Without saying anything, Jan turned to Dogety and gave him a look that said, "what the hell do you want now, asshole?"

He seemed to recognize it. "Wishart, I've been meaning to ask you something. Why do you seem pissed off all the time?"

"I am pissed off all the time, Sir."

"Why? I mean, I know plebe year sucks and all, but life isn't really that bad, is it?" Jan didn't reply. He continued, "Do you hate me, Wishart?"

"I don't like you, Sir."

"Because I did my job? Because I hazed you and made you stronger?"

"Because you're mean. Because you seem to enjoy hazing me."

"Wishart, I don't enjoy hazing...okay, maybe a little. It's what we do here, you knew that coming in, right?"

"Yes, I knew that. But you never let up. You never stand down. You never even joke with us. It's always 'dress, right, dress' with you. Sir."

He knew this was true, but hearing it from her felt like getting slapped across the face. He looked away at the trees with their new leaves. Their rustling made the only sound. Then he looked back at her for a long moment.

Dogety cleared his throat. "I liked you when I saw you on R-day, you know. I just couldn't show it." He spoke barely above a whisper. "I still can't."

She remained standing at attention, looking past him. *What am I suppose to say? What does he want from me? Is he playing games? Or is he serious?*

"At ease, Wishart." Jan relaxed her pose. He said, "After Recognition Day, I'd like to have a conversation with you, maybe over a couple beers. I'd like to hear more...of...your honest opinion. I know I have a lot to learn."

Yes, you do.

"I also know you will tell me the truth, and I'd rather hear it now before I report to my first unit and possibly make the same mistakes."

He seemed to be sincere. "Sir, you have a lot of good traits. I would be happy to advise you on a few things, if you want."

He smiled. "Thanks, Wishart."

Okay, he has potential. He's teachable. Maybe.

At 1600 hours the next day, Dogety knocked on Jan's door. Dressed in jeans, a button-down, plaid shirt, and dark brown, penny loafers, he held up a pair of black, cowboy boots. "Miss Wishart, I need your honest opinion. Should I wear the boots or the shoes this weekend?"

He had never asked her this kind of question, and she knew he was trying to turn a new leaf. She smiled at the thought of him debating between footwear. "Sir, where are you going?"

"Jackson and I are going to the city. We'll probably hit a few bars and clubs."

"Are both shoes equally comfortable?" she asked.

"Yes, but the loafers are easier to kick off." *Stupid comment,* he thought.

What's that supposed to mean? "Okay, then wear the loafers, Sir," she said with *that look.*

"No, Wishart, I only meant that after a big night of bar hopping, it's sometimes difficult to deal with boots." He was doing it again. Messing up everything that came out of his mouth. "I mean, after drinking and all....you know what I mean, right?"

"I think so, Sir. Wear the loafers."

"Okay. Well, thanks for the advice."

"Anytime, Sir."

Dear SKIP,

I thought I had found you out. But, alas, I was wrong. It's not the first time.

I don't think I want to know your identity now. If I know who you are, I might act all stupid around you. Maybe I should just stay in the dark.

Since we are closing in on the end of this year, I also think it's best to stop corresponding. This cannot go on forever, and I think the letters have served their purpose. You really helped me get through plebe year. For that, I want to say thank you. Without knowing who you are, you have been one of the best friends I made this year.

Take care,

Jan

PS. No, forget that shit. I have to know who you are.

He read her last note. It still surprised him when she wrote back. He never really expected her to respond the first time. Yet, they just kept coming.

He wasn't very good at talking to women. He always got "all stupid," as Jan had written. Even the few times he had actually spoken to her, he messed it all up. That's why he started the notes.

He wouldn't be able to hide behind "SKIP" much longer. He decided to let her know his identity on Recognition Day, although, he hoped she would figure it out on her own first. That meant he had about two weeks left to drop a big hint.

Dear Jan,

Don't worry about acting "all stupid around me." In case you haven't guessed, I have kept you "in the dark" because I'm the one who's likely to act all stupid around you. And yes, maybe these letters have run their course. But I have really enjoyed the diversion. I hope you have too.

I can't believe you haven't guessed my identity yet. I have been hiding in plain view all along. Even more this semester than last. I will definitely reveal myself on Recognition Day.

I'm sorry I couldn't get you to join our organization—you proved to be a tougher case than I thought! You've taught me a lot, too. I hope we will communicate as freely next year as we have this year, maybe even using our voices.

God Bless,

SKIP

35

Saturday, May 8, 1982
0115 Hours

The slow reaction of the Cadet in Charge prompted Jan to shout again, "YOU HAVE TO DO SOMETHING, NOW!"

That seemed to work as he picked up a field radio receiver, clicked the handle and said, "Sir, we've got a situation here. Come quickly." He put the handle back in its cradle and looked at Jan. "This better not be some kind of prank."

"It's not. Now come on. We have to get back to the Mess Hall."

"I can't go until the OIC gets here." The Officer in Charge, a Captain or Major, stayed on duty through the night at the Command Guard Office.

"Where is he? How long till he gets here?" she demanded.

"He's making the rounds over in First Regiment, but he's coming directly."

Jan opened the door. "I can't wait that long. When he gets here, run, I mean RUN, to the Mess Hall Poop Deck area." Then she took off at a full sprint back to find Kristi.

"Kristi," she whispered as she approached the Poop Deck. "Kristi."

"I'm all right," Kristi shouted from the top. "You don't have to whisper now." Jan ran up the steps, two at a time to find her roommate sitting on the floor by the doorway. It was still hard to see anything, but light from an exit sign above reflected dark stains on the front of Kristi's USMA sweatshirt. Jan assumed it was sweat.

"You must have had quite a workout," she said, "you're sweating like a..."

"It's blood, Jan," Kristi said blankly.

"Shit! Are you okay?" Jan bent down to get a closer look at Kristi.

"I'm okay, I think. Most of it's...not mine." Kristi began to stand up. "Let's get out of here."

"Oh, my God, Kristi, what happened?" Jan pulled Kristi's arms to help her stand, but she slumped back down to the floor.

"I defended myself; that's all."

"Help is coming, Kristi. I think you may be hurt." Jan suddenly felt more scared than she had all night.

"No, I'm fine, really. Just worn out. I must've hit a main artery."

Just then Jan looked toward the middle of the Poop Deck. In the darkness, she could barely make out a figure lying on the floor in what looked like a large puddle. "Oh, my God!"

36

"Encourage us in our endeavors to live above the common level of life. Make us to choose the harder right instead of the easier wrong, and never to be content with a half truth when the whole can be won. Endow us with courage that is borne of loyalty to all that is noble and worthy, that scorns to compromise with vice and injustice and knows no fear when truth and right are in jeopardy."

From The Cadet Prayer

She awoke at 0500 exactly. *Shit, shit, shit. Already late.* She flew into class uniform, brushed her teeth, and bolted out the door without even stopping to pee.

She had been up late last night. Both Dogety and Jackson, drunk from their weekend pass, tasked her with couriering an envelope back and forth between H-3 and B-1. Then they accused her of tampering with their routing envelope *with their little love notes to each other.* She could not give a damn what they were writing back and forth. She just wanted to be left alone.

Jan thought she had made some headway with Dogety. He had treated her better in the past few weeks and he seemed to actually value her opinion at times. She couldn't say she liked him, yet she no longer hated him either. Although he had made her life miserable most of the year, it's possible that he was not a bad guy if one was inclined to get to know him. She was not, however, so inclined.

Jackson, on the other hand, was a very bad guy. Dogety may have been a hard-ass, but Jackson had been a monster. Women cadets knew to steer clear of Jackson. They knew he was not someone you trusted. He wasn't someone to be alone with either, if you were a female cadet.

Jan had not always been afraid of him, like the time during Beast, when he found her alone on the Land Navigation Course. Her anger overrode any fear she probably should have felt. But as the year dragged on, after a few close encounters with the creep, and being ninety-nine percent sure he was the one who raped Debra, she developed a healthy fear of the man whom she despised more than any other cadet at West Point.

Now she had to report to his room at o'dark thirty. She hoped he would be sleeping off his drunkenness and would tell her to go away. But either way, this would be the last time she would have to deal with him. She would shine his shoes, if that's what he wanted, and she would say, "yes, Sir" about ten times, then she would be done with him for good. He would graduate in about two weeks and she would be free of him forever. *Amen.*

She softly knocked twice on his door. When there wasn't an answer, she knocked again. Finally she heard a groggy, "Come in."

She entered the room. It was semi-dark, but she could make out the form of someone lying in the left bed. The bed on the right side was not made up, no one in it. *Damn.*

"Who is it?" Jackson groaned.

"Sir, Cadet Wishart reporting as ordered." She stood just inside his door.

"Dammit Wishart, you just woke me up from a great dream."

"Sir, you told…."

"Goddammit." He rolled onto his side, facing the middle of the room. "Go get my shoes from under my desk."

Damn. She left the door open and walked behind his desk. She bent down to get his shoes, somewhere on the floor she presumed. When she couldn't see them readily, she felt around under his desk and chair for them.

Jackson sat up on the side of his bed and then walked to his door and closed it.

Jan hit her head on his desk as she came back up with the shoes. "Shit!" She stood by his desk at the back of the room with one black cadet shoe in each hand. Jackson stood by the door wearing only his underwear and a t-shirt with a hawk, wings spread in flight, on the front. Jan stared at his chest with the giant bird and "Hilldale Hawks" written above it. Jackson started walking toward her.

She threw the shoe in her right hand at him, hitting him squarely in his hawk chest. He lunged at her, but she lurched forward explosively, just like pushing off the pool floor in the Bob and Travel. He grabbed her by the wrist. She twisted away from him and hit him on the head with the other shoe. He wrangled the shoe from her left hand and it whacked her across the face, hitting her in the mouth.

"You fucking asshole!" she shouted, while turning toward the door.

He pushed her forward, knocking her into the sink counter. "Get the hell out of my room. I don't ever want to see you again in B-1!"

She flung the door open and gave him the finger before bolting out.

She kept running. She ran down the hall and down the stairwell. She ran out of Old South and away from First Regiment. She ran and ran and ran and ran.

She ran all the way up to the Cadet Chapel, where she realized her lip was bleeding. She tasted saltiness in her mouth and spit. Even in the dark, she could see the blood mixed with saliva. She walked back down to the Mess Hall and found an ice machine. Wrapping some in a cloth napkin, she held it to her lip while sitting alone at one of the five hundred or so tables. The sun had not yet come up.

"Sir, I need to talk to you." She stood at Dogety's door. It was her first free period after breakfast.

"What is it, Miss Wishart?" he asked.

She walked into his room without permission. "Jackson raped

Cadet Plowden over Army/Navy weekend. And this morning, he tried to accost me. Fortunately, I fought him off."

Dogety had been standing by his desk with an open book in his hand. He closed the book and placed it on his desk. Then he sat down in his chair. "Could you say that again? I'm not sure what I just heard."

"Sir, you heard me. And it's true. He's a threat to every woman in the Corps. And he will be a threat to every woman under his command." Jan remained standing in the middle of his room.

Sam Dogety let out a long breath. "Do you have any proof?"

Jan was afraid he'd ask that. "I cannot prove what happened at Army/Navy, but Hambin, Trane and McCarron can attest to some of it. You thought Plowden was stupid drunk, remember? Well, I'm almost positive she was drugged. She didn't have *that* much to drink." She waited for him to say something. When he didn't, she continued, "She didn't want to report it. She didn't want to relive the whole thing, so she made us promise to keep quiet."

Dogety stared at her. She couldn't tell whether he believed her or not. "And you know Jackson ordered me to report to his room this morning at 0500, right?"

"And I told you to ignore that," Dogety said angrily.

"Well, he closed his door while I was getting his shoes from under his desk." She saw Dogety grimace. "I want to have him arrested," she said. "I want his ass thrown in jail."

Dogety stood up and walked to his door, closing it. Then he walked back to Jan, facing her. "Do you realize what you're saying?"

"Yes, Sir." She stared straight at him, eye to eye. "He's got to go."

"But what proof do you have? What can you show that he did any of this?"

"I only have my word. But I'm sure there are other women." She kept her eyes with his, but she began to sense his doubt. "When I tried to escape his room, he hit me in the face with his shoe. My lip is cut."

He moved his eyes to her mouth. "Your lip looks fine. I don't see a cut."

"It's on the bottom inside of my lip. It was bleeding and I put ice on it before breakfast." She instinctively rolled her tongue over the lump inside her bottom lip.

Dogety lifted his hand. "May I touch you?" he asked.

She nodded, yes. He placed the forefinger of his right hand under her chin and gently pulled down her bottom lip with his thumb. His fingers felt soft and soothing. She tilted her head slightly back.

Dogety stared at the cut, now a red swelling just inside the lower lip. He held her lip open longer than necessary, almost mesmerized by the tender, red, moist skin of her mouth. She closed her eyes and swallowed a small lump that had risen in her throat.

It shouldn't have happened. He knew it was wrong. She had just been through a traumatic experience, and some might say he was taking advantage of her vulnerability. But he did it anyway. Softly, while his thumb still held her lip, while her eyes were still closed, he leaned in and gently kissed her.

She didn't back away. She welcomed the warm kiss to her lips. Somehow, it seemed right, although she knew they were breaking more rules. Somehow, he made her feel safe. And now that she thought about it, she always felt safe with Dogety despite how belittled he made her feel at times.

They kissed gently once, then again, then once more. She opened her eyes. "Does this mean you believe me?" she asked quietly.

"Yes, I believe you," he said as he dropped his hand and straightened up. He walked to his desk chair and sat down. "But I know Markus. He might lose his temper sometimes, but I just don't see him as a rapist. He's against women at West Point, but he's not a woman hater in general."

"How do you know? I mean most rapists don't exactly play the part, do they? He wouldn't act like one to his friends, of course."

Dogety leaned forward over his desk and shook his head. "He's my best friend. I'll go talk to him today."

"No! That's not good enough!" Jan protested. "I know what I'm going to do. I'm going to the TAC as soon as he gets in today," Jan said matter of factly. "I'm going to make a formal complaint, and I'm skipping the chain of command."

Dogety sighed deeply. "That's one way to handle it. But without any witnesses and without any other proof, I'm afraid it won't go anywhere." He picked up a pencil and began tapping it on the desk. "Of course, you can do what you think is best. But I would like to talk to him first. If I tell him I saw the cut on your lip, he may even admit to it. Then I can, at least, verify your story." He stopped tapping the pencil. "Of course, this means I will lose a lot of friends, you understand. No one is going to like me for turning on my classmate, especially for a *female* plebe."

"Even if he's a threat to women everywhere? Even if he deserves every bit of his punishment? I think most people would be happy about getting a rapist off the streets, so to speak."

"Jan," he said using her first name for the first time, "Most people won't believe he's a rapist. At best, most will think that he lost self-control for a moment, something that could happen to any of us. At worst, they will believe you seduced him and now you're blaming him for refusing your advances."

She stared at Dogety in disbelief. *What would Cadet Trane believe? What would SKIP think? Would all her classmates turn against her?* Those were risks she could accept. She didn't want Jackson getting away with this. "If you want to talk to him, go ahead. But either way, I'm going to make an official complaint as soon as I can."

Jan went by Captain Spanner's office several times, but the H-3 Company TAC was out of the office all day.

By 1600 hours, Cadet Markus Jackson filed an honor report accusing Jan Wishart of lying. The B-1 Honor Representative conducted an informal investigation the next day, May 4, 1982. Cadet Trane, Company H-3 Honor Representative, received the report at 2230 hours that evening. The next morning, Wednesday, May 5, he informed Jan that she would have to defend herself at an Honor Board which would begin the following day.

37

Saturday, May 8, 1982
0200 Hours

Major Camden, the Officer in Charge, ordered one of the cadet guards to find and turn on all the Mess Hall lights. He told the other one to call the MP's and an ambulance. He made Jan and Kristi stay seated by the upper door to the Poop Deck. He used a two-way radio to communicate with the Guard Office. "The ambulance and MP's are coming. But I need you to go to the Supe's house right now and personally wake him up. Tell him it's an emergency. He needs to get here ASAP." Then he looked at Jan, "Who else should we notify besides your TAC?"

"Please get Cadet Dogety from H-3," Jan said. "And maybe someone from JAG." Jan marveled at how clearly she was thinking. She understood right away what this would mean for both Kristi and her. "Also, send some MP's over to the basement room under the Mess Hall, level B-4. There's a young woman tied up there. She's a witness."

The Poop Deck soon erupted in chaos. The MP's took pictures, drew a chalk outline around the body, covered it with a sheet, and placed markers at every blood spot. The Superintendent stood with his arms crossed, listening to a JAG officer. Everyone seemed to ignore Jan and Kristi, still sitting silently under the exit sign.

Captain Spanner, the H-3 TAC finally walked over to the two women. "Miss Wishart, Miss McCarron, are both of you all right?"

"Sir, I think Cadet McCarron is injured."

"My wrist and ribs are sore, but I think I'm okay, Jan."

"I'm going to send one of the medics over to look at you once they finish over there," Captain Spanner nodded toward the center of the Poop Deck. "But I need you both to listen to me now. This is very important." He waited until they looked at him directly. "Do not talk to anyone before you speak to the JAG officer, Major Quiddy. Not the Supe. Not the MP's. Not even me. Once you've told Major Quiddy everything, he will advise what to do next. Be sure he reads your written statement before you sign it. Do you both understand me?"

"Yes, Sir."

About ten minutes later, a bleary-eyed Dogety came bursting up the stairs. He saw the crime scene with the sheet-covered body. "What the hell happened?"

"Sir, he came after us. He attacked us," Jan said.

Dogety stood there for a moment as if in shock. "Who came after you?"

"Cadet Trane, Sir."

Sometime after 0400 hours, they were released to Captain Spanner who ordered Cadet Dogety to escort them directly to their room. Jan didn't sleep at all, but Kristi started snoring within minutes of hitting the rack. Angel never woke up when they came in, oblivious to the whole ordeal.

The next morning, the three roommates gave each other dress-offs, before heading out to breakfast formation at 0620 hours. At 0710, they were back in the formation before classes. Cadet Dogety walked up to Jan and ordered her to follow him off to the side of the formation. They were out of earshot from the others, but he still stood only few inches in front on her. Speaking barely above a whisper, he said, "Miss Wishart, your Honor Board has been postponed until 1600 hours today.

I'm attending a special meeting of the honor committee this morning to discuss your case in light of last night's events. The Superintendent, the Commandant and just about every JAG officer are meeting with the MP's to discuss the evidence and statements. The Commandant has ordered you and McCarron to remain in your quarters at all times, except for classes, lunch and to use the latrine. You cannot speak a word of this to anyone. The family must be notified first. Do you hear me?"

"Yes, Sir." She felt as if she was in a trance. She began to understand the meaning of "out of body" or "beside yourself." For a moment, she could have sworn she had been watching everything from above.

"I will do my best to be your advocate, but I cannot promise anything good will come of this. If you're lucky, they'll just kick you out. Worst case is a murder charge. Do you understand everything I've said?"

"Yes, Sir."

"I'm going to tell McCarron the same thing I told you. Remember, do not speak to anyone about last night. This comes directly from the Supe. Finally, wait for me to come get you for the Honor Board. I have to escort you there and back. No one wants you wandering around, apparently."

"Yes, Sir."

"I don't know what else to say. You may have lost any hope of survival."

"I know, Sir, but thank you for your help."

After her second morning class, she returned to her room for free period. Only it wasn't exactly free anymore. Both Kristi and Angel had classes until lunch. She tried to study for the physics exam but it was virtually impossible. She felt some relief when a note flew in under her door.

Dear Jan,
What happened? I was ready to testify today but was told the

Honor Board is on hold. I've heard some rumors, but I don't want to speculate. Can you enlighten me? I'm dying to know the real story.

I'm actually looking forward to telling my story. I had heard Dogety and Jackson were screwing with you Sunday night and it really pissed me off, so I followed you to B-1. When you left the envelope at Jackson's door, I took it. I pulled out their notes and put my note in its place.

I thought that would put an end to the harassing, but it only made it worse for you. Much worse. So it's really all my fault you were in this mess. That's why I am so eager to be a witness at your Honor Board. I want them to know I did it, and hopefully, they will drop the charges.

Now I'm concerned I may not get the chance to testify. I've been told to wait until I'm called, but no one seems to know when that will be. Please tell me all is going to be okay. I am anxious to hear from you.

SKIP

She wrote a response and taped it to her door.

Dear SKIP,

I cannot tell you why the board is on hold, only to say that it's supposed to resume at 1600 today. I am so thankful you are willing to testify for me. And I'm glad to finally know how the note was replaced.

I'm not mad at you. I'm happy you tried to protect me. And I'm sorry it backfired.

Please pray for me. I think you have a better line to the guy upstairs than I do, and if indeed, he (or she) can do anything for me, now would be a good time. The situation has gone from bad to horrendous and it doesn't seem like it's going to get any better soon. So, a miracle would be a really nice thing about now.

If I never write again, it's because I had to leave quickly. I know how expulsions work—they don't let you hang around long. I only wish you would tell me who you are before I have to leave. Even if I never find out your identity, I will always be thankful for your friendship.

Jan

38

Saturday, May 8, 1982
1545 Hours

Cadet Dogety arrived on time. He didn't say anything except, "Let's go, Miss Wishart." She didn't ask him any questions either. They hadn't heard anything more from the Superintendent, the Commandant, the MP's or even from Captain Spanner.

She gave Angel and Kristi a hug before leaving the room. "Hold any notes for me that appear at the door."

"I will," Kristi replied. They couldn't say any more in front of Angel, who was still oblivious to the previous night's events.

Jan followed Cadet Dogety out the door.

They passed fifty or so cadets on the way to Mahan Hall. Jan felt almost all of them staring at her. She knew that at least some, maybe most, had heard about last night. Despite the "do not talk" policy, cadets talked. They always knew when something big happened, although they usually didn't know the real story. They probably heard something like, "the female cadet who's in the middle of an Honor Trial killed her Honor Representative in Washington Hall last night."

She made a conscious decision to stand tall with her head up. She stared back at every face that seemed to accuse her. She saw judgment in their eyes. She reminded herself of the resolution she had made at the beginning of second semester. Their condemnation could not, would not, penetrate her skin. At least that's what she told herself.

They approached the huge, arched doors to Mahan Hall. Cadet Dogety reached for the handle and held the door for her. The gesture reminded her of Trane. She stepped through the arch and practically bumped into Rick Davidson.

"Jan, I'll be waiting just outside the room... and I'll be praying the whole time," he said.

"What?" She stared at him wondering what he meant. "I don't need you...." *Why does he care....Oh, dear God. It's him.*

"It's okay; I don't mind waiting," Rick said.

Cadet Dogety interjected, "Go back to the company, Davidson. You're not going to be needed anymore."

But Rick followed him anyway, alongside Jan, in step—left, right, left—all the way up to the fourth floor. He waited outside while Jan and Dogety entered the windowless room.

It looked like an entirely different room. Then she realized it was because most of the honor "jury" was not there. Only Cadets Conrad, Tourney, Leavitt, Gaskins and Seymour were present. Even the bookend officers and Major Hastings were absent. The stenographer, however, was at her post.

"Sit down, Miss Wishart," Conrad said. She walked to her chair and sat down with her back straight a few inches from the chair back, chest a few inches from the table, legs at a ninety-degree angle from the knees, and eyes straight ahead. "We've spent several hours deliberating the evidence in your honor case and also in discussions with the Superintendent and the Commandant concerning the new investigation involving you and Cadet McCarron. We were not told what happened exactly, but we have been informed that the MP's, JAG and the press will be involved. We also know that these events will not reflect favorably on West Point." Jan felt her eyes glisten.

Conrad continued. "The Superintendent and Commandant indicated that the evidence thus far *appears* to validate the statements given by those involved, but Cadet McCarron's actions, at least, may be under more serious investigation." Jan saw his lower lip tighten. "I have no idea what you two have gotten yourselves into, but it's serious enough that both the Supe and the Comm felt the need to intervene in these proceedings."

Jan could tell he didn't think the Supe and Comm had any business involving themselves in the cadet honor system. Conrad felt the Honor Code belonged only to cadets and he didn't appreciate the higher-ups getting involved.

"This Honor Board has been the most irregular one in my entire cadet career. I've seen a lot of strange situations, but this one takes the prize, Miss Wishart."

Isn't the saying supposed to be 'takes the cake?'

"However, Cadet Davidson's statement explaining his role in the events of Sunday night validates your account." Conrad's voice waned after the last word. He paused before continuing, "Which means there is only the question of who's telling the truth about the events on Monday morning."

I am.

"Now," he paused, "without any other witnesses, and in light of whatever happened last night, we are in a unique situation which demands a unique resolution." He waited another moment before continuing. "Normally, we would continue the Honor Board with the facts of the case as they stand. In light of these new circumstances, however, and in consultation with the Superintendent and the Commandant," she thought she saw him roll his eyes slightly, "we have decided to take an unprecedented action."

Jan looked straight ahead, listening, but not quite hearing. The room began to fill with fog.

I am a stone.

"You need to know this was not a unanimous decision. Some on the jury wanted to continue as planned." Conrad paused again, before picking up a piece of paper that was lying on the table in front of him.

He began reading from the document. "After many hours of deliberation, and in consultation with the Superintendent of the United States Military Academy and the Commandant of Cadets, this Honor

Board has determined that the charges against Cadet Jan Wishart are insufficient in their merit, inconclusive in their supporting evidence, and are not worthy of continuing the Honor Trial at this time." Conrad placed the paper back down on the table. "Do you have any questions, Cadet Wishart?" he asked while still looking down.

She didn't exactly compute what he just read. Was it an acquittal then? Was it a mistrial? Was she free to go? What just happened?

"No, Sir."

"Okay, then there's one more thing you should know. In addition to the ongoing MP investigation into whatever," he paused, "whatever happened last night, there will also be a disciplinary hearing later this afternoon. You and McCarron will likely face serious disciplinary action. Cadets Jackson, Dogety and Davidson may also received punishment for their roles last weekend." He seemed pleased to be able to share that news. "You are dismissed."

Sam Dogety stood up, but Jan stayed seated. She looked up at him. "We're done here, Miss Wishart."

Rick Davidson stood up from his position on the floor when the door to room 413 opened. He looked straight at Jan but didn't say anything. Her eyes widened, but she made no comment either. She simply turned left. Dogety followed behind her toward the stairwell to the main arched doors.

"What happened?" Rick asked from the last spot in the procession.

Dogety turned his head and said, "All charges have been dropped."

"YAHOO!!" Rick shouted.

At the front of the line, Jan began to cry.

39

Saturday, May 8, 1982
2200 Hours

Jan, Kristi and Angel waited in their room for Cadet Dogety. He said he would come straight back with news from the disciplinary hearing. As the H-3 Company Executive Officer, he had been included in the deliberations. The Commandant chaired this committee, which included Captain Spanner, the B-1 TAC, the Company Commander and First Sergeant and a few other appointed officers.

"What's the worst that can happen now?" Kristi asked.

"They could still kick us out," Jan said.

"The most they'll do now is give you a lot of walking tours," Angel said, still not fully understanding what had transpired.

"You're probably right, Angel," Jan said.

"They might even let you off entirely, like they did with the honor charges," Angel added optimistically.

"I doubt that," Kristi said as she looked at Jan. "They will have to do something with us, I'm just hoping Jackass doesn't get off the hook."

Two loud knocks on the door caused the three roommates to jump to attention.

"Enter, Sir," they called in unison.

Dogety stood at the door in his white cadet shirt, gray trousers and red sash around his waist. "At ease," he said. The three plebes relaxed while Sam Dogety walked into the room. He sat down at Jan's desk chair and told them to take a seat. "Miss Wishart and Miss McCarron, you both have received one hundred hour slugs for being out after Taps and being off limits last night. It's a good thing you left your cards unmarked or you might be facing another honor trial. You may start walking the area next week after your exams. You can walk off as much as you want during graduation week, also. Any remaining time can be walked when you're yearlings." He took a deep breath. "Davidson's been given a twenty-five hour slug for his role Sunday night."

Jan and Kristi looked at each other, breathing a sigh of relief, knowing it could have been much worse. Jan's plan of staying out of the "Century Club" had failed. But given what she had just been through, it seemed like easy street.

"What about Jackson?" Jan asked.

Dogety breathed deeply again, letting it out slowly. "He and I have received twenty-five hour slugs, with ten hours suspended. We will have to walk the remaining fifteen hours in the next two weeks before graduation."

She no longer cared. Jackson was a jerk but not a rapist. Having been entirely wrong about Cadet Trane, it was possible she had been entirely wrong about Jackson. He made mistakes; he had been mean, hurtful, sexist and rude, at times. His version of the events on Sunday night and Monday morning differed from hers which she realized now could have been related to each one's perceptions about the other one. But he wasn't the monster she had made him out to be.

After a pause, Kristi asked, "Did they talk to the girl?"

Sam continued, "Apparently she's corroborated your story. She doesn't want to officially come forward. There's a rumor that she's part of the Mess Hall staff and doesn't want any negative attention from co-workers or cadets."

"I don't get that," Kristi said. "She's not to blame for any of this. Why wouldn't she at least publically verify her attacker?"

"If he's dead, what's the point?" Jan asked.

"What are you guys talking about?" They had forgotten Angel was in the room and she still had no idea what happened.

"Uh, Angel, we will be able to tell you all about it in a few days. But we can't say any more about it now." Jan felt badly that they had slipped.

Dogety stood up. "Miss Trane, please do not repeat anything you've heard here. Your roommates need your cooperation and silence right now. I'm sure they will fill you in when they can."

"Yes, Sir," Angel replied looking concerned.

Two days later, both Kristi and Jan were summoned to the Superintendent's office. Wearing Dress Gray, they stood at attention outside his door. The door opened from the inside. Captain Spanner told them to report to Lieutenant General (LTG) Stanton. The roommates entered the massive office and stopped five feet in front of the enormous, mahogany desk. The Commandant, Major General Mullenbehr, stood to the left and the JAG officer, Major Quiddy, stood to the right of the desk. Captain Spanner stood behind them. They saluted together. Jan said, "Sir, Cadets Wishart and McCarron reporting as ordered." They held the salute until the Supe saluted back which he did after a longer than normal pause.

"At ease," he said. The woman went from standing at attention to standing with feet shoulder width apart and hands overlapped facing outward at the small of their backs. This was "at ease," but Jan always thought it was just modified attention.

"I've served a long time in the Army. I've seen a lot of things. Nothing really shocks me anymore." He paused. "I have to say, though, I didn't expect anything like this to happen at West Point." He paused again, this time looking out his big, bay window onto The Plain.

"A few years back a cadet drowned in Lake Popolopen." He seemed to be talking to himself. "That case was shrouded in mystery for so long that by the time they determined it was murder, the story had died down." He turned back to the two women. "But this time, we have twice the scandal."

Jan swallowed. She could hear Kristi breathing. The Supe

continued, "We have a dead firstie who was killed by a plebe. We have a witness who says the firstie raped her just before he took off after you two. However, the victim does not want her identity known. She is unable or unwilling to testify further." He paused. "Yet, her statement alone appears to validate your actions, Miss McCarron. The MP's believe that you acted in self-defense and they are not planning to bring any further charges against either one of you." He paused again before adding, "I happen to agree."

Jan and Kristi simultaneously sighed. "However," he continued, "we still have the problem of explaining to the Corps, and the general public, how a firstie was killed by a plebe. First, let's talk about the dead man." The Supe lifted a piece of paper off his desk and read from it. "Cadet Bill Trane is admired and respected by everyone. He is considered a role model and an inspiration to all who know him. Bill serves as the H-3 Company Honor Captain and his reputation is beyond reproach. He is a good man with a very bright future in the Army." LTG Stanton placed the paper back down. "This was written about Cadet Trane in his last peer evaluation."

The Supe leaned back in his big leather chair, placing his hands on his face and then brushing them up through his gray, but still thick, head of hair. "Cadet Trane had an unblemished record. He had good grades, he was a good athlete...he seems to have done well in every area as a cadet."

I thought he was perfect, too.

"It turns out that Cadet Trane *did* have one problem, however. One that no one knew about. Not his girlfriend, not his friends, neither his subordinates nor his superiors—no one seems to have known about Cadet Trane's problem."

Rapists don't usually share that information....

"He was an alcoholic." The Supe leaned forward in his chair and stared straight at Jan and Kristi. "We searched his room and discovered a stash of liquor in his footlocker and behind the wall of his bottom closet drawer."

Trane never seemed drunk to me....

The Supe continued, "It appears that his drinking problem very likely clouded his judgment on several occasions."

And no one ever noticed before?

"What we have here, Miss McCarron and Miss Wishart, is a situation where a good man went bad because of alcohol abuse. Do you understand what I'm saying?"

"Yes, Sir," Kristi answered for both of them.

"Cadet Trane is dead, so he cannot speak for himself. Everyone who knew him thought he was a great guy. He had many friends. A family has lost their son and their brother who was just a couple weeks away from graduating from West Point."

Jan couldn't fathom the grief Trane's family must be experiencing. All she knew was that it could have been her family or Kristi's family instead. And in Kristi's case, there had already been enough grief for one year.

The Supe continued speaking. "We are going to have a memorial service at the Cadet Chapel for Cadet Trane, for the fine young man everyone knew. We are also going to talk about the dangers of alcoholism and how it can affect the mind, making otherwise good people do some very bad things." He sat back again in his big leather chair. "Miss Wishart, I understand Cadet Trane was your supporting cadet at your Honor Board."

"Yes, Sir," she almost whispered.

"So even you must have thought very highly of Cadet Trane, correct?"

"Yes, Sir."

"What I'm saying to both of you is this: Cadet Trane did a terrible thing when he was drunk. But otherwise, he was a good man who was loved and will be deeply missed. We have to handle his death with sensitivity and dignity for the family and all who knew him."

Jan didn't have a problem with that part. She figured funerals were for the living anyway. "Yes, Sir," they both replied.

"Good, now let's talk about you two."

Jan flinched slightly.

"What we have here is a situation where you defended yourselves from your attacker. You did what anyone in that situation would do.

Miss Wishart, you went to find help while Miss McCarron stayed behind with a weapon, correct?"

"Yes, Sir," Kristi answered.

"Okay, so help me understand one thing. Miss McCarron, why didn't you also go get help with Miss Wishart? Why did you stay behind with the knife?"

Jan felt Kristi flinch this time. "Sir, I was afraid Cadet Trane was going to catch up with us. He had closed the gap by the time we had reached the Poop Deck. I felt one of us had to run for help and one of us had to stay and either fight or hide."

"So why was Miss Wishart the one who went for help?"

"Sir, she's the better runner." Kristi said it with all seriousness, but Jan found it slightly humorous. "And Sir, I thought I could hide better."

"But he found you, didn't he?"

"Yes, Sir. I tried to hide, but when he got close, I decided the best defense was offense, so I jumped out. We struggled for a little bit, and I could tell he was going to take the knife, which I had in my right hand, so I jabbed him with it." Kristi re-enacted the jabbing motion which looked like what they were taught in bayonet training. "I was just trying to hurt him enough so I could get away. But I had no idea I cut his brachial artery." They both had learned a new lesson in anatomy.

"I see." LTG Stanton looked down. "Do you think he might have killed you if you hadn't had the knife?"

Kristi lifted her chin slightly. "Yes, Sir, that's what I assumed."

The Supe took a deep breath and leaned back in his chair again. "Okay, here's what's going to happen. I'm going to address the entire Corps of Cadets about the situation. I'm going to explain Cadet Trane's alcohol addiction and how it affected his actions that night. I'm also going to explain that you both acted in self defense—the MP investigation as well as our internal one validates your actions that night." He leaned forward again. Looking straight at Kristi, he continued, "However, you must know that there will be some, perhaps many, who will feel that you committed murder and got away with it."

The room fell completely silent. No one moved or spoke while LTG Stanton let his words sink in to Jan and Kristi's psyche. Then he added,

"Furthermore, no one can protect you from the fallout that may come from this. Some will never accept you, some may silence you, and you may find yourselves as the brunt of jokes, snide comments or other verbal assaults. There's nothing I, or anyone else, can do to keep these things from happening."

Jan and Kristi had already thought about that. They already felt the stigma.

"If you were my daughters, I would advise you to resign." He said it softly but deftly.

Another long moment of silence ensued. Jan began to understand the point of this meeting. *He wants us out.*

"Sir, may I ask a question?"

"Yes, Miss Wishart?"

"Sir, what would you advise if we were your sons?"

Jan saw him flinch. He sat back again in his chair, interlocking his fingers behind his head. He waited another moment before answering. "That's a good question, Miss Wishart." He looked up to the trey ceiling before looking back at Jan. "I'd probably tell you to stick it out. You were out after Taps and in an unauthorized area. You're not the first nor the last cadets to be guilty of that. But if you hadn't been out, we might never have discovered Cadet Trane's propensity for evil." He paused again. "Don't get me wrong, I wish you had not gone out that night. But in doing so, we've solved..." He abruptly stopped speaking.

Solved what?

The Superintendent leaned forward in his chair. "Anyway, it's done now. There's no way of knowing what might have happened if you had not gone out that night." He seemed a little flustered.

"Sir, what do you mean?" Jan hoped it wasn't what she thought.

"Nothing that can be changed at this point, Miss Wishart."

"Sir, are you saying there have been other rapes?" Jan began to feel the rage rising again.

"I didn't say anything of the sort." He stared directly at Jan. She didn't flinch. "I'm saying we are hopeful that there will not be any more incidents like this one."

"Sir,..."

"Miss Wishart, there's a lot you don't know. We do not share everything with the entire Corps of Cadets. It would not be prudent or helpful to do so. But, yes, there have been a few incidents over the last few years which yielded no evidence and only reluctant victims. Without proof and without witnesses, there is nothing to do but wait and hope. There's no point alarming everyone." His voice indicated the end of the subject.

Jan didn't say any more. This wasn't her fight. *Not every battle is Armageddon.*

LTG Stanton told them to think about their options and that he would support whatever decisions they made. They were dismissed.

40

Jan \jan\ as a girl's name (also used as boy's name Jan), is pronounced jann, Feminine form of John. As a girl's name, also a short form of Janet and Janice. It is of Hebrew origin, and the meaning of Jan is " God is gracious".

Wednesday, May 26, 1982
1300 Hours

Eternity finally arrived. Recognition day began with the last parade of the year—graduation parade. It was like every other parade, only this time, the Corps of Cadets minus the firsties passed in review of the graduating class. The cows in charge led the parade like they were old pros, which tends to happen after three years of practice. Each company presented arms when passing the firsties, and then each company returned back to their formational areas for recognition of the plebes.

The acting Company Commander ordered the plebes of H-3 to fallout in a wide U-shape. But the Army doesn't do soft corners, so they formed up in a three-sided rectangle. The yearlings started the procession, each one coming down the line of plebes, introducing themselves by first name. The plebes also offered their first names, while sounds of joking and laughing went up across the Academy.

The night before, the Superintendent called a special session to address the entire Corps of Cadets. They had marched to Ike Hall where he spoke about "an incident involving the death of a first classman." This young man, he said, while a model cadet in many ways, had a serious alcohol addiction which explained why he might have acted violently. He never used the word "rape." The investigation into these events would continue, LTG Stanton said, but the cadets involved were not to blame. All the evidence to date, he said, supported the female cadet's decision to defend herself from a perceived and real threat. Any rumors to the contrary were false. These cadets, he stressed, deserved acceptance and treatment in the same manner as any other member of the Corps. Additionally, he reminded them that the deceased firstie had a spotless reputation prior to this incident and that the Corps should also remember him that way. Since the young man was no longer here to defend himself, no further judgment could be made about his character other than what was previously known about him.

Jan and Kristi sat stone-faced and still in their seats for the whole lecture. Angel looked over at them a couple of times, still disbelieving what her roommates had been through. Even though their names were never officially mentioned, most everyone knew who was involved. They went to bed hoping the Supe's words would be taken seriously.

They didn't have to line up in height order, so Jan, Kristi and Angel stood next to each other. Each upperclassman congratulated them and most seemed genuinely happy that the three women had made it. Although, a few came through the line and refused to shake Kristi's hand. One or two only nodded at Jan, never greeting her formally.

Kristi's first semester Squad Leader broke the ice, "Well, you certainly finished plebe year with a bang, Kristi."

"Yes, Sir." She looked down.

"Hey, none of that anymore, I'm Ken now." He smiled at her.

"Thanks, Ken. I wish it could have been very different."

When Cadet Meyer stepped in front of Jan, he said, "You were squared away first semester when I was your Squad Leader, Jan." He smiled, "I'm Steve."

"Actually, I was a mess first semester—intra-murder soccer, blueberry pies and diet tables—you remember?"

"Okay, but those were nothing compared to..." he seemed to think twice about his comments, "well, you know what I mean."

Jan smiled back. "You were the first upperclassman to give me a compliment. I really appreciated that."

"I did? I don't remember..."

"Yes, you did, I remember it well."

"Well good luck at Camp Buckner."

"Thank you, Sir...I mean, Steve."

With each Yearling who congratulated and called her "Jan," she felt more secure in her place in the Long Gray Line. She was now a full-fledged member of the United States Corps of Cadets. They confirmed it. They called her Jan. At least most of them did.

Then the cows came through the line. She greeted Cadet Rallins, "Thank you for the iron, Jean. It really helped with my wool trousers that time."

"Oh, I felt so bad for you, Jan. That was such a hard night."

"Yeah, but you made it easier. You saved my pants from the trash can." They both laughed.

"And I guess it was easy in hindsight...I mean...now..."

"Yes, Jean. Looking back, it was.... easy."

The cows finished filing through, then the firsties started coming. She saw Dogety approaching in the corner of her eye, but she didn't look at him. Thankfully, Cadet Holdern came first.

"Congratulations, Jan. No matter what anyone else says or thinks, remember that you and Kristi both deserve to be here. Hold your heads high. "

I'll try. "Thank you, John."

"And you will always have the notorious distinction of digging Harold's grave." He winked, but Jan wished he hadn't mentioned that last word.

"It was an honor."

He lowered his voice, "And nothing will ever seem too difficult after what you've been through."

"You're right about that."

A few more firsties came through the line. Jan saw Dogety getting closer—only two people away. Then, he stood in front of her. She took a deep breath while an awkward silence hung between them. She decided not to speak first.

"Congratulations, Jan." He held his hand out to shake.

She took it and they shook slowly, deliberately. "Thanks, Sam." She could not think of anything else to say.

"I'm really sorry for all the trouble I put you through. You've taught me more than I could possibly have taught you." He looked in her eyes.

"You've taught me well. Everything you put me through helped me to survive the... that last thing." She looked back at him, eye to eye. "You prepared me to face this...situation."

"Well, I am truly, deeply sorry for getting you into this whole mess." He looked down now.

"I am sorry we couldn't get to know each other more. But I wish you all the best in the Army, and beyond." She meant it.

"Thanks, Jan. I wish you the best, also. Goodbye."

"Goodbye, Sam."

Jan looked down the line of plebes and saw Rick greeting everyone with a smile and a handshake. She never would have guessed *him.* This cocky, prior service, good at everything, Mr. Know-It-All could not possibly be the same sensitive, funny and spiritual pen pal she had come to know. But he was indeed the very same person. She realized how little she knew about anyone. Hell, she didn't even know much about herself. Although, she knew quite a bit more now than a year ago.

She wanted to hug him before everyone scattered for summer leave. She contemplated how best to approach him when he looked up and caught her eye. Jan wanted to tell him how much he meant to her. She wanted to tell him she loved him. But what did he think about her now? Now that she had been involved in Cadet Trane's death would he still want to be her friend? She looked away.

The line finally finished. The plebes of H-3 were officially recognized and dismissed to begin packing. She walked back to her room. Kristi and Angel were packing their green duffle bags. Jan flopped down on her now stripped bed, putting her feet up and falling back on the pillow. She felt like she had just been released from prison.

"Oh Jan, I almost forgot. You got another note taped to the door." Kristi handed Jan a folded piece of paper.

Jan took the note and brought it close to her face. She unfolded it and read.

Jan,

I really enjoyed helping you in Calculus. You always made me feel so smart. (I know you think you were terrible at it, but you were not that bad really.) And yes, I enjoyed seeing you in Drowning, also.

I am so thankful that the honor charges were dropped. And deeply thankful that you were not blamed for what happened on that other night. I don't think I've ever prayed so hard in my life. And it looks like God may have been with us after all. `

I'm sorry we haven't connected very much in the last couple of weeks. With exam week, moving to Camp Buckner, graduation week activities and walking area tours, we haven't had any time to catch up. I'm sure you've had even less time, given the extra hours you have to put in on the area.

Anyway, I was hoping to spend a little time together before summer leave. But it looks like we'll have to wait until Buckner to actually speak again. I am looking forward to it.

I hope I won't get "all stupid" around you then. If I do, give me a chance to make it right, please. Surely you can tell by now that I'm a nice guy.

Rick (aka SKIP)

Jan folded the paper again and held it against her stomach with her left hand. *I thought Trane was a nice guy, too.* She covered her eyes with her right hand. She suddenly felt so tired. So goddamn tired.

Angel and Kristi continued packing. Jan began to nod off when

Kristi said, "Jan, do you mind if I come to your house again in, like, two weeks?"

Jan felt like she needed a break from everyone, even Kristi, but two weeks should do it. How could she say no to the one friend who risked her own life for Jan's? "Yeah, that's fine. Just let me know when you're coming."

"I'll call a few days ahead. You can pick me up at Logan, right?"

"Yeah, Kissy, no prob." Jan didn't want to think about two weeks from now. She just wanted to sleep. She turned her head toward the wall on the uncovered pillow, closed her eyes and fell asleep.

The West Point Class of 1982 graduated the next day. Senator John Tower (R-TEX), Chairman of the Senate Armed Services Committee, gave the commencement address. Jan wondered if the firsties felt a little ripped off since the previous year's graduation speaker was President Ronald Reagan. The thousand or so classmates, including Dogety, Conrad and Jackson, threw their hats at "Class Dismissed."

Everyone was free to leave after the two-hour ceremony. Jan's parents didn't come for her this time. Instead, she took a late afternoon Greyhound bus from the nearby town of Highland Falls. *Fitting name for the bus out of West Point.*

She stared at the gray face in the window while the bus rolled down the interstate. She studied the unfamiliar reflection staring back at her and spoke out loud to it.

> *I saw you on R-day, in the mirror.*
> *I knew you then.*
> *But who are you now, Gray Girl?*
> *I don't know you.*
> *I don't...*
> > *Recognize you.*

Rick checked his mailbox before leaving. A single envelope with *SKIP* written in large letters lay on its side. He braced himself for what could be a sort of *Dear John*. She had not spoken or written anything to him since he revealed himself to her on that second Saturday in May. He had hoped they could speak at least once since the Superintendent's lecture about what had come to be known as "The Incident." But there just hadn't been any time.

He unfolded the note and recognized her handwriting. He inhaled deeply and read Jan's last note to him.

Dear Rick,

Even though I have been a "tough case," I hope you won't give up on me just yet. Thanks for everything. I mean, everything. Especially the prayers.

See you at Buckner!

Jan

POSTSCRIPT

Any inaccuracies regarding the buildings, grounds, rules, uniforms, training, sequence of events, etc. are entirely my own fault. I didn't worry about getting all the details straight and I purposely changed a few of them.

Even though Jan and I share some of the same characteristics, I was never charged with an honor violation, nor fraternized, nor involved in anyone's death. Jan and Kristi do not exhibit the level of fear that we experienced as plebes because I wanted to make these characters bolder, smarter and more empathetic than we actually were at that age. I wish I could have been more like Jan Wishart when I was a cadet.

Finally, I want to express my deep appreciation for my West Point experience. It may be the only college you grow to love long after you leave. Very few of us loved it while we were there. Yet, USMA gave us more than it took away. Despite, and perhaps because of, its harsh nature when we were cadets, most of us have become proud members of the Long Gray Line. I feel blessed to be among the men and women who have experienced something that is not comparable anywhere. We share a bond. I feel this ever more deeply with each passing year, especially among my classmates and women who were once cadets.

ABOUT THE AUTHOR

Susan I. Spieth graduated from West Point in 1985 and served five years in the Army as a Missile Maintenance Officer. After completing her military service, she attended Seminary where she earned a Master of Divinity degree. She is an ordained clergywoman in the United Methodist Church, having served five churches as Pastor/Associate Pastor for seventeen years. Susan and her husband have two children and live in Seattle, WA. This is her first novel.

Made in the USA
Lexington, KY
29 July 2014